# LAKE

Catherine Cooper is a journalist specializing in luxury travel, hotels and skiing who writes regularly for national newspapers and magazines. She lives near the Pyrenees in the South of France with her family, cats and chickens. Her debut, *The Chalet*, was a top 5 *Sunday Times* bestseller. *The Lake* is her sixth novel.

𝕏 @catherinecooper
▣ @catherinecooperauthor

Also by Catherine Cooper

*The Chalet*
*The Chateau*
*The Cruise*
*The Island*
*The Penthouse*

# THE
# LAKE

## CATHERINE COOPER

HarperCollins*Publishers*

HarperCollins*Publishers* Ltd
1 London Bridge Street,
London SE1 9GF

www.harpercollins.co.uk

HarperCollins*Publishers*
Macken House,
39/40 Mayor Street Upper,
Dublin 1
D01 C9W8

First published by HarperCollins*Publishers* 2025
1

A catalogue record for this book is available from the British Library

ISBN: 978-0-00-867258-4 (PB)

Typeset in Sabon LT Std by Palimpsest Book Production Ltd, Falkirk,
Stirlingshire

Printed and bound in the UK using 100% Renewable Electricity by
CPI Group (UK) Ltd

MIX
Paper | Supporting
responsible forestry
FSC
www.fsc.org
FSC™ C007454

In memory of Pickle xxx

It is wonderful that five thousand years have now elapsed since the creation of the world, and still it is undecided whether or not there has ever been an instance of the spirit of any person appearing after death. All argument is against it; but all belief is for it.

Samuel Johnson


I look for ghosts; but none will force
Their way to me. 'Tis falsely said
That there was ever intercourse
Between the living and the dead.

William Wordsworth

I planned it all carefully.

Watching the flames envelop the castle from my boat on the lake, I haven't felt such peace for a very long time.

He deserves it.

I am not sorry.

I have done what I needed to do.

It is finished.

# Part One

# Creaglie Castle

**8 November 2025, 8 p.m.**
Amelia

Creaglie Castle is barely recognizable since the last time I was here. There's now a huge glass cube just outside – the new spa, apparently. And inside, there are rows of soft slippers adorned with the family crest lined up on a heated rail for the new paying guests' use in the vastly smartened-up boot room.

Some of it is still the same. The portraits of all the miserable old Creaglie duffers who stretch back years – to the sixteenth century no less – still hang on the walls. Those vile animal heads with eyes which seem to follow you around the rooms are still there, as well as the crossed swords in the hallway which always gave me the creeps – they look so sharp and heavy. Horrible.

But the castle has also been cleaned up and renovated, as it would have to have been anyway after the fire, and many of the fixtures and fittings have been modernized and upgraded now that the family is opening it up as a luxury resort.

Who would have thought? I can't imagine that was the brainchild of Alistair – or the Nineteenth Laird of Creaglie, to give him his full title. Perhaps it was the new young wife, Lady Tabitha of Creaglie. Wife number three for him. It's possible the family has fallen on hard times, though I find that difficult to imagine. Maybe Tabitha is demanding a new sports car or diamond ring.

Or perhaps opening the castle to the public was Alistair's son Joshua's idea. About 30 years old, and quite good-looking in a posh-boy kind of way, if you like that kind of thing, Joshua seems like he might be the entrepreneurial type – fresh back from some American university and bringing all these big ideas with him, like the annexe which has now been built. It's a flashy glass cube housing an indoor–outdoor pool with a Jacuzzi and water jets – totally modern and should be at odds with the mishmash of architecture that constitutes the rest of the castle but, somehow, it works. I went to have a look earlier.

Many of the ancient, worn and dusty rugs have been replaced with ones which look like they are antique but probably aren't, and there are definitely some similarly pretend-old new pieces of furniture.

I didn't expect to be invited to this weekend, to the opening to the public, but as I was, I thought it only polite to accept. It's interesting to watch the people around the dining table and how they behave – you can see who is used to opulence and relaxed about it (Alistair and his son Joshua, his wifelet Lady Tabitha, though she makes the odd slip-up as she's clearly newer to this), and those for whom it is novel and a bit over-whelming (everyone else except me).

Alistair is quite old, even frail-looking, these days. Nothing like last time I saw him. He clears his throat.

'Good evening to you all and many thanks for coming all this way in this awful weather we're having,' Alistair says. Even though this is their family home, none of the family sounds Scottish as they're always sent off to posh boarding schools almost as soon as they can walk. 'I would love to tell you that it is unusual for the time of year, but that would be a lie,' he continues.

A ripple of polite laughter goes around the room. I discreetly roll my eyes. Clearly an easily pleased crowd.

'I don't want to hold you up; most of you have come a long way to be here, and I'm sure you're desperate to get on with the no-doubt delicious meal which our staff has prepared for you. I'm going to hand you over to Lady Tabitha of Creaglie,' he indicates Tabitha next to him, absolutely stunning and easily young enough to be his daughter, probably even granddaughter, 'my beautiful wife, who is much better at this kind of thing than me.'

The sequins on her dress sparkle as she stands. She wouldn't look out of place on the red carpet at a film premiere. She must have married him for his money. Absolutely must have. Simply no other possible reason.

'Thank you, Alistair,' she says smoothly. 'I am indeed Lady Tabitha of Creaglie officially, but we don't stand on ceremony here and during your stay you must call us Alistair and Tabitha, please.' She smiles warmly.

'As you know, these next few days are about investigating the castle's ghosts, which have become quite famous over time, though this is the first time the Creaglie family has allowed people in to explore freely, so it is a very rare privilege indeed. Silas, on my right, is a professional ghost hunter. Some of you may recognize him from his online channel and, without meaning to be indelicate, the older ones among you may even remember his TV programme, which was extremely popular in its time, I believe.'

Well before she was even born, I'm sure. Silas smiles modestly. I smile back at him. 'It was a great programme,' I say. I used to like it a lot.

'He will be filming for his online channel "Is There Anybody There?"' Tabitha continues, 'and if things go well, there may even be bigger things in the pipeline on that front, but,' she taps the side of her nose a couple of times and winks, 'I'm afraid that has to remain confidential for now.

'I believe you have all signed waiver forms giving your permission to be filmed. If you have any questions about this, he or I will be happy to answer them. Other than that, I invite you to simply relax and enjoy the surroundings, as well as having a bit of spooky fun.'

She smiles briefly before continuing in a more sombre tone. 'As you will have noticed, the weather was already pretty inclement when most of you arrived a couple of hours ago.' There's a general murmur of agreement. 'It has become worse, and I'm afraid it has made it currently unsafe to bring the rest of the guests,

6

who arrived in Glenvraith across the lake a little later than you. Guest safety and comfort is our priority, so for now we have found rooms on the mainland for them and hopefully they can join us as soon as the weather abates.

'But for you lucky ones who made it,' she continues, her voice becoming warmer, 'you'll have plenty of time to get acquainted with each other over dinner. Most of you have already been shown your rooms and we very much hope you're happy with them; they are beautiful rooms.'

'Stunning,' I agree.

'Your bedroom is your own private space,' Tabitha assures us, 'and no one may come in without permission, except for Butler Donald should you need him, our head housekeeper, Mrs Laroche, and her assistant, Irina, assuming she eventually makes it across with the rest of the guests.

'We obviously want you to enjoy your stay and feel at home, so there aren't many house rules. You may go anywhere you like in the castle, except through doors marked "Private", which are rooms reserved for myself, Alistair and the staff. Nowhere is simply randomly off limits – there are no secrets here. You are our guests, and we want you to feel entirely at home, to behave exactly as you would if you were staying with a beloved family friend.

'Silas will be carrying out various tests, and I believe will be happy to talk to you all about his work. If any of you experiences anything supernatural while you are here, which we very much hope you do, I'm sure he would love to hear about it.'

Silas nods sagely.

'We have planned a few ghost-themed events, which you may attend or not as you wish,' Tabitha explains, 'and we have invited a world-renowned medium to be with us, who won't be joining us for dinner this evening as she is currently upstairs recovering from jet lag.'

A medium! Amazing. What an absolute load of nonsense.

'Most importantly, we want you to simply experience the castle and tell us, and in particular, Silas, about anything unusual you might feel or see. You'll find that while you will experience every modern comfort and convenience, in many other ways, we have not moved into the twenty-first century. There is no mobile signal or wireless internet, partly because of our remote location, but also because we want this place to be a true retreat from the world, the way it always has been for Alistair and his family through countless generations, dating back to the sixteenth century. There *is* a landline, which you may use if you need to contact anyone urgently, though it is located in our quarters so you will need to let us know.

'In summary, we would like you to enjoy the castle and the grounds, though perhaps – given the terrible weather – it might be better to postpone your exploration of the grounds.' Cue another ripple of polite laughter.

'Silas will be working with his camera to record what

you see and do, and he asks that – unless he is interviewing you or asks you a direct question – you try to ignore his presence as much as possible.'

Silas nods again.

Tabitha casts her glance around the table. 'Right! I think that's my spiel done. Thank you for listening and please don't hesitate to ask if you have any questions. We hope you'll bear with us if some things are a little makeshift at some points; we're a couple of staff members down, as I mentioned. We're very much looking forward to getting to know you over the weekend.'

## 8 November 2025, 8 p.m.
Kayla

I don't think I've ever experienced a dinner quite like the one we are being served this evening.

A gong sounds before the starter is brought in. Each course is announced in great detail by Alistair or Joshua Creaglie, who both apologize profusely in advance for the lack of staff. The under-butlers, who would usually tell us what we are eating, are also, apparently, stuck on the other side of the lake, along with the chef. But fortunately most of this evening's meal preparation had been done in advance, Alistair explains. And you'd certainly never guess that the chef was absent.

The announcement of each course is hardly necessary anyway, as the menu is printed out in elaborate cursive on thick pieces of creamy gilt-edged card, placed between the shiny rows of cutlery at each place. I am glad that I learned at some point you start with the outer set of cutlery and work inwards, though I spot one of the other guests, an older lady whose name I've forgotten, glancing around the table at the others before picking hers up to check she is aiming for the right ones.

Somehow, even without their usual complement of staff, what they have produced is absolutely incredible. Our starter is a chicory and chestnut winter salad, all produce from the castle's own vegetable garden and orchard. 'We aim for eighty per cent of the food that you eat during your stay to come from our own land,' Joshua says.

The main course is a haggis, 'piped in' by multi-tasking butler Donald, who seems to be something of a dab hand at playing the instrument. Haggis is actually much less unpleasant than you might imagine that something made of a sheep's stomach would be. Alistair proudly informs us that the entire dish comes from sheep raised on the island, which I know in theory is a good thing, low food miles and all that, but somehow makes me feel a little queasy. Dessert is several giant chocolate fountains placed on the table, with platters of fruit and marshmallows (homemade, of course) for dipping.

I am seated next to Ben on one side, a travel writer for one of the national papers, here to experience the hotel, and apparently not interested in the ghostly side of things at all. On my other side, and much more interesting to talk to, is Silas the ghost hunter, who is sweetly humble and earnest and speaks softly about the 'honour' of coming to investigate the ghosts of Creaglie Castle.

11

'You'll know the stories, of course?' he asks quietly.

I shake my head. 'I don't,' I lie. I have actually researched the Creaglies very thoroughly, and in doing so couldn't help but come across the ghost stories. But I don't want to talk about that. 'I came mainly for the spa,' I add, also a lie, though it is a nice added extra and I am definitely planning to use it. 'And I was hoping to do some hiking. But looking at the weather, I don't think that's likely to be possible. So maybe I'll get involved in your . . . ghost things after all.' I don't really want to, but neither do I want to offend him. He seems nice.

'I see,' he says earnestly. 'But when it comes to the ghosts . . . you're a believer?' he asks.

I've never thought about it in any great detail but, being put on the spot, I think I'd be inclined to say I *didn't* believe in ghosts. However, this gentle, bearded man seems to have devoted his life to the supernatural, and it would be churlish to say that I think he is wasting his time. So I prevaricate. 'I think, like many, I'm on the fence. Perhaps I'll learn more while I'm here and, who knows? I may even be able to decide one way or the other.' I pause. 'I'd love to hear about the stories that are told about the castle,' I add, because, why not? What's the harm? 'What kind of things have happened here? Do they know who the ghosts . . . are?'

He takes a mouthful of the meat and chews thoughtfully. 'Well,' he says, 'there have been many, many reports of ghosts in Creaglie Castle going back hundreds of years. The fantastic thing about a property like this place, one which has stayed in the same family for many, many generations, is that there are plenty of records. Family bibles, family trees, diaries and journals, records of births, deaths, marriages and christenings, as well as, of course, simple legends which are passed around orally, and down through the generations. So sometimes it is a little difficult to know which are myths, and which stories come from actual experiences.'

He becomes more and more animated as he talks, clearly warming to his theme. 'So for now, so as not to bore you, I'll stick to the ghosts which have been experienced several times. The first are the cries of a child, a girl, usually experienced at night. They seem to have started at some point in the sixteenth century, almost as far back as the castle records go.'

Well, that could easily be a fox, I think to myself.

'And sometimes she is heard singing a nursery rhyme to herself,' he adds.

Yikes. That's a bit more creepy. Though also a little clichéd.

'The second is a grey-clad lady who appears to descend a stairwell which is no longer in existence,' he says. 'Legend has it that she is a maid who was made pregnant by the master of the house in the late 1600s, and then killed by him to cover up their affair.'

In spite of myself and the heat of the room with the fire blazing, I shiver. 'Wow, that sounds eerie. And – erm – criminal.'

He nods. 'It does. Though according to *official* records, as far as I understand, the lady in question died naturally of influenza, and there is no record of her being pregnant at the time. So it may simply be a myth, and the grey lady may be someone else entirely. If,' he pauses, 'she exists at all, of course.' He looks thoughtful as he takes a sip of his wine.

'Just because I happen to believe strongly that there is something out there beyond death, and that there are presences which return to visit us from beyond the grave, it doesn't mean that I also believe every tale I am told. Unlike some of my colleagues,' he adds, chuckling lightly and sighing gently to himself. 'Either way, I am very much hoping to see the grey lady during our stay but . . . well, visual apparitions are the most rare, so I don't hold out too much hope.'

He takes another bite, chews and swallows before continuing. 'There have also been reports of a poltergeist which throws things down the main staircase, and some attribute that to the same spirit. There was once a large portrait of her alleged abuser hanging above the staircase, which fell, badly injuring a member of the family. I believe that's where those particular rumours started.'

'Wow. Interesting,' I say, sincerely. I don't believe a word of it, but I always love listening to anyone who is passionate about something.

'There are, of course, other explanations as to how things might come to fall, for example, an old picture might come loose from a potentially crumbling wall,' he adds, and momentarily I feel bad because I wonder if he has sensed my scepticism, 'and they may have value, of course. But equally, the possibility remains that there *is* something supernatural going on here. We should come with open minds, and be here to investigate all possibilities.'

I like Silas. I didn't expect to, I thought he'd be some kind of tin-hat-wearing lunatic, but he's actually really interesting. He takes another mouthful and swallows. 'Mmmm. This is good, isn't it? As long as you're not a sheep,' he adds, chuckling to himself again. He finishes the last of the food on his plate and places his knife and fork neatly together.

After dinner I am shown to my room by the uniformed housekeeper, Mrs Laroche. I was last to arrive; the others were already heading to the table as I came to the door and I didn't want to hold things up. I'm in the Red Room – all the rooms are named after colours – and I see my luggage has already been brought up and unpacked for me. There's a double four-poster bed with twisted wooden posts spiralling upwards and heavy brocade drapes, which are tied back with large swags of the same material. The room is wood-panelled and the floor-length curtains, which are in the same pattern as those on the bed, have already been closed against the dark and rain. A fire is crackling away in the fireplace and for a second I wonder if there is no central heating, but a quick glance around the room shows a couple of those old-fashioned radiators attached to the wall. I walk over to one and place my hand on it – it's warm. I'm relieved, because it was absolutely freezing on the journey here and I'm pretty sure a few fireplaces wouldn't be enough to keep a place this huge toasty – I hate the cold.

'The bed is original, and Queen Victoria once slept in this very one,' the housekeeper tells me. 'But you'll be relieved to hear that all the mattresses have recently been upgraded and are now hotel quality, plus the beds have goose-down mattress toppers and duvets. We will light the fire for you every morning and, with your permission, will come in at intervals throughout the day to keep it stoked. We have central heating now, of course, but the rooms are large and we feel the fires make them feel cosier. Everything you need has been provided, though,' she indicates a pile of logs to the side of the fireplace, 'should you wish to tend to the fire at any other time yourself, or you can always summon someone to do it using this bell.' She indicates a button inscribed with the word 'HELP' in capitals to the right of the mantelpiece; it is thoroughly modern and somewhat at odds with the rest of the room.

I follow her as she walks over to the far corner where there is a panelled wooden door.

'This is your bathroom,' she says, opening the door. It's beautiful, if somewhat impractical, with a large marble plinth set with twin sinks, their gold taps shaped like dolphins, and an enormous clawfoot bath, which looks as if it would take days to fill, in the middle of the room. Unless it's tucked away somewhere, there's no shower.

'It all looks lovely,' I say. 'Thank you.'

'I'll leave you to get settled in here,' the housekeeper

says. 'If you need anything, the easiest thing is to press the help button to let me, Donald or the housemaid know, assuming she actually gets here,' she adds, in a tone which seems to imply that the housemaid is simply using the weather as an excuse for bunking off work. 'Otherwise you can leave a note in your room to be picked up during your daily clean. Do you have any questions?' she asks, somewhat brusquely.

I shake my head. 'Thank you. No, that's all very clear.'

'Good. Like I said, if there's anything you need, just ask. The first ghost hunt is later tonight. As you know, attendance is not obligatory, but if you'd like to come along, and we very much hope you will, we'll be meeting in the entrance hall at midnight.'

## 8 November 2025, midnight
Ben

I don't believe in ghosts; I mean, really, who does? But I'm here to research a piece about the castle and its new offering, so I will need to go to the ghost hunt to write about it for those who do believe in that kind of stuff. I don't mind, I've done far worse on trips in my time, and this place is at least a fabulous place to stay, so there's that too. But my job isn't exactly secure at the moment, and the paper I work for loves minor nobility – in fact, for all I know, the laird is quite possibly an old friend of the paper's managing director or some such, so I need to do a good job. I'm told the family asked for me especially, which is nice. But it's not as if I'm going to be able to write about the deer-stalking and hiking as planned, the weather being the way it is, and I will need to make sure I meet my word count somehow.

I make my way to the hallway, down the enormous wooden stairs with their plush carpet, literally as the clock strikes midnight. There are two suits of armour at the base of the stairs, a stuffed stag's head above the main door, and a couple of crossed swords on display on another wall, along with various pictures of people who I assume are the Creaglie ancestors. They all have an expression like someone has farted near them and they think it is probably you.

There is no electric light on in the hallway – instead a couple of large flambeaux in metal holders are burning either side of the huge arched and wooden-studded double front doors. A candelabra hangs from the ceiling, which they surely must have had to use a ladder to light, and there are enormous votive candles burning on every surface. It's pretty dramatic-looking – I hope they've got some good pics they can let me use. I imagine they have – Tabitha seemed pretty savvy with her marketing when we were arranging the details. I wonder if she worked in PR before she married the old guy? I was meant to be with a photographer, but he got stuck on the other side of the lake. Which again makes me wonder if part of my assignment is to do the castle a favour – there's not usually a budget to send a snapper on trips like these any more.

With a wind howling outside which makes the candles flicker and sputter – the castle is draughtier than you'd expect, given it's so luxe – the effect is already pretty spooky. Perhaps they've sneakily left a window open to add to the atmosphere. The Laird and Lady of Creaglie must be delighted that the storm turned up today – you can't pay for that kind of backdrop.

I look down to see who else has turned up for this evening's main event – looks like it's just about everyone. I hope Kayla is going to come. We had a chat at dinner and I think she fancies me. She's a single mum and I hate kids, but it's not like we have to get married, is it? Might be nice to have some fun together this weekend to pass the time, as it looks like we're all going to be stuck inside.

Tabitha looks up at me from the hall – she's still in the tight black dress she wore at dinner and is fit as. She must have married the laird for his money, surely? He's not even one of those old guys who looks like he still runs marathons or anything; he's skinny, a little stooped, kind of shuffles rather than strides. She must be way less than half his age and could have anyone she wants, looking like that. I certainly wouldn't say no in any other circumstances. But my editor had words with me after what happened on the last trip and told me that if any similar stories reached her I would very much not be working for them any more, so I won't be going there.

'Ben!' she calls up at me, smiling; did I catch the hint of a mischievous glimmer in her eye? 'There you are. Are you joining us this evening? Hurry up, we're about to set off.'

I saunter down the rest of the staircase and head over to her, taking one of the small black torches she is handing out to everyone and making sure I 'accidentally' brush her fingers with mine (because there's no harm in a bit of flirtation, is there?) as I take one. I'm sure she noticed, even though she was pretending she was checking everyone had their torch and knew how to work it – you twist the top, it's not exactly rocket science.

That beardy ghost-hunter bloke is fully kitted out in sensible walking boots and a woolly jumper which looks like his wife or mum probably knitted it, and he has all sorts of things hanging around his neck which look like tape recorders only a bit different.

The Laird of Creaglie – or Alistair, as I need to remember to call him; I'm not impressed by people because they're posh, of course I'm not – walks up the staircase a few steps and clears his throat. 'Ladies and gentlemen, I hope you enjoyed your dinner. Thank you once again for your company here tonight – I'm thrilled that so many of you have turned out for the first ghost hunt of your stay. We are aware that it has been a long day for you all, and for that reason we are going to keep this one short. Joshua will be talking a little about the history of the house and the ghosts which are believed to reside here with us, and Silas will be happy to explain some of his craft as we go for anyone who is interested. As I'm sure you will all know, supernatural beings are a law unto themselves and nothing can ever be guaranteed, but given the plethora of spirits we have here in the castle, I think it's likely that some of you will meet some of them in some form or another during your stay. Thank you again for coming. I'm going to hand you over to Joshua now.'

'Thank you,' says Joshua. 'Right, if everyone is ready,

we're going to start with the cellar tonight. Can I please ask that you stay together as a group? If you feel frightened or want to leave at any time and relax upstairs or go back to your room, of course that is fine, but please tell myself, my father, Tabitha or Silas first so that we can be sure that no one gets lost – it is very dark and a little bit of a warren down there. We would ask for quiet where possible, to ensure that we can see and hear anything which might occur, though please do ask any questions at any time as you wish.'

He pauses and casts his eye over the small assembled group. 'Ready? Then let's begin.'

A hush falls as Joshua Creaglie leads us out of the hallway and along a corridor which is dimly lit by candlelight. As we reach the end, he stops by a large wooden door and we all follow suit and come to a halt.

'I would ask you to switch on your torches now,' he says in a low voice, 'and be careful where you tread on the way down – the stairs are steep, and the steps are not always regular.

'Our cellar is quite famous, not only for its ghost, but for the wine. We have eight hundred bottles down here and some are more than a century old. That is why there is no artificial lighting – it can damage the wine.'

I make a mental note to mention this in my article – our readers love that kind of thing.

'If everyone is ready, we'll go downstairs.'

The large door creaks as he opens it. As we descend the stairs, the ceiling ahead gets lower and the temperature drops. At the bottom of the stairs I feel my heart start to beat faster. We walk in a line along a narrow, damp-smelling corridor, which eventually opens out into a large dome-shaped room, lined with wine racks laden with bottles.

And then I feel it. As I step into the centre of the room, a sense of dread, pure evil. I've never felt anything like it before. I gasp and look around at the others; I am quite clearly not the only person feeling uncomfortable.

'I don't like this,' says a dowdy-looking woman in a voice which is barely more than a whisper. I think she said her stay had been given to her as a birthday present, and maybe her name is Rosie or something like that. I don't know – she's old and I wasn't really listening to what she was saying. 'I'd like to go back upstairs now.'

'Not a problem,' Tabitha says smoothly. 'I'll come with you. I know many people find this room particularly unsettling, even those who are quite used to the castle. Anyone else want to bail out now?'

The rest of us glance nervously at each other. I really, really want to go back upstairs, get away from this awful, awful feeling, but I don't want to look like a twat. I take a deep breath. I'm being ridiculous. There is no such thing as pure evil, no such thing as ghosts. I need to stay here, otherwise I'll look like a knob in front of all these people. And who knows, someone on the travel desk might eventually watch Silas's video thing and know that I was practically wetting my pants over the prospect of something a bit spooky.

Joshua clears his throat. 'Right. As you will have

23

noticed, this room very rapidly makes many people feel extremely uncomfortable.'

Christ. That's an understatement. My heart is racing, sweat is prickling in my armpits. I feel like I might throw up or pass out.

'Some find it difficult to stay in the room at all,' he continues, 'as you saw with our friend Rosemary feeling that she needed to leave. So, tell me, what are you feeling at the moment?'

'Anxious,' someone says.

'Scared,' says someone else.

Evil, I want to say. I feel the presence of evil. But I don't want to look like a dick, so I say nothing.

'It's not a surprise,' Joshua says. 'No one likes to spend too long down here, which is why we thought we'd keep this visit very brief, a taster to launch you into the theme of the weekend. Take a look at these.' He swings his torch around so that its beam falls on the bare stone wall behind him. 'What do you see?'

'Iron rings,' someone says.

'Indeed,' he agrees. 'This was once the castle's dungeon, in medieval times before the castle belonged to our family. The island had more of a population then, because the castle had more staff and there were also tied cottages, which have since fallen into disrepair or been repurposed as outbuildings. And going even further back, before the castle was built, some of the worst offenders from the mainland were imprisoned here in a much simpler building, due to its inaccessibility. Legend has it that some were put in a small cavity right

24

beneath this floor, and simply,' he pauses for effect, 'left to die.'

The dark room is silent. I take a deep breath. I'll grant him this, he's a good storyteller, but I'm not sure how much longer I can bear being down here.

'We don't have full records of exactly who was kept here as a prisoner, or why,' he continues, 'but we do know that some people who came in never left again, except to be tossed in a pauper's grave – without cere- mony – at the edge of the island. If the weather abates, I can show you where some of the bones were found.'

Another awful silence fills the room. I glance around me. No one looks like they are enjoying this, apart from Silas, who is looking at Joshua with rapt attention, as if he has never heard anything more fascinating in this life.

'Right!' Joshua says in a more upbeat tone. 'I think that's probably enough for the time being. How about a nightcap?'

## 9 November 2025, 12.05 a.m.
Amelia

'How are you feeling?' Tabitha asks. The three of us are sitting on a vast, sagging sofa in a living room next to the dining room we ate in earlier. Rosemary picks up the brandy in a huge balloon glass that Donald placed in front of her at Tabitha's insistence, in spite of Rosemary's protestations that she didn't want to make a fuss or cause a scene and she doesn't much like brandy anyway.

'I'm fine, thanks,' I say. 'I'd just had enough of being in the cellar. I didn't leave because I was scared.' I'd followed Rosemary up when she left because I was bored of listening to Joshua pontificating and I knew there was nothing interesting to see down there anyway. 'How about you, Rosemary?'

Rosemary's hands are still shaking as she takes another sip before replacing the glass on the low wooden table.

'I'm a bit embarrassed, to tell you the truth,' she says.

26

'I'm not someone who likes to make a fuss or draw attention to myself. I don't know what came over me. I'm not usually easily frightened. But something about that room . . .' She shudders. 'I don't know. It somehow felt wrong.'

Honestly. Some people are so easily scared. 'There's nothing down there that will hurt you,' I say.

Tabitha rests her hand lightly on Rosemary's arm for a couple of seconds and then removes it. 'Please don't be embarrassed,' she says. 'That room has affected a lot of people in that way; there are plenty of staff – and even family members – who have refused to go down there. It's not that surprising given its history, I guess . . .' she tails off. 'But as you've already clearly had quite a shock, I think that might be a story for another day.'

Rosemary takes another sip of the brandy and smiles weakly.

'This is the first time we've invited the public in, let alone run a ghost hunt so we're still finding our way a little,' Tabitha continues. 'I *did* say to Joshua and Alistair that I thought starting with the cellar might be throwing guests in at the deep end to too great a degree, but they both grew up here and seem almost immune to the creepiness of the castle. They know there are ghosts, of course, but they're so used to them they don't bother them at all. In fact, Alistair says that when he looks back at his childhood, he sometimes finds it difficult to know for sure which of his playmates were imaginary friends and which ones were actually ghosts.'

'He said the same to me,' I say. I had thought Tabitha would be snooty and aloof when I first met her, but she's being really kind to Rosemary after her funny turn and is a much warmer person than I had expected.

Even if she is a gold-digger.

Rosemary takes a final sip of the brandy, draining the glass. 'And what about you?' she asks Tabitha. 'Do you find it creepy?'

She nods slowly, several times. 'When I first came here, very much so. But now I'm more used to the place, not so much. Most of the . . . presences seem pretty benign. They wander around, make a bit of noise sometimes, throw the odd thing, but in some ways they're like children. If you don't pay them too much attention, they soon give up. We rub along fine together. The way I try to look at it is they've been here longer than I have, and they have as much right to be here as I do. But I won't allow myself to be scared by them.' She smiles to herself. 'But enough about me. What about you? How did you come to be here?' she asks.

'My daughter bought me the weekend in a charity auction. She knows I've always been fascinated by other planes, especially since my husband passed and I've been so lonely. This was a birthday present. It was very sweet of her, and I've been really excited about it but, well, I guess I didn't expect to feel quite so alarmed.' She pauses. 'It seems silly now that we're up here just chatting and everything is fine.'

Tabitha shakes her head. 'Not silly at all. I totally understand. Would you like another brandy? Or perhaps something like a herbal tea? If you're sure you're feeling better, I should probably get back to the others, check everything's going OK.'

'I don't want anything else, thank you. I think I'll go to bed, stop being a silly old woman getting in everyone's way.'

Tabitha puts her arm around Rosemary's shoulders and gives her a gentle squeeze. 'You're doing nothing of the sort,' she says. 'I'll get Mrs Laroche to accompany you up to your room to check you find your way OK, if you like?'

She shakes her head. 'No that's fine. I've taken up enough of your time. I'm feeling much better now. I'll see you in the morning.'

**9 November 2025, 9 a.m.**
Kayla

'Did you sleep well?' Alistair asks, buttering a slice of toast.

The breakfast spread is amazing – there are stacks of pancakes with maple syrup, a beautiful platter of cut fruit, smoothie shots, piles of bacon and sausages made from free-range acorn-fed pigs, smoked salmon scattered with chives, plus homemade granola and bircher muesli. Eggs (from the castle's own free-range chickens) are made to order, of course – I asked for mine poached and they arrived perfectly cooked; not a hint of clear white but the bright-orange egg yolks perfectly runny. The other guests who were stuck on the other side of the lake don't seem to have arrived yet, so I guess the chef didn't either. I can only assume that this has all been put together by Donald and Mrs Laroche. Pretty impressive.

'I slept very well, thank you,' I lie. In truth I actually ended up sleeping with the lights on because – even though I don't believe in any of this ghost nonsense they are trying to sell – the house is spooky as fuck and every noise and creak freaked me out.

'That's good to hear,' he says, taking a bite of his toast, a drop of butter running unpleasantly down his chin.

'I'm looking forward to today,' I add. 'What's the plan?'

'We thought we'd do a treasure hunt,' Tabitha says. 'It's a good way to get everyone to explore the castle and learn a bit about its history, hopefully having some fun along the way.'

'That sounds like a good idea,' says the older lady who freaked out in the cellar yesterday – Rosemary, I think her name was? 'I have to admit, the castle feels like a different place in the daylight. I'm so embarrassed about my meltdown yesterday, I must apologize. It's extremely unlike me, honestly.'

Tabitha touches her arm lightly. 'Please don't give it a second thought. We're very aware that the place is creepy, which is exactly why we thought we'd open it up to the public in this way. We know that a lot of people are interested in the supernatural, but perhaps we need to warn people a little more strongly about what to expect. Make sure people are prepared.'

'Did your instruments show up anything last night, Silas?' I ask brightly, fully expecting him to say 'no'. Of course people felt freaked out, Joshua was laying it on pretty thick. But it doesn't mean that anything was actually happening down there.

Silas frowns. 'Well, there was definitely a drop in temperature, but that's to be expected in a cellar, of course. The EVP recorder didn't pick up anything definite, but it wasn't very quiet as Joshua was recounting the history of the place and there were general noises of people moving about, so we might not have noticed if—'

'What's EVP?' I ask.

'Electronic voice phenomena,' intones Silas gravely. 'An EVP recorder can pick up voices from beyond the grave.'

I can't hold in a smirk. 'Seriously?' I ask. 'You actually hear things on it? Like a radio?'

He nods. 'Yes. It can pick up noises outside of what a normal tape recorder would, or what the human ear can discern. So, though we didn't hear anything specific last night, that isn't hugely surprising with so many people there and all the hubbub which was going on. But I left it behind once we'd finished and haven't had a chance to listen back yet. I've left one in my room today too; if I left it on overnight, I fear all I'd hear is my own snoring.'

He chuckles to himself.

'I have to admit, though, having been a paranormal investigator for more than thirty years now, that presence is one of the strongest I've felt for a long time. And not a particularly pleasant one at that. I'm looking forward to the séance later, see if we can learn more about who or what is behind it.'

'The séance?' repeats Rosemary. 'That's still on the agenda?'

'As with everything during your stay, there's no need

32

to take part if you don't wish to,' Tabitha reassures, 'but I know Silas is very keen that it goes ahead. Séances are very popular with his viewers, apparently.'

'But what if it . . . stirs up evil spirits?' Rosemary asks. 'After how I felt in the cellar last night, I'd be worried that something might . . . harm someone.'

She looks down at her plate and pushes her scrambled egg around it.

'What do you think, Silas?' I ask.

'Spirits can be frightening, there's no doubt about that,' he replies, in a measured tone, 'but I can't think that there are any cast-iron instances of them causing actual physical harm to anyone.' He pauses. 'None whatsoever; at least, none where it has been proved that a supernatural entity was the cause.'

'Yes, but . . . being frightened can be a form of harm, can't it? Mental harm?' Rosemary persists.

'I lived with these spirits for years as a child and, believe me, they're all talk and no action,' Joshua says. 'You get used to them after a while, banging and bumping around. Sometimes knocking things over or blowing windows open, that kind of thing. They never actually do anything meaningful or even very frightening, honestly.'

He takes a bite of his avocado toast. 'But you absolutely don't have to take part in the séance, Rosemary, if you don't want to,' he continues, 'and if you're feeling uncomfortable, I'm quite happy to try to arrange an early departure for you – our aim is certainly not to make anyone unhappy. Though given the weather . . .'

he glances out of the window where the rain is still falling heavily, 'it wouldn't be possible yet. As you will have noticed, our other guests still haven't been able to get here, so it's unlikely it would be deemed safe to take you off the island unless it's a true emergency.'

Rosemary looks out of the window and sighs. 'I'm sure you're right. And, as you say, I've no real option but to stay. Though I feel much calmer now than I did last night, and I think I would still want to stay even if leaving were possible.'

She turns back to Silas. 'I was planning to try to contact my late husband again during the séance, and I know the medium they've invited has done some amazing work. But with that . . . presence there, the one I felt in the cellar, I'm not sure I want to. I'd be worried in case whatever I felt, it—'

'The one thing I would say,' Silas interjects, 'is that we have very little control over when and how the spirits choose to appear. If your dear departed husband feels that this is the right time and place, you might find he reveals himself to you anyway, séance or not. It might not be via a physical entity, a voice, or anything like a séance. It could simply be a sign, a smell or a feeling. Many people find it a comfort, a blessing. Given that the castle has a history of hauntings, it would seem it is a place where the spirit and the living world are close – a thin place, if you will. So it's perhaps more likely that he would make his presence felt to you here than when you are at home, as it is probably less closely connected to the spirit world.'

'Thank you,' Rosemary says. 'I have visited a couple of psychics and tried to contact him but, so far, nothing has worked. If you think it's safe, I would like to try again here.'

Silas pats her hand in an avuncular way. 'I guarantee it will be safe. Spirits can't hurt you. And the medium is world-renowned, she's come in especially from America. We'll all be here to support you, and you'll be in very good hands.'

**9 November 2025, 10 a.m.**
Ben

The treasure hunt is quite fun – I make sure I'm paired up with Kayla. We are about the same age and she's pretty fit. Clearly looks after herself.

I flirt gently with her as we solve the clues to retrieve objects and trinkets from around the castle. I think she likes me. I know I need to behave myself this week-end – this is work, after all – but there's no harm in having a little bit of fun, is there? And no one will know what we get up to in our bedrooms, should it come to that, will they? I push the thought away. I need to behave myself.

I'm relieved that we're not sent back to the cellar again today. Not that I'd admit it to anyone, but I don't think I'd go back in there if you paid me. The trail takes us through the vast kitchens to retrieve a lemon, into the boot room to grab a walking stick, along to the library with its impressive floor-to-ceiling book-shelves to find an ancient copy of a play by Shakespeare, who is, apparently, rumoured to have once stayed here, which is a nice detail for my article. I read the latest clue aloud to Kayla:

> *Draw close and listen, gentle soul,*
> *Your search continues with noble goal;*
> *To find a shoe, so tiny and neat,*
> *expressly made for dainty feet.*
> *White slipper soft, of thread and lace,*
> *Is put away in a tranquil place;*
> *Where children play and take their rest,*
> *Can you solve this puzzling test?*

'A baby bootee!' Kayla cries. 'Got to be. I know where the nursery is! It's just up the stairs from my room. I saw it when I was having a look around the place yesterday – I'll show you.'

We go up the main staircase, along the corridor and then up a narrower set of steps which leads into a small room in the eaves.

As soon as we step through the door, I feel the temperature drop. There's an atmosphere – not as strong as it was in the cellar, but it's there even so. I glance at Kayla, who seems entirely unbothered and is happily drifting around the room, lifting pillows and moving toys, looking for a bootee.

The room is dim, its only windows small and high up so you can't see out. Their glass looks thin and old. The windows are not double-glazed up here as they are in other parts of the castle, and the room is draughty.

There's an old-fashioned crib in the centre, all made up with white baby bed linen and topped with a white steeple-shaped canopy. There's a steely-eyed rocking horse in the corner and I feel my heart rate quicken – it looks like the kind of thing which would start moving on its own in a horror movie. I take a deep breath – that's not going to happen, I tell myself. It's all fine. Let's find the bootee and get out of here.

'Help me look!' Kayla cries – she seems to be really starting to enjoy this, to the point of actually getting quite competitive about it – and I force myself to get out of my zoned-out state and start moving. The quicker we find this thing, the faster we can get out of this room.

I open a cupboard and yelp as, I kid you not, a toy which is basically a Chucky doll from that ancient horror film appears to launch itself at me.

'Fuck's sake,' I mutter, picking it up and flinging it back onto the top shelf of the cupboard. I can't let Kayla see how freaked out I am by this whole thing, it's not a good look on any level. But it's pretty hard to keep how I feel under wraps – I'm not enjoying this at all. I scan the rest of the cupboard. On the shelves sit a series of eyeless ceramic dolls in Victorian dresses, which do nothing to help my state of mind, but no bootees.

I open the next cupboard which, thank Christ, is full of frilly white and pink clothes and spot a line of tiny soft white boots on the bottom shelf.

'Got one!' I say, grabbing it. 'Now let's go.'

'Brilliant!' Kayla smiles. 'I was tempted to bunk off and go to the spa this morning, but I'm glad I didn't – this is fun, isn't it?'

Fun? No. It's horrible. I wish with all my heart I could be out doing the fifteen-mile hike I was meant to be doing – if the weather had been even slightly less horrendous, I would be out there sucking up the cold, but it's dangerous and irresponsible to hike in this kind of storm, especially alone. I can't go back to my editor with nothing though, so I'm going to have to throw myself into this awful ghost hunting. I thought it would simply be stupid and pointless, but it's actually really creeping me out.

'What's next on the list?' I ask. 'What's the next clue?' I don't actually care. I just want to be away from this room, which seems almost as bad as the cellar, for reasons I can't quite put my finger on. Ideally I'd like to be away from this castle, basically anywhere at all, but there's no chance of that right now.

There are a few moments of silence as Kayla fumbles in her pocket for the sheet of paper. The wind continues to howl outside, and the leaking thin windows are making the curtains move in the draught. What a horrible, horrible room for a baby. Surely you'd grow up traumatized after sleeping in a room like this as a child? Sweat starts to prickle on my forehead.

And then I hear it.

The breathy sound of a child singing.

Kayla and I look at each other and bolt from the room.

39

We charge down the stairs and along the corridor, passing Joshua and Rosemary, who look at us in surprise, only stopping when we get to the top of the main staircase.

'What the fuck was that?' I say, trying to keep the wobble out of my voice. 'You heard it too?'

She is wide-eyed. I wonder about putting my arm around her, but perhaps it's too soon.

'Yeah. I heard it. Creepy as,' she says, nonchalantly.

'Do you think it was . . .'

She laughs. 'A ghost? No. Of course not. Probably one of the others playing a trick on us.'

The ghost-hunter guy is at the base of the stairs and looks up at us. Maybe sensing that something is going on, he heads up towards us. 'Did something happen?' he asks.

'Yes,' I say, at the same time Kayla says, 'No.'

He raises an eyebrow.

'It sounded like a child singing,' I say, 'but perhaps it was one of the others messing about.'

I don't tell him about the feeling I had there. It wasn't as strong as what I felt in the cellar, nowhere near, but there was definitely something unsettling about that room too. But I'm not going to ruin my chances with Kayla by saying something like that in front of her. And now that I'm away from it, perhaps it was just the creepy dolls, the storm, the Chucky toy. They probably set it up like that to give us a scare. That's all it was. Nothing.

'Interesting,' Silas says. 'I'm going to go and take a

look and do some general shots of the room and then Ben, maybe I can interview you in the nursery about what you think you heard?'

'Yep, no problem,' I say. 'I'll come back up with you now.' I don't want to go back in the room at all, but I'm not going to say that. I'll look like a total dick, and look at Kayla! She didn't appear to be bothered by it at all.

'No, you go on and finish the hunt,' Silas says. 'I don't want to interrupt your fun.'

Fun! Hardly.

'I'll get my room shots now and we can do the interview there later on,' he continues. 'It'll be better in the dark. I'll put you in a spotlight. More atmospheric. The viewers love that.'

I hadn't thought this through – I don't want to have to go back into that creepy room in the dark. That sounds way worse.

Fuck.

**9 November 2025, 9.30 p.m.**
Kayla

I'm surprised to see that absolutely everyone has turned up for the séance this evening. I had thought that people might have had enough of ghostly stuff after Rosemary freaked out in the cellar last night, and then the weird singing in the nursery, but apparently not. Everyone is here.

I watched over Silas's shoulder when he was listening back to the interview he did with Ben. The vague, indistinct voice in the nursery we heard had somehow become an entire nursery rhyme by the time of the interview, as well as a doll flinging itself across the room and even a window blowing open.

The singing . . . yes, it happened. I think. It was spooky, but there is always a rational explanation for these things. The doll and the window, I don't remember. Part of me wonders if Ben is padding his part a little so he has something interesting to write in his feature. And I get the impression from a few things he alluded to earlier that he's on somewhat shaky ground at work. So he'll be keen to come up with something good.

The séance is taking place in the library. A red cloth has been placed over a small round table. The room is lit only by candles – they must be singlehandedly keeping the beeswax industry in business here – and there is so much incense burning it's making my nose itch. We are seated close to each other at the table, and in the centre there is a wooden board with letters, and the words 'yes' and 'no' on either side.

The medium is a complete cliché, a huge woman apparently named Elvira (yeah right; real name probably Elsie or Elaine or something like that). She is dressed in robes and has a black scarf tied around her head with little gold moons and stars woven into the tassels. She looks very different to when I saw her talking to Tabitha in the kitchen yesterday, just after her arrival and before she retired upstairs to 'prepare and to tune in to the spirits', as I overheard her say. Then she was dressed in unflattering jeans and a pastel rainbow jumper, and had been complaining to Tabitha about what a nightmare it had been getting here through the snow, and how badly she was suffering from jet lag, and thank God she'd insisted on staying the night both before and after the séance as part of the package as there was no way she was risking trying to get back to the airport this evening in such awful conditions.

Now she is sitting up straight in her chair, eyes closed, and the rest of us are gathered around the table in silence. She opens her eyes.

'Everything is set, and I am ready to receive the spirits,' she says in an American drawl which sounds like it's from the Deep South. 'Can I ask that y'all join hands, and then we'll begin.'

We lift our hands onto the table and join them in a circle. I am next to Ben on one side, and Alistair on the other, whose hands are too soft and small for a man's as well as unpleasantly damp.

I'm surprised to see Rosemary has come along for the séance tonight – I guess she has decided that she is more interested in contacting her late husband than she is worried about evil spirits. Silas's camera is on a tripod, set to record the action. There was a lengthy discussion before we all sat down, as Silas wanted to stand up and be behind his camera so he could see what he was filming and observe what was happening during the séance impartially, as he apparently usually does in his videos, but Elvira was adamant that no one could be in the room who was not participating in the séance.

'It's extremely disruptive for the spirits,' she says. 'They can be very temperamental. They need to know that everyone present is ready to accept them and ready to listen, otherwise they might not appear at all.'

In spite of Silas's generally mild-mannered demeanour, you can almost feel his annoyance radiating off him as he sets up his camera on a tripod and fiddles about with it. He arranges a few other instruments on a nearby surface and eventually takes his place at the table.

Elvira starts making a low humming noise in the back of her throat, the windows rattle and a draught

44

blows through the room, extinguishing a couple of the candles.

I glance around the table. Most of the guests except Silas are looking a little uncomfortable, but Rosemary looks absolutely terrified.

Elvira stops humming and her eyes snap open. 'I feel a presence,' she says. 'I would ask y'all to unclasp your hands and each rest one finger on the planchette on the spirit board,' she says, lifting her arm slowly in an over-dramatic gesture to rest a pudgy finger with a purple-painted nail on the flat, triangular wooden object in the middle of the board.

She closes her eyes again and takes a deep breath in through her nose. 'Is there anybody theeeerrrrrre?' she intones in an almost comically deep voice. 'Is there anybody theerrrrrrrre?' The room is silent. Nothing happens. I hold my breath, not entirely sure what I feel about this. It's not exactly scary, but it's definitely weird, and if I'm honest with myself, I do feel a little nervous.

And then, I feel a movement. Rosemary lets out what sounds like a small squeak as the flat wooden shape begins to move, slowly but surely towards where 'yes' is written at the edge of the board and then back to the centre.

I look up, wondering who is moving it, but everyone is staring at the planchette, some in what looks like simple surprise, others (especially Rosemary and Ben) in horror. Except Tabitha. She holds my gaze, expressionless, for slightly longer than feels comfortable or natural, and then looks down at the centre of the table.

45

Perhaps she is moving the thing?

'Do you have a message for somebody here?' Elvira asks in the same spooky-sitcom tone. Again there is a brief pause before the planchette makes its slow journey over to 'yes' and back again.

'You have a message, spirit, and we are ready to listen. Can you tell us your name?'

The planchette starts to move, faster now. 'D. A.', it spells out. I have to admit, I am mesmerized, and my legs feel weirdly wobbly, even though I am sitting down. Rosemary's free hand flies to her mouth, but her other finger remains on the planchette, which is still moving as it points out 'V' then 'E'.

By now every single person around the table, even Tabitha, is wide-eyed. 'Welcome, Dave,' Elvira intones, closing her eyes again. 'We are listening. Who is your message for?'

'It's my Dave,' Rosemary squeaks, tears running down her cheeks. 'He's here. I knew he'd come back to me.'

## 9 November 2025, 10 p.m.
Ben

Fucking hell. I didn't think I believed in any of this, but right now I feel like I might throw up. This is absolutely terrifying. I will someone to make a joke, to break the tension, but nothing happens, everyone is completely silent. Should it be me? Should I say something? I don't think I can. I feel like I might burst into tears if I open my mouth.

I take a deep breath. Don't be ridiculous, I tell myself. This is all a show. Think of it as immersive theatre. I wasn't pushing that wooden thing, but chances are someone else was. Maybe Rosemary, who's so desperate to speak to her dear departed husband that she might be moving it without even knowing she's doing so. That could happen, couldn't it? Or this mad old bat Elvira might be doing it because she knows she's more likely to get another booking if she delivers the goods, and the Creaglies have probably got a bit of money to shell out on these weekends to make sure they're a success.

Maybe Silas, to make his video more interesting. Or one of the hosts to make their inaugural ghost weekend properly spooky. Any of the others just for fun. Could be anyone. I glance at Silas, who probably looks the least shocked of everyone, but I guess this is all in a day's work for him.

'Is everyone OK?' Tabitha asks softly. 'If anyone is feeling uncomfortable then say the word and we can step away and—'

'No!' Elvira shouts, making everyone around the table visibly jump. 'We do *not* walk away from the spirits when they want to converse. There is nothing to fear. Stay seated and calm and I will continue the session.'

Christ. Who does she think she is, bossing everyone around like that? I swallow hard, willing myself not to cry. I am hating this.

Tabitha whispers 'sorry' in a barely audible voice and sits up a little straighter.

'If y'all can put your fingers back on the planchette,' Elvira says, 'then we can continue.'

I fight down the urge to simply leave – I'm an adult, after all, and can surely do what I like? But then I might look like I'm scared, and anyone watching Silas's video could think that and if it gets back to my editor that I've caused a scene then . . . no. I need to stay. Man up, I tell myself. I put my finger back on the planchette.

'Dave,' the woman intones in a deep, serious-sounding voice. 'We welcome you. You are among friends. Do you have a message for someone here today?'

There is a sharp intake of breath around the table as the wooden thing moves towards the 'yes' point and then back to the centre. I look at Rosemary, who still has tears coursing down her cheeks.

'Is your message for Rosemary?' Elvira asks in the same stupid, melodramatic tone. This time the thing moves in the opposite direction, towards 'no'.

Rosemary starts to cry harder. 'But why would . . .?' she starts to ask, plaintively, before being abruptly shushed by Elvira. I see Tabitha check that Elvira's eyes are still closed before letting go of the planchette and giving Rosemary's arm a gentle pat.

'The spirits move in mysterious ways,' Elvira snaps, her eyes still closed. Poor Rosemary stares in horror as the thing moves back to the centre of the table. I glance around the room at each person in turn. I try to concentrate on the movement of the thing. Does it feel more like it's being pushed or pulled? Is there any way of telling where the pressure is coming from?

Elvira starts up with some kind of humming sound. Her eyes are still closed. Rosemary is now quietly sobbing. Alistair glances at his watch. Silas looks over his shoulder at his camera and then back at the table. Everyone else is still staring vaguely at the table with fairly neutral expressions.

Christ. Am I the only one other than Rosemary who feels at all freaked out by this?

Elvira starts to sway as her hum becomes more akin to a groan. She lifts her finger off the planchette and we all follow suit.

Is it my imagination, or has the room suddenly got colder? I feel a draught on the back of my neck and notice that the window has blown open. Or has it been open all the time? I can't remember. I feel hot and clammy and wipe my hands on my trousers before sliding them under my thighs to stop myself fidgeting. I can't wait for this to be over.

Elvira makes a sudden high-pitched noise and everyone turns to look at her.

'Someone here has been wronged,' she growls, and for a few seconds I honestly think I might wet myself. She doesn't sound like she did before; her voice is deep and manly, like the ones which do the voiceovers for trailers in the cinema. Everyone is paying attention now. Rosemary has stopped crying and is now staring at Elvira in what looks like terrified awe.

'And somebody must pay.'

**9 November 2025, 10.30 p.m.**
Amelia

I look around the room. I'm amazed that everyone is taking this so seriously.

'Oh come on!' I say, throwing my hands up in the air. I mean, this is a joke, right? No one actually believes any of this, do they? The old lady in all her robes and that stupid deep voice, swaying and moaning, straight out of central casting. Utterly ridiculous.

But everyone else seems to be in varying degrees of shock or terror. Rosemary is now sobbing so hard her shoulders are shaking. I notice Tabitha glance at Elvira with what I take to be a 'what the fuck, why are you upsetting our guests like this? – this is not what you are being paid for' expression, which she quickly re-arranges into something more bland. Even Silas the ghost hunter looks pretty unsettled, and surely he should be used to this kind of thing?

Rosemary makes a noise somewhere between a cry and a yelp, gets up and darts from the room.

'DO NOT BREAK THE CIRCLE!' Elvira booms in that stupid voice again.

'Fuck this, someone should go and see if Rosemary's OK,' Ben mutters, ignoring Elvira completely and standing up.

'I'll go,' Tabitha says, also rising, 'I know she was feeling a bit shaky last night, and this is not going to have helped.'

Elvira opens her eyes and looks around the table. 'The spirit is unhappy that the circle has been broken,' she intones. 'It has gone from me, but I feel it is still in the room. I feel their business here is not complete.'

This is ridiculous.

'I think that's enough for tonight, isn't it?' says Kayla. 'I for one could do with a drink anyway.'

'Definitely,' I agree.

'I'm just popping upstairs for an instant to use the facilities,' says Alistair, 'but in the meantime, Mrs Laroche, could you organize some drinks?' The house-keeper seems to have appeared from nowhere, perhaps alerted by the commotion of Rosemary rushing out.

'Have we got any amaretto?' Tabitha asks from the doorway. 'I fancy something like that.'

'And perhaps some of our house cocktails?' Joshua suggests. 'Why don't we all reconvene back here in about ten minutes?'

'If you'll all excuse me,' Silas says, 'there were some very interesting phenomena going on there and I'd like to go somewhere quiet to check my recordings and instruments. And to watch all that back to see if I can see . . .' he glances at Elvira, 'see . . . anything.'

Obviously he means he's going to see if he can work out who was pushing the wooden thing around the board. Because clearly someone was. Things like that don't move by themselves.

Do they?

## 9 November 2025, 10.45 p.m.
Kayla

Before I know it, everyone has left the library except for myself and Elvira. I get up and pretend to be looking at the books because I don't want to have to try to make conversation with her – I've no idea what I'd even say. I don't think she realizes that I'm still looking at her. Now that everyone has gone it's even more obvious, to me at least, that the whole thing was a performance. She's gathering up her board and all its accoutrements, her flowing robes and stupid turban thing she's wearing looking faintly ridiculous as she moves like a normal person, instead of all that swaying, grunting and groaning she was doing before. She's probably an out-of-work actress.

The next time I glance at her, she happens to be looking straight at me. It feels rude to look away again, so I say: 'That was all quite . . . interesting. I've never been to a séance before. Is it always like that?'

I see her instantly snap back into character, her movements becoming more fluid and exaggerated, her voice,

54

while no longer the manly boom she was doing a minute ago, deeper than you'd typically expect for a woman. 'The spirits are extremely capricious, my dear,' she says, holding my gaze for too long so that it starts to feel a little uncomfortable. She's probably doing it deliberately. 'One can never presume to predict what will happen,' she adds.

'Don't you find it scary, though?' I ask, warming to my theme. 'I mean, when that man's voice was speaking through you – what does that feel like? Is it like someone's . . . possessed you?'

She gives me a somewhat patronizing smile. 'Not at all. Possession is very, very different, and can be extremely dangerous. I am not possessed. I am a mere channel, through which the spirits communicate. And as I never have any memory of it, it is not frightening, no.'

No memory of it! Yeah, right.

'In fact, I see it as a privilege,' she continues. 'I can allow spirits who have passed over but have unfinished business here on earth to gain closure, as I believe the fashionable expression is now. To help them move on to their next stage, to find peace.'

'But . . . what if they're here to cause harm?' I don't believe anything she is saying for a minute, but I'm interested to hear what she'll say about this. 'I mean, that woman Rosemary, she looked really scared when you were . . . doing the thing. And you said, I mean, the spirit said, that someone had been wronged and that somebody must pay. Isn't that going to be pretty alarming for anyone? Especially when she was just hoping to have a nice reassuring chat with her late hubby.'

She looks at me in what appears to be genuine surprise. Guess I was right about her being an actress – her expression is actually pretty convincing. 'Really, dear?' she asks. 'That's what the spirit said? I am surprised. That is most unusual.' She pauses. 'But very interesting too, as you say.'

'And poor Rosemary genuinely seemed to think it was her husband who was speaking . . . through you.'

'That's not unusual. The spirits often return to give messages to loved ones. Many find it a comfort.'

'She didn't look very comforted to me. She seemed distraught. And the spirit – Dave – said he wasn't here to talk to her anyway. So you'd understand why she'd be upset – he's apparently come all the way back from the dead and it turns out it's not actually to speak to her at all. And he was being pretty threatening.' I'm not going to let this woman get away with randomly distressing some defenceless old woman and making out it's nothing to do with her.

She sighs theatrically. 'Sadly, though it is thankfully rare, that can also happen. But as I said before, the spirits are capricious and I personally have no control over what they say, or how someone might react to it.'

'Riiiiiight,' I say, entirely unconvinced and not afraid to show it. Elvira puts the last of her stupid séance things in a large bag covered with little fragments of mirrors, I imagine to indicate that this is the end of the conversation and that she doesn't wish to continue it. But I'm not going to let her off the hook that easily.

'So, if you were to hazard a guess about what he – it – the spirit – meant by "somebody must pay", what do you think he might have meant?'

She picks up her bag and gives me a withering look. 'I am not here to interpret the spirits.

'As I already said,' she continues, in the kind of tone I imagine she might use to speak to a child asking the same question over and over again, 'I am merely here to act as a conduit through which they can communicate.' She looks at the window where the wind is really howling now, and you can see the rain glinting in the light as it falls. 'It's been lovely chatting with you, dear, but channelling spirits is extremely draining, as I'm sure you can imagine, and I need to go and rest now. I have a long journey ahead of me tomorrow.'

And then there is a scream.

## Silas's voiceover

The year of death was 1830.

The Twelfth Lady of Creaglie was a vain woman, who loved nothing more than importing jewels and elaborate dresses from far-off lands.

She employed several ladies-in-waiting, who were tasked with dressing her every day, arranging her wigs and painting her face. Even though the family rarely had visitors, she would insist on being immaculately attired every single day, with her hair and make-up just so too.

Her husband, the Twelfth Laird of Creaglie, had a dalliance with one of her dressers but then quickly cast her aside.

The Twelfth Lady of Creaglie was never aware of the brief affair, but the dresser became extremely jealous. She encouraged her mistress to whiten her face each day using Laird's Bloom. 'It's what all the high-society ladies in France are using now,' she told her. 'You'll be the envy of all of society.'

But the dresser had a brother who was a chemist. He had told her that some had started to suspect that Laird's Bloom was in fact toxic because of some of its ingredients. The Twelfth Lady of Creaglie eventually died of what is now believed to have been lead poisoning.

She can be seen in a portrait on the second-floor landing, perfectly dressed and made up, as she was in life, and some believe she is one of several ghostly figures who still wanders the castle.

She could, of course, simply be a figment of their imagination, a trick of the light, or the cause of her death could even be a myth.

We'll probably never know for sure.

## 9 November 2025, 11 p.m.
Kayla

'What the hell?' I yelp, the first time I've actually felt properly alarmed since my arrival. That was a real, blood-curdling scream, not someone messing about. There is a male voice shouting and then a woman shrieking.

Fuck. I start to head to the door when Elvira says, 'Wait, no, it might not be safe!'

I ignore her – she really is pathetic. And someone might need help. I walk towards the hallway where I can now hear someone – maybe Tabitha? – crying. Ben is in the hallway holding his phone up in the air, frantically jabbing at it and frowning, clearly trying and failing to get a signal. Others are at various places on the stairs and around the first-floor gallery where our bedrooms are, looking bewildered. As I get to the hall, I see that Rosemary is standing behind Tabitha, holding her shoulder, the other hand to her mouth, while Tabitha is bent, wailing, over a figure lying prone on the floor.

## 9 November 2025, 11 p.m.
Amelia

There suddenly seems to be a lot of noise: people either shouting instructions to someone else, anyone, or screaming, or crying.

I stand there uselessly, frozen to the spot, looking at Tabitha weeping and keening over Alistair, who is lying on the flagstones with, I can see now, blood pooling from his head.

Donald rushes through the hallway – the first time I've seen him look anything other than entirely un-ruffled – and stops at Tabitha's side.

'The landline seems to be down,' he says. 'It must be the storm.'

'I can't even get a bar of signal,' Ben says, still waving his phone around.

Kayla arrives at my side. On seeing Alistair on the ground, she rushes over and crouches down by him, the only person who actually seems to be trying to do anything useful.

'Get me something to stop the blood!' she yells, looking up at Donald. 'Some towels or something. Quickly!'

He races off. Meantime Kayla feels for a heartbeat, clearly finds none and calmly starts CPR. She's impressively composed – much more than just a pretty face.

Tabitha is still wailing and randomly pawing at Alistair, trying to hold his hand. It's quite touching – as if she genuinely loves him. She might be young, but perhaps I've got her wrong. Maybe she's not a gold-digger. Though I'd be surprised – she's gorgeous and, apart from his money, Alistair isn't exactly a catch. Especially these days.

Kayla looks up, appears to cast around the room for who is looking the least useless.

'Ben,' she says, 'can you please look after Tabitha? I need some room,' before continuing her chest compressions and breaths while the rest of us stand around in different degrees of shock and dithering.

Ben steps forward and gently puts his hands on Tabitha's shoulders. 'Tabitha. Let's step back and give Kayla some space, shall we? She's trying to help your husband.'

She lets out another wail, and for a second I think she's going to refuse to let go, but she surprises me by turning around and throwing herself into Ben's arms. I sneak a look at Alistair. His face is grey and there is so much blood. Kayla is continuing with her efforts valiantly, but surely there's no point? He's quite clearly dead.

Donald arrives with a stack of white tea towels. 'Put them under his head,' Kayla barks. 'Apply some pressure.' Donald does what he's told but the towels are soaked through in seconds.

'I told you that the malevolent spirit was still present,' says Elvira, who has appeared seemingly from nowhere.

Tabitha lifts her head and pushes away from Ben to shout: 'What the fuck are you on about, you stupid woman? No "spirit" did this!'

There is a beat of silence as everyone stares at Tabitha, open-mouthed.

'How very dare you!' Elvira shouts.

'Give her a break!' I exclaim. 'The poor woman's husband has just died.'

Elvira starts muttering something along the lines of 'never in my life have I' but thankfully quietens down, while Tabitha, who has by now collapsed to the ground again, ignores us both, looking up towards the galleries. I follow her gaze and can see that a section of the top banister is hanging down, broken. 'He must have fallen from up there!' she shrieks.

Ben is hovering nervously near Tabitha, clearly not knowing whether to go back to her since she pushed him away, but seemingly wanting to help, bless him. Rosemary, who is by now looking much more composed than she was at the séance when she believed her dead husband was talking to her, touches Tabitha's arm and says: 'Let's go to the kitchen, my dear. Get you away from here and make you a cup of tea.'

Tabitha allows herself to be hauled up and led away

by Rosemary, still sobbing as Alistair's blood pools further away from his head.

'I feel his spirit in the room,' Elvira says. 'It is still here, watching. But it has gone from his body.'

Everyone ignores her.

Silas moves forward, with his camera on. 'Silas. Stop filming, mate,' Joshua says evenly, though the anger in his voice is clearly evident. 'Have some respect. My father just died.'

Silas gives a sideways look and reluctantly switches his camera off. Kayla is still frantically pumping at Alistair's chest and blowing into his mouth, but anyone can see from the amount of blood coming out of his head that he's not coming back. 'Kayla,' Ben says quietly, touching her shoulder. 'I think you've done all you can.'

She shakes her head and carries on.

'Kayla, Ben's right. You need to stop now,' I say, gently.

Ben approaches her and takes her shoulders in the same way he did with Tabitha a few minutes earlier. 'Kayla. Come on. Please. He was just too injured.'

She carries on pumping for a few more beats, gives him one final large thump on the chest and then stands up and flees from the room.

Donald removes his hands from Alistair's head, placing it back down gently on the stack of towels and closing his eyes.

'If the landline is down, at least one of us is going to have to go for help,' Joshua says. 'And given the circumstances, I think it should be me. Donald, can you please prepare the boat?'

Donald eyes the window. 'I'd strongly recommend waiting until morning, Mr Joshua. It is sadly too late to do anything for your poor father now. And I wouldn't want you to put yourself in danger.' As if to emphasize the point, there is an extra-loud clap of thunder and a bright flash of lightning. 'As you know, it's very dangerous to be on the water during an electrical storm.'

Joshua looks at the prone body and sighs. 'You're probably right,' he agrees. He rubs at his chin and swipes at his eyes. 'We can't leave him there though. Shall we—'

'I think we should leave him where he is,' Mrs Laroche says. 'We don't know what's happened here and it may be that the medics or police might need . . . things left as they were. Donald, perhaps you can get a sheet to cover him with, and we can leave him here until the morning, when hopefully we can alert the necessary authorities. If it is safe to leave by then, of course.'

We look at the window where the rain couldn't even be described as falling – it's sheeting horizontally.

'No,' Joshua says. 'I'm not having my father left on the floor like a piece of rubbish with everyone having to walk by him all night, pretending he's not there. It's undignified. We'll move him into the snug with as little fuss as possible. Then at least he will have some privacy. Donald, you can help me do that please.'

Mrs Laroche is probably right that he shouldn't be moved, but at the same time I can entirely see why

Joshua doesn't want him simply left there. Dignified or not, it would be weird for everyone.

'Why don't you all go through to the library,' Donald says, addressing the rest of us, 'while Mr Joshua and I sort things out here. I'm sure most of you could do with a stiff drink. Mrs Laroche can arrange those while I deal with the Laird of Creaglie. I will sit with him until morning. He was a good employer, God rest his soul, and it seems only right.'

## 9 November 2025, 11.30 p.m.
Ben

As the others file through to the library, I go up the stairs to check on Kayla. She's sitting in the small open-plan salon at the top of the stairs on a ruby chaise longue, head in her hands. She hasn't reappeared since dashing from the room after trying to restart the old guy's heart.

I sit down alongside her. 'Kayla? I came to check if you're OK. But if you'd rather I leave you alone, just say the word and I'll go.'

A moment or two passes and then she lifts her head and looks up at me. She looks pale and tear-stained and I want to give her a hug but, given that I was flirting with her earlier and the current circumstances, I'm not sure if that'd seem inappropriate.

'You were amazing down there,' I say softly. 'You did everything you could. I don't think anyone or anything could have saved him.'

She gives a kind of modest half-smile. 'Thank you. But it's still so . . . upsetting to lose someone like that.'

'You did more than the rest of us,' I add. 'I'm quite ashamed that I stood there and did nothing. It was just such a . . . shock. And I don't know how to do CPR or anything like that. You've made me think I should learn.'

We sit together in silence for a few moments. To my surprise she shuffles closer and leans her head against my chest. I put my arm around her and squeeze her shoulder gently, trying to push away the inappropriate lustful feelings that are rising.

'Everyone reacts differently in these situations. It's nothing to be ashamed of,' she says, somewhat generously, I think.

'I feel a bit freaked out by everything that went on downstairs though,' I admit. 'What do you think happened?'

I feel her chest move against mine as she takes a deep breath and then sighs. 'I don't know. I didn't look closely – I was concentrating on doing what I could do. Tabitha seemed to think he'd fallen from the gallery.' She sits up and looks at me, her thigh still pressed against mine. 'Maybe he had a heart attack and lost his footing?' she suggests, her eyes wide. 'The balustrades aren't very high. I guess that could happen?'

God. It feels wrong to be speculating about this.

'Maybe. All that blood,' I add, pointlessly.

'He hit his head on a hard floor from a height. Heads really bleed,' she says. 'But it could just have easily been a heart attack that killed him rather than the fall. The fall could have happened because of something like that.

68

Or a stroke. He could have been dead before he even hit the ground.' She pauses. 'He was quite old. Didn't look in the best of health, did he? These things happen, sadly.'

There is silence again for a few seconds.

'Has someone called anyone?' she asks. 'Even if they can't get out here to actually do anything, it feels like something . . . someone should know?'

'Phone's down, apparently,' I say. 'And no signal, as you know.'

She sighs again. 'Shit. Really? So what's going to happen now?'

'They were discussing it when I left. Josh wanted to try to go and get some help, but Donald has persuaded him to wait until the morning because it's too dangerous to cross the lake. Rosemary was looking after Tabitha somewhere. Donald said he was going to stay with the . . . Alistair. I think the rest of them were going back to the library and someone was sorting drinks.'

She nods. 'OK. I don't think I can face going back down right now. I think I might try and get some rest. Will you send my apologies for me? Obviously if there's anything I can do to help, then someone should come and get me, but I think I've done all I can. I'd rather take a sleeping pill, go to bed and get the night out of the way, until we can get off the island.'

I squeeze her hand. 'No problem. I'll do that. Hope you get some sleep.'

\* \* \*

69

As soon as I leave Kayla to head downstairs again, I can hear that there is a row going on beneath us.

'I will not be spoken to like that!' a somewhat operatic, female voice is shouting. Elvira. Of course. 'Never in my life have I—'

'Please, can I ask that you try to compose yourself,' a woman says in more measured tones. 'A man has died, it's only respectful that—'

'His spirit is around us!' Elvira booms. 'It remains here. In this room. We should help him move on, the poor soul. We should . . .'

As I get to the top of the stairs, I can see that almost everyone is in the hallway, most of them shouting at each other.

'This isn't the time, Elvira,' Silas says, softly. 'Whatever your beliefs, any further intervention from you this evening is going to be extremely upsetting for Alistair's poor bereaved wife. And his son. The meteorological conditions being as they are, it's going to be impossible for anyone to leave tonight.'

She snorts. 'More's the pity.'

'We're all going to the library,' Silas continues. 'Mrs Laroche has kindly already brought some drinks through for us. Mrs Laroche, perhaps you could go and find Rosemary and Tabitha and see if they'll join us? It's very possible that the Lady of Creaglie would rather be by herself at this tragic time, but if she would prefer to have company, we can try to be some kind of comfort.'

Elvira gives Silas a filthy look and then stamps off into the library.

The others in the hall look at each other before following him in, while Mrs Laroche goes back towards the kitchen.

I'm almost tempted to follow Kayla's example and go to bed, but I feel like I should at the very least pass on her apologies. I go down the stairs and head into the library with the others.

## Silas's voiceover

The year of death was 1534.

The Second Laird of Creaglie was considered extremely handsome, one of the most eligible bachelors of the time. His portrait hangs in the dining room, and while his cartwheel neck ruff, padded hose and feathered hat may not be considered manly or attractive today, his chiselled cheekbones would surely be the envy of many a modern-day model or film star.

But his parents – the First Laird and Lady of Creaglie – despaired because, while he loved to go to parties, dine and carouse, he seemed entirely uninterested in taking a wife.

When he reached the age of forty, in desperation a marriage was eventually arranged with a young girl from a 'good' family but, after several years, no heir was forthcoming. She eventually confided in her lady's maid, Hannah, that the marriage had never been consummated, and that she had caught her husband looking at sketches of naked men in 'unnatural' embraces.

Hannah attempted to blackmail the Second Laird of Creaglie with this knowledge, threatening to reveal publicly what she knew. But the laird was confident that the maid, who was known to be a gossip, would not be believed. He simply called her a liar and dismissed her from her post for disloyalty.

The maid fell into penury and died of typhoid a few months later. Her ghost is believed to haunt the old kitchen and laundry room, causing pots and pans to fall from shelves, food to spoil and milk to curdle. Several future ladies of Creaglie would come to warn their children, 'Old Maid Hannah will come and visit you at night if you tell lies', if ever they caught their children making up stories.

Then again, Old Maid Hannah could, of course, simply be an entirely fictional cautionary tale used by mothers to encourage their children to tell the truth.

We'll probably never know for sure.

## 10 November 2025, midnight
Ben

Rosemary and Tabitha join the rest of us in the library, led by Mrs Laroche who is carrying a tray of drinks. 'Brown Derbys,' she announces. 'Somewhat of a Creaglie signature cocktail here – bourbon, grapefruit juice and honey. Comforting as well as restorative, I think you'll find. But if you'd rather have something else, that can of course be arranged.'

Another tray of hot drinks has already been placed on a low table – looks like she is covering all bases. Tabitha is still snivelling but looks a little calmer than earlier, while Rosemary, who it turns out is a former nurse, seems to have taken everything in her stride. She has risen to the challenge of fussing around Tabitha, sitting her gently down, getting her to drink something and talking to her in a low, calming voice.

Mrs Laroche hands the cocktails around. I accept one and take a sip. It's good – the same as we had before dinner, I think.

'I'd like to leave now, please,' says the hammy psychic huffily, downing her drink in one. 'This is not what I signed up for, and I no longer wish to stay overnight as planned. I've done what I was contracted to do, the séance. I don't want to spend any more time here than I have to.' She shivers. 'This place has extremely bad energy. And I should know.'

'I'm sure none of us is especially keen to stay now, given what's happened,' Silas says patiently. 'Alistair's wife – widow – and son in particular, I'm sure, would prefer that he is . . .' he glances at Tabitha, who doesn't appear to be listening, '. . . dealt with in a more digni-fied manner than is possible at the moment. But given the weather, staying here is what we must do. Surely you can see that? Hopefully, by the morning, the storm will have abated and we can alert someone to what's happened. Then the, erm, body can be dealt with in the correct manner and everyone can get on their way.'

Elvira gives Silas a look, as if he's dog shit on her shoe. 'I do not wish to be treated like a child and told what to do,' Elvira spits back spikily, her wafty persona of earlier all gone.

Tabitha still has tears streaming down her face and a distressed, almost vacant expression. She lies down on the sofa and closes her eyes. Rosemary puts a cushion under her head and pats her shoulder.

I'd assumed, as I think we all did, that Tabitha had married the old guy for his money, given her youth and looks, but she seems genuinely and deeply upset. Guess it goes to show you shouldn't judge people by appearances. Or that some people are very good at acting.

'It's not right, leaving my father there like that, like a piece of meat on a butcher's block,' Josh says sadly. 'I'm going to have a proper go at finding a phone signal. Perhaps if I can get through to the police, the powers that be can . . . I don't know . . . send someone. Somehow. Even if crossing by boat isn't an option. Maybe there's something else that can be done.' He holds up his phone. 'Sometimes, on a good day, I can get a bar or two if I stand in the right place.'

He walks out of the room, staring at his phone. Poor guy. I can't see they'd be able to get anyone here in this weather, but I suppose trying to do something might help him feel better.

'The spirit of the Laird of Creaglie is still with us,' Elvira says in a stupid, wavering voice. 'He has not yet left us.'

## 10 November 2025, 12.30 a.m.
Amelia

We are all sitting in silence in the library. Bloody hell, this is not the weekend I was expecting. I'm sure none of us were.

'I'm going to go and find a blanket for the Lady of Creaglie,' Mrs Laroche says. 'I'm worried she's going to get cold lying there.'

She leaves the room and silence falls again. When she returns, she tucks the tartan blanket lovingly around Tabitha before suddenly leaping back in alarm, shrieking.

'She's not sleeping! She's freezing cold! I think she's dead!'

## Silas's voiceover

The date of death was 1592.

The Fourth Laird of Creaglie married a French noble-woman, renowned throughout France for her incredible beauty, and especially for her youthful appearance.

The Fourth Lady of Creaglie attributed her smooth, perfect skin to a daily tincture of gold chloride, mercury and diethyl ether, which she drank every day with break-fast, along with what we would perhaps today call a smoothie, except for the fact that – along with the metals and compounds – it also contained frogspawn, earthworms and scorpion oil.

Several hundred years later, a lock of her hair was found in a keepsake box in the castle by one of her ancestors and tested in a laboratory. It was found to contain five hundred times the normal level of gold.

On brighter days, as the sun goes down, her portrait, which is displayed above the fireplace in the morning room, is said to glow as the Fourth Lady of Creaglie likes to remind whoever is the current Lady of Creaglie that she is equally as, if not more beautiful than her.

Or then again, perhaps it is simply the way the sun shines through the window at that time of day.

We'll probably never know for sure.

**10 November 2025, 12.35 a.m.**
Ben

Rosemary leaps up from her place at Tabitha's feet and springs into action. She gently touches her forehead, lifts her wrist to take her pulse and lays her arm gently back down at her side.

'She's not dead,' she proclaims. 'A little cold perhaps, but . . .'

Thank Christ for that. Rosemary tucks the blanket more closely around Tabitha and then taps her two cheeks in turn, hard enough that her head moves from one position to another. 'Tabitha! Tabitha! Wake up!'

She doesn't stir. Her skin is grey and waxen. She looks dead to me.

What the fuck is going on here?

Rosemary frowns. 'However, there's clearly something wrong. I can't wake her. She's not just asleep, she's unconscious.'

'I noticed she had quite a few cocktails earlier.' I ask, 'Might it be that?'

Rosemary shakes her head. 'No. I saw enough drunk people in my time in A&E to know that's not the issue here. We need to get her some help.'

'But . . . the storm,' I say. 'Donald said that it's too dangerous to try to leave until it abates.'

On cue, there is a particularly loud clap of thunder and the lights flicker. Bloody hell – the lights going out is surely the last thing we need. But thankfully they steady and come back on.

'What do you think, Mrs Laroche?' Silas asks. 'If Tabitha needs medical attention, then getting away from here is a little more urgent. What are our options? Is there anything we can do?'

The housekeeper frowns. 'I don't think it'll be possible for anyone to leave right now. But let me go and get Donald to come and speak to you. He's been here much longer than me and will have a better idea.'

She scurries away, seemingly glad to escape from the library where now everyone is staring at Tabitha in horror, except Rosemary who is perched on the edge of the sofa holding her hand. I guess as an ex-nurse she is more used to this kind of thing. Certainly more used to it than I am, anyway.

Donald comes in and stands over the sofa, looks at Tabitha and frowns. 'What happened to her?' he asks. 'Is she all right?'

'We don't know what happened,' Rosemary says, 'but no, she's not all right. I can't wake her.'

'Could it be . . . the shock of what happened?' he asks.

'Something like that? Is there anything we can do for her here?'

Rosemary shakes her head. 'I don't think the shock would affect her in that way. At least, not directly. I've never heard of anything like that. And as I don't know what's wrong with her, I don't know what we can do for her. She needs to get to a hospital. Or at the very least be seen by a doctor.'

Donald peers at Tabitha again. 'I understand what you are saying. But we never go out when the storm is like this. It's too dangerous to cross the lake in this kind of weather and – even if we did get across the water – the mountain road is likely to be blocked with fallen trees.' He pauses. 'I'm not sure even a helicopter would be an option but, as you know, the telephone line appears to have been damaged and so we are unable to contact the mainland to call one anyway.'

'Can we not even *try* to leave?' Rosemary suddenly wails, more desperately.

Donald looks at the window again. 'I will go and check the conditions,' he says. 'But I think it's very likely to be too risky to leave until the wind drops. Obviously we want to do our best for Lady Tabitha, but we certainly don't want to be putting anyone at risk. Some poor unfortunate souls have drowned in the lake before in much more clement conditions than this, after all.'

He gives a little bow and leaves the room.

**10 November 2025, 12.45 a.m.**
Ben

Time passes slowly as we sit in silence. Clearly suggesting a game of cards or similar would be totally inappropriate, and even trying to make conversation seems wrong, but I'm not sure how much more of this I can stand.

Silas is fiddling with his phone, which is strange as there's definitely no signal down here. Perhaps he's got some app which monitors ghostly activity or something.

Rosemary looks around the room. 'Joshua has been gone a while,' she says. 'I wonder if he had any luck trying to find a phone signal?'

'I'll go and look for him,' I say. I can't just sit here doing nothing, when eventually I'm clearly now going to have to write about all this and I don't want to admit that I was too freaked out by the castle to make the effort to do something useful. I need to man up. I'm going to go and find Josh, see if he's managed to find any signal. I'm not going to let some supernatural beings – which probably don't even exist – scare me or stand in my way.

Or at least, that's how I feel when I'm in the library with the others, but somehow as soon as I step out into the hallway, the temperature seems to drop, the draughts are more evident and the noise of the wind much louder. I glance into the snug where I see the body – Alistair – has been covered by a sheet. I can't see Donald from where I am. In spite of being called a snug, it's actually a big room, not snug at all. He's probably tucked away in a corner I can't see, and I don't want to disturb him by putting my head around the door. It would feel voyeuristic, interrupting this seemingly very loyal butler in his grieving. And surely Josh isn't going to be there anyway – didn't he say he was going to the top of the castle? That would seem to make more sense if you're looking for phone signal anyway.

I start walking up the stairs. Even though it's not exactly a party atmosphere downstairs for obvious reasons, as soon as I'm on the first landing and can no longer hear the quiet murmur of conversation from the library, it feels too silent and much more eerie. 'Josh?' I call out, partly so that there is some sound, even if it is coming from me, 'Are you there?'

All of the doors on this landing are closed, and I probably shouldn't be going into people's private rooms anyway, so I carry on up the next flight of stairs, which is smaller, up to the scary nursery that freaked me out so much earlier.

Not scary, I tell myself. An ordinary nursery. I was

primed to be scared. That doll had probably been left placed deliberately to fall out of the cupboard and make me jump. Probably even bought especially for the purpose – what person in their right mind buys an awful Chucky doll like that for a child? And someone was probably singing that nursery rhyme to take the piss. I bet it's Silas's people, wanting to make his video more interesting. Or maybe the Creaglie family have set a few things up, making sure the punters get the scares they're after. Yes, it'll be that. At least, that's what I'm going to tell myself.

But it's definitely getting colder as I ascend.

'Josh?' I call again. I walk past the nursery, along the uncarpeted corridor, which has a low ceiling and doors on either side, much closer together than on the floor below. I guess this must have been the servants' quarters – perhaps it still is. An image of a corridor filled with blood from a film pops unbidden into my mind and I push it away.

Is this where Donald sleeps, I wonder? Or Mrs Laroche? Or the other staff who are apparently still stuck on the mainland? Christ, I envy them. I'd much rather be in some bland three-star hotel enjoying mass-produced food than being scared witless in this awful castle. 'Is anyone there?' I ask.

I can see there's a door ajar at the end of the corridor, and I take a deep breath as I push it wider open and flick on the light.

## 10 November 2025, 1 a.m.
Ben

'Josh? Are you there?' I call.

I gingerly push open the door, only to find that there's not actually a room behind it at all, just a staircase. I reach around the door to feel whether I can find a light switch, but I can't feel anything there, so I switch on the torch on my phone, which I've been carrying around with me, so far uselessly, out of habit.

But Josh will know this property well, having grown up here, so hopefully he's correct in his thought that it's possible to find some signal here. And I guess it makes sense that he appears to have gone up high.

The light from my torch shows a spiral stone staircase winding upwards in a narrow turret. Judging from the cold air blasting down it, it's probably open at the top. I don't relish the idea of going outside in this weather, but we need to try to get help for Tabitha. I should have got Silas to come with me, he'd love the chance to explore a spooky tower like this, surely? Then anyone watching his film later would see that I'm doing something useful, playing the hero. I push the thought away. This is about Tabitha, not about me, I tell myself. I am a better person than that.

'Josh? Can you hear me?' I call again.

There is no answer, but something is rattling and banging higher up. I take a deep breath and try to be rational. There is nothing to be scared of here. Ghosts do not exist. But I feel my heart beating too fast and my breath catching in my throat.

I push the door wider and see quite how narrow and steep the staircase is and feel another jolt of adrenalin. I'm quite claustrophobic, even at the best of times.

'Fuck's sake. Get on with it,' I mutter to myself. 'Calm down.' I take a few deep breaths and wish I'd bothered trying those yoga classes my ex was always trying to get me to go to – I always took the piss out of her going on about her 'breathwork' – after all, even babies are born knowing how to breathe. But right now I feel like whatever she was talking about might have been a skill I could use.

I go through the door and put my foot on the first tread, which is stone and smooth as the baby's proverbial bottom. I wish I'd worn trainers rather than the impractical dress shoes I've got on which are too tight and have no grip – somehow I thought they were more suitable for a castle than my usual trainers. Seems ridiculous now.

What if I fall? I could really hurt myself. 'I'm coming up,' I call out again. I'm not sure why. I hope Josh is up there. I don't want to do all this for nothing.

The stone steps spiral up and up. As I get higher the wind gets stronger and louder. I wonder if I should go back and get someone to come with me, but no, I can't do that. Silas might make me look pathetic on screen.

Eventually I reach an opening which is too small to call a door, squeeze through it and then I am out in the cold, entirely exposed to the elements, on top of a tower. Christ. I should at least have put a coat on. Why didn't I think of that? 'Josh?' I call again, but he is nowhere to be seen. Huge fat raindrops are blowing straight into my face. I look around and there is literally nothing but blackness – no lights to be seen anywhere, and the stormy skies mean there are no moon or stars to be seen. Never been anywhere like it, but it doesn't feel like a good thing. Like an omen. I push the thought away. Get a grip, Ben. Get on with it and get out of here.

I hold my phone up in the air to see if I can find a signal, my wet hands already stinging from the cold. I guess if it's going to work anywhere, it would be here, up high, both in the open air and outside the thick walls, but there is nothing. No bars at all. Part of me thinks I should explore up here a little more – try some different areas of the top of the turret maybe. Or should I look over the edge, in case Josh has come up here and fallen over? Could that have happened? It's so windy I'm too nervous to go too close to the low wall which encircles the top of the tower – it's too dangerous, surely? Plus, it's fucking freezing – I can't stay out here any longer. And Josh isn't up here. I'd see him – it's not very big. I tried this way almost at random because there was an open door, the castle is huge, there are probably several towers like this, and he could be anywhere.

I go back through the hobbit-sized door into the turret, and it's an instant relief to be out of the wind, though I'm now soaked through, even after that short time outside. I'll need to go back to my room and get changed – I'm already starting to shiver. Fucking hell, this is so much not the weekend I had thought I was signing up for. I shine my torch down at my feet as I start to descend the staircase again, because the steps are small and smooth and sloping downwards as well, for fuck's sake, and now that my stupid impractical shoes are wet too, I don't trust myself not to slip. It seems to take for ever, and I feel my heart rate increasing as I slowly circle down and eventually reach the heavy door I came through.

It's closed. Did I close it? I don't remember doing that. I feel a sick surge of adrenalin as I go to try to open it, somehow already knowing what's coming. I scan the smooth wooden door for a handle: there is none. I push it and it doesn't budge. I shove it harder with my hands, and then with my shoulder, but it doesn't move. I look at my phone again, in case by some miracle the signal has returned, but of course it hasn't.

I hammer on the door with my fist. 'Help!' I shout. 'I'm stuck!'

But I'm a long way from the library where everyone else is still gathered, as far as I know.

No one is going to hear me.

## Silas's voiceover

The year of death was 1695.

The Seventh Laird of Creaglie was a man of considerable wealth and influence, but was not a physically attractive man, and was known to have an eye for the ladies.

Among his staff was a young maid named Mary, known for her gentle demeanour and striking beauty. Whispers among the servants hinted at secret meetings between Mary and the laird, suggesting a clandestine affair.

Then one day, without warning, Mary disappeared without a trace. It was rumoured that she had become pregnant and that the laird, desperate to avoid scandal, had taken drastic measures to silence her.

Some said that she was buried in the cellar. Others that he had drowned her in the lake. The laird and his wife told the household that she had left the castle of her own accord, having become pregnant by a local blacksmith. And that he, on learning of her condition, abandoned both her and the town, and that Mary herself had since died of influenza.

Over the centuries, people have claimed to have seen a grey lady float though thin air where there was once a servants' staircase. Some say that Mary can never be at rest, endlessly searching for her unborn child who died inside her.

Then again, it could be a simple trick of the light.

We'll probably never know for sure.

## 10 November 2025, 1.15 a.m.
Ben

'Help!' I shout, again and again, hammering so hard on the door it is making my hands hurt. 'I'm stuck! Let me out!'

I lurch at it with my shoulder but it doesn't budge. I feel myself starting to hyperventilate and remind myself to breathe slowly, rein it in, calm down. I take a few deep breaths to steady myself and then shoulder the door again, when it abruptly opens I land with a thud on my right side, ending up sprawled on the floor.

Josh, who must have opened the door, is staring down at me with a puzzled expression. 'What's all the shouting about?' he asks.

I sit up and rub my arm. 'I was looking for you,' I say, sounding somewhat whiny and petulant even to my own ears. 'I went up to the top of the tower, because I thought that's where you might be trying to find some phone signal, and then someone locked me in.'

He pulls a face. 'Really? I'm sure no one would have deliberately locked you in. The door must have shut behind you. Or maybe someone closed it without knowing you were there to keep the draught out which,' he pauses, closing the door, 'I'm going to do now because it's fucking freezing.'

'So did you find any phone signal?' I ask. I really hope he has. I've had enough of being here, stuck in the stupid castle in the middle of a stupid lake halfway up a bastard mountain. This place is freaking me out on several levels. I just want to leave. Whatever Donald says, maybe they can send us a helicopter. Those big ones with the two sets of rotary blades can go out in almost any weather, can't they?

But the phone line is down and there's no way to communicate with anyone. Which is why I ended up in the tower in the first place.

Josh offers me his hand and I take it to haul myself up to my feet. I brush myself down. I'm aching all down one side where I fell but I don't say so, I've already lost enough dignity as it is.

'I didn't find any signal,' he says. 'On a good day you can get a signal in the old nursery sometimes, but obviously today isn't a good day.'

'So you weren't up the tower?' I ask. 'I thought – as it's so high – that might be where you went.'

He shakes his head. 'No. And now you mention it, I don't even know why this door was open. No one should be up there, it's not safe, especially on a day like this.' He examines the door. 'I'll make sure we get a lock put on this before we have any more guests staying here – I don't want anyone else going up there.'

'So what now?' I ask. 'Is there anywhere else we can try to get some phone signal? Rosemary seems quite worried about your, um, stepmother.' It seems weird to call Tabitha his stepmother when she's probably younger than he is. I should have just said Tabitha.

His expression changes. 'Don't call her my stepmother,' he snaps. 'My mother was worth twenty of her, God rest her soul.'

I hold my hands up in a gesture of surrender. 'Sorry, I didn't mean . . .'

His expression changes back to the genial host one he's been wearing most of the night and he claps me on the shoulder. 'Sorry, mate. Don't mind me. I'm a bit overwrought after . . . well, you know. Tabitha'll be fine, I'm sure – probably just looking for attention. I'm not worried about her at all. But my father deserves better than lying on a cold, hard floor draped in a sheet. I want to get the right people here so that he can be dealt with in a way befitting a man of his station.

'So mark my words, I'm doing my best to sort this out. I want to get in touch with the mainland just as much as you do, believe me.'

I nod. 'I understand. No offence taken. Rosemary wanted to know if there's any other way one of us could try to go and get help. Did Donald speak to you about it?'

He shakes his head. 'Not yet. I haven't seen him. But

there's no way anyone should be going out in this kind of weather. I won't have anyone putting themselves at risk simply because Tabitha's taken a bit of a funny turn. She's probably just annoyed all the attention isn't about her for a change.'

I'm a little surprised to hear him talk that way about her so openly, but I try not to let it show – it's none of my business. He seems to realize he was perhaps a bit too forthright as he continues:

'But I'd be grateful if you didn't mention any of what I said about Tabitha to anyone else, please? Just a heat-of-the-moment thing. Grief, shock and all that. Does funny things to you. I guess. I didn't mean it. In all honesty, she and I have never seen eye to eye, but she's my late father's wife whether I like it or not, and I need to respect that.'

'Yeah. Course.' I get why he doesn't want me to say anything, but he very much sounded like he absolutely meant what he said.

## Silas's voiceover

The date of death was 1764.

The Tenth Laird of Creaglie was a gourmand and loved nothing more than hosting huge feasts for his friends and associates. Creaglie Castle was never livelier than during his tenure, when he would regularly invite guests to stay for weeks at a time and enjoy his hospitality.

He loved to eat and drink, while the Tenth Lady of Creaglie wished to stay slim and did not want to join him in his lavish meals. 'But we have guests!' he would allegedly exclaim. 'They will think we are mean if we don't feed them well!'

According to the lady's journals, she believed that the constant procession of guests was simply an excuse to allow the laird to eat enormous lavish meals in the way that he craved. And chances are, she was right.

Almost every night he dined on an eight-course meal of dishes such as caviar, lobster, suckling pig, venison, truffles, brioche, wine, champagne and always several helpings of dessert.

He died aged forty-two, weighing more than twenty-eight stone. His official cause of death was given as over-eating.

Today, if food goes missing in the castle, it's sometimes said that the Tenth Laird of Creaglie has taken it for himself.

Then again, perhaps it could simply be a greedy dog, a child, or even a hungry house guest to blame.

We'll probably never know for sure.

## 10 November 2025, 1.45 a.m.
Ben

I drink a lot of whisky over the next couple of hours even though I don't particularly like it and by the time dawn starts to break, I am feeling quite drunk, and not in a good way. My eyes are sticky and gritty. I am alternately shivery and sweaty and definitely in need of a good scrub and some clean clothes. I feel like I've been awake for days and think longingly of the giant claw-foot tub in my bathroom upstairs.

Until now I felt too freaked out by the events of the night – the séance, the old guy dying, whatever it is that's happened to his wife now – to even consider being on my own in my room for longer than necessary. But as the night goes on and I get more and more exhausted, the prospect of going to bed becomes increasingly appealing. It would feel wonderful to freshen up and get some rest. The storm still doesn't show any sign of abating.

Everyone apart from me, Rosemary, Tabitha and that

awful psychic woman seems to have gone elsewhere – I must have nodded off at least briefly as I didn't notice most of them go – so it doesn't look like I'd be the first to go to bed anyway. The four of us have been sitting in silence for what feels like hours anyway and it makes no difference to anyone if I'm here or upstairs, I'm sure. No one seemed to mind when Kayla decided not to come down again after she'd tried to resuscitate the old guy. I stretch my arms out above my head and yawn extravagantly.

'I think I'll head up for a while if no one minds,' I say. 'Doesn't feel like there's anything else to be done until the storm eases.'

'I'm going to stay here and keep an eye on Tabitha,' Rosemary says. 'I think someone needs to as we don't know why she won't wake up and she might take a turn for the worse. There's no way I could sleep, anyway, with all this going on.'

I get up from the sofa. 'You know where I am if you need anything, Rosemary,' I say. 'Do you want me to get you a drink or anything to eat before I go up? Some water maybe? Or a hot drink? I could find Mrs Laroche and see if she could make you something?'

She smiles gratefully and shakes her head. 'No thanks. That's kind but I'm fine. Hope you can get some rest.'

I leave the library with a feeling of relief but, as before, as soon as I'm alone, I start to feel creeped out and uneasy. Almost like I'm being watched. But no. No, I tell myself. You're tired, overwrought and imagining things. Some sleep will do you the world of good.

'Get a grip,' I mutter to myself as I climb the stairs. While part of me is desperate to have a bath and get into that lavish, comfy bed, another part of me is dreading closing the door behind me and being all alone.

Reaching the top of the stairs, I turn to walk along the landing towards my room. The floorboards creak and groan, which doesn't help with my growing unease. And something definitely seems strange now. Like something's changed since last time I came up to my room.

Smoke. It's smoke. Perhaps it's from the fireplace downstairs? Yes. Must be that. Old places like this with all the fireplaces always smell smoky.

Don't they?

I walk further up the corridor and then I see it. At first I think I'm imagining it, but no. Smoke is drifting from under the last door on the right.

I run the short distance along the corridor, fling open the door and huge plumes of thick grey smoke instantly fill the air. 'Help me!' I yell. 'Donald! Josh! There's a fire!'

Shit, shit, shit. I've no idea where anyone is or if anyone can hear me, so I'm going to have to go in. Covering my mouth with my arm, I run into the room and throw open the two sash windows I can just about see. The through-draught pulls most of the smoke out of the room, although it's still billowing from the fireplace in a way it shouldn't be, especially as the fire burning in the grate has now almost burned itself out. I look around for some kind of receptacle that I could fill with water from the bathroom maybe to try to put

101

it out, but then I notice that there's a figure in the bed, motionless. Getting them away from the smoke is surely more urgent so with no real thought for their modesty, I pull the covers back and try to manhandle them out of the bed. It's still pretty smoky in here and they're wearing an eye mask so it's not immediately obvious who it is – the castle is enormous and I'm not sure whose room is where.

I manage to get whoever it is off the bed and onto the floor where they land on their back with a thump. I put my hands under their armpits and drag them out into the hallway, where I'm met by Donald, red-faced and carrying a fire extinguisher.

'I think the chimney's blocked or something,' I splutter, 'the room's full of smoke. I've opened the windows.' Donald rushes in, and a few seconds later I hear what must be the sound of the fire extinguisher squirting.

I look down at the figure on the floor and, now the smoke has cleared, I can see who it is.

# Part Two

# The Nineteenth Lady of Creaglie

## 1983
The Nineteenth Lady of Creaglie

Having grown up in a series of foster homes, the last place I'd ever have expected to end up living is a castle in the Highlands of Scotland.

Creaglie Castle has been in the family for about a million generations, and it's the castle of every girl's dreams – Sleeping Beauty's Castle, except halfway up a Scottish mountain and in the middle of a lake.

Legend has it that it was won by the Creaglie family in a duel in the sixteenth century. Though some say it was a wedding gift from one rich family to another. There are other stories too. It depends which book you read or whose account you believe. These days, I have a lot of time to read. But luckily the library is very well stocked.

It's one of those places where even the staff have been here for generations, and at least one of them clearly disapproves of me. The housekeeper Morag, though she can't be all that much older than me, is very

Mrs Danvers about it all. There's no former wife, though Alistair is a bit older than me (twelve years, to be exact), but she makes it clear that she doesn't consider me a suitable match for him in the slightest.

And I get it. Alistair, or the Nineteenth Laird of Creaglie, to give him his full title, will have been expected to marry some wide-hipped Hooray Henrietta, ideally with a matching title and probably some family money of her own too. I read somewhere that back in the day, marriages were more like business arrangements than being about love. Morag obviously still subscribes to that theory. She never says so explicitly, obviously, but she's made it very clear.

Alistair totally swept me off my feet. I'd never met anyone like him before.

Alistair and a group of his rah friends, all men, came out to stay in the high-end lodge where I was working for the hunting season as a live-in kitchen assistant, waitress and housekeeper, basically because the job came with accommodation, and it felt like an easy option on leaving care. No expense was spared as Alistair and his friends spent their days hunting and shooting and their evenings eating and drinking. I cleared up vomit more than once and put up with a lot of leers and stupid comments and, given that these were all men in their thirties or so with high-flying jobs, and some with wives and kids, it was pretty pathetic. But then when one of them took things further and groped my arse, Alistair stood up and said: 'Steady on, Tarkers, that's not OK,' and the filthy fucker left me alone after that.

106

But I didn't think any more of it. As the lone female working in that environment where most of the guests were rich and entitled men, I was pretty used to it, and simply happy to see the back of them when they left at the end of the week. But then the biggest bunch of flowers I'd ever seen arrived from Alistair with a note which said he had a place nearby, asking if he could invite me for dinner to apologize for the appalling behaviour of his friends.

I remembered him standing up for me against his friend, but I didn't remember much else about him other than that, of the group, he was clearly 'the quiet one'. No one had ever sent me flowers before, and when I looked at the address on the note, Creaglie Castle, with a time and date, I decided to agree, mainly out of curiosity.

When I rang the number on the card, it was a woman who answered the phone with simply the words 'Creaglie Castle' in a clipped accent which I couldn't quite place.

'Um . . . I'm calling to speak to Alistair?' I'd said. I had no idea who this was. His mum? Sister? Girlfriend? Wife, even? Surely not, otherwise why would he be inviting me?

'The Laird of Creaglie is not currently at home. Can I take a message for him?'

Laird? He never said anything about that.

'Uh . . . yeah. Yes. Please. I'm, um, from the hunting lodge he stayed in last week. He sent me . . . um, well, I wanted to say thanks for his dinner invitation and that I'd like to accept. Please.'

There is a moment's silence and for a couple of seconds I think I might have been cut off, until whoever the woman on the phone is continues: 'I will pass that on. Will there be anything else? We will send the driver for you as we are quite difficult to reach independently.'

'Oh, I um, gosh, thank you. That's very kind.'

'We have your address?'

It's '*we*' now? So odd.

'Uh, yeah. I stay at the lodge he stayed in last week. He sent flowers so . . .' Why am I telling her all this? I don't even know who I'm speaking to. 'So, yes, he has the address.'

'Very well. I will send Donald one hour and a half before your appointed time for dinner. I would recommend dressing warmly. Thank you for your call.'

'Will he also . . .?' I start to ask, wondering how I'm going to get home if it's so remote, before the phone abruptly goes dead. I look at the receiver in bemusement, as if it might have some answers as to what all that was about: the weird formality, the woman not telling me who she was, taking a message as if she was Alistair's secretary. And even telling me how to dress! Part of me wonders if this is an elaborate wind-up or practical joke.

Working in the middle of nowhere in the Highlands of Scotland and not being a 'smart clothes' type of person anyway, I don't have anything which feels remotely suitable for a dinner date in a castle with one of the poshest people I've ever met. I settle for a decent pair of black jeans which look like they could be actual trousers at a push, and an 'out on the pull' top which I never have the opportunity to wear any more. But it's freezing and there's no way I can go out like that and, mindful of the warning to dress warmly from the woman on the phone, whoever she was, I pull one of my least bobbled jumpers on over the top.

On the dot of 6 p.m. the lodge doorbell rings and I head out to find a uniformed driver waiting for me. Uniformed! What is this?

'Miss Beddoe?' he says. 'My name is Donald. I'm here to take you to Creaglie Castle. Are you ready to go?'

'Yep, ready, thank you,' I reply, grabbing my some-what overly glitzy gold and black company-logoed jacket because it's the only really warm one I've got. I feel a lurch of unease at not knowing exactly where we are going. But I have Alistair's details on the lodge's booking form and I have given them to the chef I work with 'in case I'm murdered and never come back,' I joked. But somehow I think I'll be OK. Alistair seemed very polite and entirely harmless, especially compared to the awful mates he was with. My upbringing along-side some fairly rough kids in many of my foster homes means I'm pretty good at looking after myself. And apart from all that, I have barely left the lodge beyond going for the occasional hike since I arrived in Scotland as I have no transport, so it'll be good to get out.

Given the uniform the driver is wearing, which I was surprised to see, I'm expecting the vehicle I get into to be something lavish like a stretch limo, but it's actually an enormous all-terrain vehicle with giant wheels. The driver opens the back door and flips out a couple of steps, offering me his gloved hand which I take as I climb up.

The inside is kind of like a London taxi, only bigger, with two black leather sofa-style seats facing each other, with fur throws on both of them.

'The Laird of Creaglie asked me to offer you some champagne,' he says, still standing in the snow outside. 'I have brought small bottles, suitable for drinking with a straw if you would like? The road to the castle is quite rough and winding, and not entirely conducive to drinking from a glass. Would you like me to open one for you?'

'Oh . . . yes, why not? Thank you.'

He raises the steps, closes the door and gets into the driver's seat. I see him reach down into an insulated box and, a few seconds later, hear the sound of a cork pop. He turns to pass the little bottle complete with pink straw over to me. It is glistening with condensation and ice-cold as I take it.

'Journey'll be about an hour and a bit, miss, an hour in the car and then about twenty minutes by boat.'

*Boat?* Where are we going? I feel a lurch of alarm but push any worries away – it's not as if he's trying to hide anything, is it? I'm sure it'll be fine and I don't want to look stupid by asking.

'If you get travel sick at all, I'd suggest keeping your gaze out of the window for the last half-hour of the journey,' he continues. 'And if you'd like more champagne or some water, let me know.'

He starts up the huge vehicle and we head down the mountain. This is the first time I've been any distance from the lodge since I arrived. The lights of the other few hotels and lodges look cosy against the dark of the night and it has started to snow. I take a sip of the champagne which is fizzy and a little acidic – it's never been my favourite drink, not that I am offered it very often. I'd have preferred a beer or something, but it seemed impolite to say so.

We turn right onto the valley road, drive for about ten minutes and then turn left and start ascending again.

At night, when I can see the lights twinkling on this side of the valley from the chalet, the little groups of lights look like small, cosy hamlets, but as we start up the windy road, passing through tiny villages with a small cluster of street lights, I see that many of the buildings are shuttered and abandoned, and those that aren't look pretty dilapidated.

The 'villages' become fewer and further between the further we ascend, and I am starting to feel a little queasy. I swallow down a burp. Perhaps that champagne wasn't the best idea. The road becomes increasingly steep and narrow, and I hear the gear change to a lower one. It's now very clear why the mystery woman on the phone offered a driver – there's no way even most four-by-fours would make it up here.

It's snowing harder now, and for the last ten minutes I haven't seen anything other than trees either side of the winding road as it gets steeper, more narrow and more bumpy as we ascend. As well as feeling quite car sick, I'm also starting to feel a little uneasy. Should I have insisted on bringing someone with me on this dinner date? Is this safe? If I don't come back, how quickly will my colleague let someone know? Should I have called someone else too? But like who?

I'm starting to contemplate opening the door and throwing myself from the car, even though we're in the middle of nowhere and it's absolutely freezing, when suddenly the trees thin and I see a huge lake glinting in the moonlight.

The driver hops out of the car and opens the door. A blast of cold air whooshes in.

'I'd put your jacket back on, miss,' he says. 'The boat has a cabin but it's not heated and, on a night like this, it's pretty chilly.'

'Boat?' I repeat, gormlessly. My catastrophizing during the drive had almost made me forget that Donald had said that part of the journey would be by boat.

'Yes, miss,' Donald replies patiently and without even a hint of snark, or at least none that I can make out. 'Creaglie Castle is on an island in the middle of this lake. You can't quite see it from here as it's behind the next headland.'

I'm not sure if I fancy Alistair or not but, on the off chance that I do, I don't particularly want to greet him in my gaudy coat. Needs must, though, I guess. Equally, if I'd known this 'date', or whatever it is, was going to involve a trip across a lake in the dark, I'd probably have at least thought twice before accepting – I'm not exactly a water baby. My fractured childhood and several different schools has meant I've never learned to swim.

I haul the jacket on and zip it up. Donald holds out his hand and I see the steps down from the giant car have reappeared as if by magic.

'Take care, it might be slippery,' he says, which does nothing to increase my confidence.

Once out of the car, I see we are by a wooden jetty which has a small boat tied to it. I feel a lurch of alarm, but I can hardly back out now and say I'm not sure I want to go after all, can I?

'I'll get onto the boat first and help you on,' he says. 'There are some blankets and things inside to help keep you cosy. Even though it's not the best weather tonight, there's no wind, so it'll be a nice smooth crossing.'

'OK,' I say, trying to sound more confident than I feel.

He's holding a large torch and leaves me on the jetty as he steps onto the boat. I'm relieved to see that once he's aboard, he switches on a light in the cabin – I was envisaging crossing in the dark. Then he comes back and helps me on before getting me settled inside.

The 'some blankets and things' turn out to be velvet seats and fur throws, so I'm at least cosy, even if more than a little nervous. I glance around the interior and can't see anything that looks like a life jacket and am too embarrassed to ask. But Donald isn't putting on anything like that and he said it would be calm . . . I'm probably being ridiculous. You don't see people wearing life jackets on things like pleasure boats, do you? I'm sure I'll be fine.

'Can I get you anything else to drink before we set off? Another champagne?'

I shake my head. 'No. I'm good thanks.' I'm actually feeling a bit sick and tempted to ask for some water, but I'm also now starting to need the loo. I doubt there's anything like that on board and again I'm too embarrassed to ask.

'OK. Wrap up warm and we'll be across in no time.'

He heads into a little booth and I hear the engine start up. I pull the fur around me tighter as it does start to feel a little cold but, as he promised, the ride is pretty smooth. I wonder if he senses my nerves and is taking it extra slowly but, if that's the case, he is polite enough not to say so. And after about ten minutes, I manage to start relaxing into the journey. The snow has stopped and between the clouds I can see the moon is full and reflected on the lake. It's beautiful.

And then the castle comes into view. Wow. It's almost like a gothic version of Sleeping Beauty's Castle – with turrets and spires but without the pink and blue, lit by a couple of spotlights even though there's no one to see it apart from me and Donald. The boat pulls up next to another wooden jetty and he switches the engine off. 'Give me a second while I tie up the boat,' he says, 'And then we'll get you inside and warmed up.'

Once he has helped me off the boat, we pass through a couple of huge gateposts, flambeaux blazing, and a uniformed woman opens an enormous door as we

114

approach. How did she know we were there? Perhaps she was looking out of the window for us.

'Miss Beddoe? The Laird of Creaglie is waiting for you. Please come this way.'

All this 'laird' stuff seems weirdly formal and old-fashioned, but maybe that's just how they act in these kind of places. I've never been anywhere like this before.

I walk up the steps and in through the enormous doorway, which has two more flambeaux either side. The hallway is incredible, a large wooden staircase with a red carpet runner in front of me, which splits into two towards a wooden gallery that runs around the first floor, with a second wooden gallery above it. Hanging from the ceiling is an enormous chandelier, which brings to mind the one which fell in that recent *Only Fools and Horses* episode. There's a fire crackling in a huge stone fireplace and above it, the head of a stag with enormous antlers. Its eyes have been replaced with glass and seem to look at me.

'Can I take your coat for you, Miss Beddoe?' asks the woman who brought me in. She looks me up and down disdainfully and puts a disparaging emphasis on the word 'coat'. I wonder if she's the woman I spoke to on the phone? 'And then I'll take you through to the snug where the Laird of Creaglie will join you.'

'Great, thank you,' I reply, shrugging off my lurid jacket, which looks ridiculously garish in these ancient and classy surroundings. She passes it to a man who seems to have appeared from nowhere; he must surely be her brother, judging by how similar they look.

'This way please,' she says.

I'm expecting a snug to be a small room, but I'm led through a doorway to the left into a huge sitting room with another fire blazing. The walls are covered in portraits of what look like people from different centuries, and above the fireplace there is another animal head – this time a boar with giant tusks and the same spooky glass eyes. Guess Alistair's family and their ancestors have always enjoyed their hunting.

'If you'd like to take a seat by the fire, I'll let the laird know that you are here,' she says, looking down her nose at me again, as if she thinks I might be about to steal something.

I settle into the sofa. In front of it there's a bottle of champagne on ice and a couple of glasses on a coffee table.

Of course there is. Suddenly I feel quite nervous. The usual 'dates' I've been on have usually consisted of a few drinks at a local pub and a kebab on the way home if I'm lucky. I've never been anywhere as grand as this, not even as a paying visitor, bar on a couple of school trips. Growing up in foster families means you don't tend to be a 'visit a National Trust property at the weekend' type of person.

I barely remember anything about Alistair from his stay at the lodge, other than him telling his friend to leave me alone. Is that a good enough reason to agree to spend the evening with someone in the middle of nowhere, with no means of getting away if I change my mind? And whoever the woman I spoke to on the phone was, she wasn't exactly joking when she said the access was 'tricky' – there's no way I could get back from here on my own.

I realize that I never got a reply about whether the driver will take me back at the end of the evening. Surely he will? So far everything has been . . . well, a bit strange, I guess, but that's only because I'm not used to this kind of treatment.

'You came!' The voice jolts me out of my thoughts. Alistair is now standing by the sofa – I hadn't noticed him arrive. 'I'm so pleased,' he continues. 'I wasn't sure you would. Thank you so much for coming all this way in this hellish weather. I hope the journey was OK and Donald ensured you were comfortable? I made sure he had some champagne for you and told him to take it easy on the lake – he can be a bit of a demon with the boat, left to his own devices.'

Alistair is better looking than I remembered: dark hair, dark eyes, clean-shaven and, I'm delighted to see, dressed simply in jeans and a jumper. Given the grandeur of the surroundings and the formality of everyone I've met here so far, I was worried he might be in a three-piece suit or something and I'd feel woefully underdressed. Even my gold jacket doesn't seem so embarrassing now, so I don't know why the maid or housekeeper or whoever she was had such a stick up her arse about it.

He looks nervous too, which I find somehow reassuring. 'The journey was fine, thank you. This is quite a place!'

He sits down next to me, smiles modestly and lifts

the bottle from the silver ice bucket. 'Would you like some?' he asks. 'Or I can get you something else if you prefer?'

'Champagne's lovely. Thank you,' I say. 'Is this where you . . . normally live? Or is it, um . . .' I'm not even sure what I'm asking here – is it *what*?

'Yes, I live here full time now, since my father passed a few years ago.'

'Oh . . . I'm sorry.'

He nods tersely as he deftly unwraps the foil from the top of the bottle, pops the cork off, fills the two glasses and hands me one. 'Thank you. We were never exactly . . . close, but it now falls to me to look after this place. Anyway, cheers.' We clink glasses and I take a sip.

'So you grew up here?' I ask.

'Kind of. I was mainly at boarding school. Back here in the holidays. Or, at least, some of the holidays. If I could get away with it, once I got into my teens I'd mainly stay in the London place if I was allowed, or with a mate, some of whom you met at the lodge.' He pauses. 'Sorry again for the way Tarkers behaved towards you. He can a bit . . . much, but underneath it all, he's all right.'

I shrug and take another sip of the champagne, which is growing on me. 'That's OK. I've got quite used to that kind of thing since I've been working there, to be honest. But I appreciate you standing up for me.'

'My mother brought me up to respect women,' he says. I wonder where his mother is now – was that who

I spoke to on the phone? Or is she dead too? But now doesn't seem to be the time to ask. 'So tell me about you,' he continues. 'Is this the first season you've worked at the lodge?'

'Yep. Just fell into it, really. I, um, grew up in care, and when I turned eighteen, I didn't know what to do next. The job came with accommodation, and I've always liked cooking, so . . . yeah. I thought it was worth a go.'

I don't usually tell people I barely know so much about my background, but something about Alistair makes me want to confide in him. Or maybe it's the champagne. I wave my hand. 'Sorry. Oversharing.'

He smiles. 'Not at all. And the job . . . are you enjoying it?'

'Yeah. Mainly. It's OK. Bit lonely, I guess. But it's not for ever.'

'I'm sure it's not. Someone like you, I imagine you could do anything you want.

I blush. 'That's very kind. But I don't know. I've never been very career-minded. Didn't do that well at school because I moved around a lot. And I'm not really good at anything except cooking.'

The door opens and the same man who took my coat appears again. To my astonishment, he bangs a little gong. 'Dinner is served.'

## 1983
The Nineteenth Lady of Creaglie

The butler insists on me leaving my glass on the coffee table, so he can then move it onto a silver tray as he leads the way to the dining room, and finally replace it on the table in front of me. I thought my boss at the lodge was stuffy about the way things are done, but this takes it to another level.

The dining room is beautiful, like the snug but even more grand, with yet another blazing fireplace and dominated by an enormous table which must be able to seat at least twenty people. It is set with five candelabras along its entire length, but I'm relieved to see that the only two place settings are opposite each other at one end. So it will just be us. I won't have to make conversation with any random family members I haven't yet met, and there won't be any of Alistair's knob-end friends joining us.

Another uniformed man who I haven't yet seen comes in and pours wine, offering a lengthy description of where it is from (in a nutshell, a vineyard somewhere in France), which grapes it is made of, what type of soil it has been grown in, along with a description of how it will taste. I smile politely and let what he's saying wash over me. Red or white is about as far as my wine knowledge goes, and that's always been enough for all except the most pretentious of the lodge guests.

There are various elaborate *amuse-bouches*, each described in minute detail by the man serving, followed by a tiny and exquisite bone-broth soup with julienned vegetables, then whole quail stuffed with sage and wrapped in bacon, followed by an incredible dark chocolate dessert with a melty centre.

And Alistair is sweet. So polite. Asks questions about me, listens when I speak, tells me stories about school and his travels. We drink a lot of wine and before I know it, the huge grandfather clock is striking eleven.

'Gosh is that the time?' I ask, genuinely surprised. 'I didn't ask but . . . I assume your, uh, driver guy can take me back?'

'Of course. You are very welcome to stay if you like – I had Morag make up a room just in case.' He glances out of the window. 'The weather out there is still pretty grim, but I'm guessing you have to get back for work?'

I do indeed have to get back for work, but what stands out to me most in his statement is that he had a room made up for me. All this, the driver, the champagne, dinner, the evening, was not aimed at simply getting me into bed. And I would absolutely love to see what the room is like – I bet it's amazing. But sadly . . .

'That's so kind. But I have to be back to do breakfast at the lodge. Another time though . . .' I add, instantly embarrassed, because who's to say he wants me to come another time?

'I would love that,' he says, to my relief. 'I'll call Donald for you now.' He says a few words to the waiter who scurries off. 'I'm sorry I didn't realize it was so late,' he adds. 'You'll be tired tomorrow.'

''S OK. I'm used to it.' The waiter reappears and announces that Donald is ready to take me back, before helping me with my chair.

Alistair leads me from the room and back to the front door, where someone hands him my coat and he holds it out to me to help me put it on. 'Thank you so much for coming tonight. It was a lovely evening.'

'It was,' I agree, somewhat breathlessly. Suddenly, more than anything, I want him to kiss me. But there's still a butler guy hovering and I don't know if . . . Alistair leans in and kisses me on the cheek.

'Safe journey home. I hope to see you again soon.'

The next day, another huge bunch of flowers arrives, along with a note saying: 'Same again next week? How about arriving before lunch so we can spend the day together? Call and let me know?'

I call straightaway to accept, speaking to the same woman as before, who I now know is Morag the house-keeper. She is no less snooty and unwelcoming than the last time, but whatever, I don't care.

And then after that things start to move quite quickly. The next time I visit, it's an unusually cold crisp day with blue skies – the kind of weather which almost never happens here. So, after a quick lunch which is much less formal than the dinner we had, we go for a hike in the forest which surrounds the castle. We end up at a hunting lodge, where tea and cake has been set out for us, before hiking back. Hot chocolate has been prepared for our return.

Alistair shows me to 'my' room which has been made up, even though he knows I can't stay. He wanted me to be able to 'freshen up', as he put it, in peace and comfort before dinner. The room is about the size of most of the houses I've lived in. In the centre there is a huge canopied double bed, with twisted thick wooden posts and brocade curtains. These are pulled back to reveal a tapestried bedspread and plump white pillows. It looks so inviting that I totally wish I could stay the night.

When we come back from our hike, Morag runs me a bath which is scented with God-knows-what oils; it is heavenly. She has left a stack of white towels on top of the old-fashioned radiator along with a spa-style robe. And because my clothes got wet in the snow, Alistair also asked her to find me something 'comfy' to wear. I was imagining something like some old track-suit bottoms and a sweatshirt, but hanging up in the window as I have my bath is a long bright-red velvet gown with a deep V neck and similarly plunging back. It looks like it would generally be very far from my idea of comfortable, but when I put it on, it's silky soft, the heavy fabric is warm and drapes beautifully.

It's actually pretty comfortable plus, even if I say so myself, it really suits me.

Given that there don't appear to be any women at the castle other than Morag, who I can't imagine wearing a dress like this let alone agreeing to lend it to me, I wonder who it belongs or belonged to. Perhaps his mother? Or a sister?

I'm guessing Alistair knew what I was going to be wearing tonight, as this time he is in a dinner jacket. Perhaps so that I don't feel overdressed, but maybe because he knows he looks pretty hot in it.

Dinner is a lot more flirty on both our sides than last time, and it quickly becomes very clear where this is leading. Suffice to say that I don't make it to my room, though I do make it to his. But Donald still takes me back in the early hours because I have to work in the morning. He remains as polite and courteous as ever, with no innuendo or knowing looks, even though he must know exactly what's been going on.

One month later, on our by-now-weekly Thursday date, when Alistair and I are lying in bed after dinner and I'm trying to gather the energy I need to get out of bed, get dressed, and start the long journey back over the water and down the mountain, Alistair takes my hands and says: 'I don't want you to go. Please stay.'

'I can't,' I say. 'I have to help with breakfast at the lodge. Otherwise I'll get sacked.'

He props himself up on his elbow and looks down at me. 'I know.' He strokes my cheek gently. 'I mean stay properly. Stay for good. Or at least for a while, see how you feel. You don't need that job. Don't go back. They'll manage. Stay here with me. We make each other happy. We have fun. I have easily enough money for both of us.'

I sigh. 'It's tempting but . . .' I sit up. 'I can't let them down like that.' I ease myself off the bed and start to put my clothes on.

'OK,' he agrees. 'I understand. I admire your . . . well, work ethic or whatever. But promise me something . . .'

I pull my jumper over my head. 'What?'

'When your contract finishes, come here and stay for a while. As long or as short as you like. Come and spend some time with me, here, so we can get to know each other properly. Let me look after you.'

No one had ever offered to look after me before, unless they were being paid to do so. And given that I would no longer have a home in two weeks' time when my job finished, it was a very tempting offer.

So I agreed. I moved to the castle. And that was that.

If only I'd known how much things would change.

# 1985
## The Nineteenth Lady of Creaglie

To start with, it is all amazing. We have a lavish, if small, summer wedding at Creaglie Castle, followed by a honeymoon in Italy, as apparently is the tradition in Alistair's family. Almost all the guests are his extended family and friends, though in truth he doesn't seem to have many of either. I try to invite my last foster parents, but they are too busy with their new foster children, and it would be a very long journey to the castle for them. I feel a pang, like the one I always did when I moved homes, because people in my life have always been so temporary. But I push the negative feelings away. I am marrying Alistair now, I will have a husband, and probably, in time, a family. Things aren't going to be temporary for me any more. So on my side, guest-wise, it's only the chef from the lodge and his partner. They come along for the party and I think to have a nosy around, because it's rare to get an invitation to Creaglie Castle, according to what he told me when we were still working together. But I don't imagine we'll stay in touch.

For the first year or so, I love playing lady of the manor. Alistair and I do loads of hiking, have loads of sex, go on lots of holidays all over the world, and have great food when we are at home. Plus I never have to lift a finger – absolutely everything is done for me.

We are having such a good time together that it takes me a while to realize that we never spend time with anyone else.

'Why don't we have some people over?' I suggest one night over yet another elaborate dinner just for the two of us. 'Why don't we have a party? It seems a shame to have this place all to ourselves and never show it off to anyone else.'

Alistair clears the last of the food from his plate and puts down his knife and fork. 'We could consider doing that. Who would you like to invite?'

'Um . . .' I don't have an answer. I don't have any close friends. Or any friends at all, for that matter, now that I think about it. I made friends over the years as a child and teenager, of course, but it's hard to stay in touch when you move around so much. There were people I wrote to and received letters from for a while, and talked to on the phone now and again, but the calls and letters always petered out after a few weeks or months. These days, we're so remote that I never meet anyone except when we're travelling. And Alistair isn't the sociable type, so we're not the kind of couple who strikes up conversation with another couple in a resort and arranges to have dinner with them. He'd always prefer it was just us.

'Well, I don't know . . .' I say, 'but you know lots of people. What about those guys you were at school with? The ones who you were at the lodge with when we first met? They seemed . . . fun?'

They didn't. They were awful. But by this point I can barely remember when I spoke to someone other than Alistair or one of the housekeeping staff. I was never the most sociable of people either, so initially, I didn't mind. I even thought it was quite cute that my new husband wanted his blushing bride all to himself.

But it's starting to feel quite claustrophobic now. It's not that we've exactly run out of things to say to each other – we haven't – but I'm twenty years old and in spite of all the luxury trappings I have around me, I feel like I need something else. That something is missing. And apart from anything else, it's starting to make me a little uneasy.

'Them?' he says, dismissively. 'I'm not really in touch with *them* any more. I feel like I've outgrown them, now that I have you. They were mainly people I used to stay with in the holidays at school.' He pauses. 'When I wanted to avoid coming back here.'

'You've never really told me why you avoided coming back here in the holidays. It's such a beautiful place. And now it seems to be your pride and joy,' I say, cautiously. Now and again, Alistair has alluded to problems in his childhood and his relationship with his parents, but only in fairly vague terms.

He takes my hand. 'My father was controlling and my mother did nothing to protect me from him when she was alive. It's different now that you are here, but back then, the castle was a joyless place. I don't think it's going too far to say that it was even somewhat frightening.'

I squeeze his hand. 'And your parents . . . what happened to them?' I ask. I've tried to ask several times, but he's always avoided the subject.

'There was an accident,' he says stiffly. 'While I was away at school doing my A levels. No one bothered to tell me for two days. Not even my sister.'

Sister? This is literally the first time he's mentioned a sister. 'You've got a sister?' I ask. 'Where is she now?'

He takes a large slug of wine and slams the glass back down. 'We're estranged,' he says. 'She brought shame on the family. Or she would have done if . . . if we'd let her. It wasn't a good time for any of us. She's no longer in my life. My parents disinherited her shortly before they died. She has no claim on . . . anything, due to her . . . choices and, quite frankly, I'll be quite happy never to see her again.'

He looks down at his hands and I see his expression harden. He rests his fingers on the edge of the table and takes a deep breath in and out, before looking back up at me, his expression neutral, saying: 'Do you mind if we talk about something else?'

## Silas's voiceover

The year of death was 1863.

The son of the Fourteenth Laird of Creaglie and a servant child, with whom he had struck up a close friendship, were playing hide and seek.

The young noble was delighted with the excellent hiding place he had found, a trunk with a heavy lid in the attic of an obscure, little-used wing of the castle.

After half an hour of fruitless searching, the servant boy, who was not officially allowed to play with the six-year-old future laird, was called away to his task of lighting fires in the bedrooms and abandoned the game. Fearing he would get in trouble if he admitted to playing with the 'upstairs' boy, he told no one.

It was only some hours later that it was realized that the boy was missing and a search launched, and several more hours before his body was finally found. He had suffocated in the trunk, unable to open the heavy lid.

The servant boy never admitted to their game, but

carried the guilt throughout his life, finally confessing on his death bed and being absolved of his sins by a priest.

Throughout the decades since, servants in the East Wing have claimed to hear small footsteps running across floorboards in the attic above their heads as they sleep. Legend has it that these are the footsteps of the two boys playing, reunited in death, still friends enjoying a game of hide and seek, in spite of one causing the demise of the other.

Then again, it could be mice.

We'll probably never know for sure.

## 1988
The Nineteenth Lady of Creaglie

Things didn't change overnight, of course. It was a gradual slide. We started to travel less, and Alistair was away from home more often 'on business' – always a little vague about what he was actually doing, but it was made clear he felt that I didn't need to know.

I began to get itchy feet. I tried to take up hobbies, more gardening, more baking, more reading, but none of those things interested me and I quickly tired of them. I was always bored and unfulfilled. I didn't know what I wanted, but I knew it was more than this. I had everything I could possibly want materially, of course, but absolutely nothing to do.

I suggested to Alistair that I get a job in one of the lodges again – nothing fancy; maybe something seasonal like I had been doing before. Something to help pass the time, let me get out and about to meet people. But he said it was unseemly for a lady of my position to be doing menial work. Plus, realistically, it would be at least an hour there and an hour back, probably more; most of the available jobs would require long hours; many would require staying overnight. None of which Alistair would countenance. And apart from anything else, we absolutely didn't need the income.

'You're bound to get pregnant soon,' he'd say. 'And then you'd have to give up work anyway. You need to be here for our child. It's the way the Creaglies do it. Always have done, always will do.'

'You said you had a nanny from when you were a baby and went to boarding school aged eight,' I had countered one evening while we were having yet another dinner for two. 'And that you had a terrible relationship with your parents. That your father was controlling and your mother did nothing about it. You're completely estranged from your sister. That's not what I want for our child. It's not like I had the best childhood either, and I have no family apart from you, as you know, so I'm keen that for our child, or hopefully children, we—'

He'd slammed his hand down on the table, making me jump. I had been seeing this side of him more and more lately, and I didn't like it. It scared me.

'That is utterly beside the point,' he'd said, evenly. 'Mama might have been weak, but she was always here for us. She wasn't away somewhere cleaning toilets like a . . . well.' He'd looked up at me, his expression hard and unsympathetic. 'I'm sorry. It's just that . . . I was hoping that by now we'd have that heir on the way.'

God. This again, I'd thought. As soon as we were married, Alistair had talked me into stopping taking the pill. 'Imagine,' he'd whispered as we lay entwined in bed one night, 'a little you or me, made from our love. How amazing would that be?'

And when he'd put it like that, it did sound amazing. Growing up in foster care, I had no siblings and had never known either of my parents, or ever truly felt loved. A little person of my very own! Who would love me unconditionally. Made of me and Alistair. It did sound wonderful. A mini miracle.

At the beginning, like most couples I imagine, we'd had a lot of sex. I thought it would happen in no time. We were young and healthy, at it like rabbits, but nothing happened.

I'd suggested we both go for tests. But he was having none of it.

'It takes time sometimes,' he'd said. 'It'll be fine.'

Five years on, we still have regular sex, but it has become almost mechanical, an ordeal. When Alistair is at home, we do it every three days, without fail, wherever I am in my cycle, as he's read somewhere that that is the best way. I get it over as quickly as possible. He no longer bothers to make sure I enjoy it like he used to in the past. We've even taken to sleeping in different rooms, him using the excuse that I read too late in the night and he gets up earlier than me, so it's better for both of us.

In the beginning, I used to join Alistair on his trips to London. We'd try out all the latest restaurants, maybe see a couple of shows. Once we even went to a night-club, though he hated it and we left early. But whatever we did, it was always just the two of us. Growing up in the north, and not staying in touch with anyone anyway, I don't have any friends in London, but I thought we might see some of his at least. I craved new company. But no.

I used to enjoy shopping, even if alone, while he was in his various meetings, marvelling at the window displays in places like Selfridges and Liberty. Trying on the clothes. Buying myself things which in the past I could never even have dreamed of affording. But Alistair would make his disapproval very clear at items he deemed 'unsuitable' – basically anything that he considered too short or too tight, or in any way 'tarty' or even 'slutty', as he would put it.

'You are the Nineteenth Lady of Creaglie!' he would shout. 'You will not dress like a cheap whore! My family's reputation is everything to me and I will not have you cheapen it like my sister tried to!'

Over time, I tempered what I bought and shopping became less interesting. And then he started to accuse me of meeting other men while I was out shopping, and didn't want me to go out alone at all. Once or twice, when he wouldn't believe me about where I'd been, he'd hit me – but then been full of remorse and begged and cried and bought me presents, often very expensive jewellery, and promised it would never happen again. And mainly, it didn't. But perhaps that was because I started trying very hard not to accidentally provoke him.

It became easier simply to agree not to buy the clothes

135

he didn't want me to wear, or not to go to the theatre alone because he would always accuse me of secretly meeting up with someone. Eventually it became easier not to go to London with him at all; it was too exhausting trying to convince him I could be trusted when I was out alone. By then we had dogs at home, and I made the excuse that I wanted to stay with them. The staff were perfectly capable of looking after them of course, but I'm sure it was a relief for both of us that I decided to stay behind. Alistair didn't want me with him in London. For all I knew, he might even have another woman there, but even if he did, I wasn't sure I actually cared all that much. It was clear that we were already growing apart, if we'd even had anything in common in the first place. Apart from anything else, it meant having some time away from that awful, perfunctory sex we were having.

I should never have married him – I realize that now. I was too young, dazzled by the opulence of his life, too insecure, didn't know any better. I consider leaving, of course. But where would I go? I have no money, no friends, know no one. And I know that Alistair would never allow it. He would see it as bringing shame on the good name of the Creaglie family, which was the most important thing to him, above all else. He has never been explicit about what his sister did, but the alleged shame she could have apparently brought on the whole family is clearly almost the worst thing in the world to him. I assume she got pregnant by someone deemed unsuitable, unless she did something like join a commune or become a drug addict.

I wonder about trying to get in touch with her. Perhaps she could shed some light on why Alistair is the way he is? Perhaps I could even encourage him to forgive her for whatever she did. But I wouldn't know where to begin to look for her. I don't even know her first name, Alistair refuses to ever speak about her. It's entirely possible that she's dead – Alistair has never said that she isn't.

No Creaglies have ever divorced, Alistair has proclaimed before, several times. He is very proud of that fact. He is also a rich and powerful man and would rather see me dead than allow me to leave him, I am sure of it.

Even so, I am intermittently considering leaving as a possibility. Sometimes I feel brave and try to start planning. But most days, it seems like an impossibility.

Today I am weighing up the options as I plant yet more flowers. I have absolutely no interest in the garden, but am simply trying to make the boring and lonely hours pass faster.

It is probably too late for me to leave. I should have made my escape when I was in London back when he still took me with him. He would be too suspicious if I asked to join him on a trip now. And the logistics of getting away from this place are a nightmare. I can't operate the boat. And even if I could, and I could get across the lake, it's a six-hour walk to the main road. I can't drive. I have no access to any money. I don't have a bank account of my own, or even a cash card, because I never go anywhere alone. He has made me powerless. He has done it deliberately.

Suddenly my situation seems absolutely desperate. I put down my trowel, stop digging and sit down on the ground. I don't care about growing things! Stupid hobbies that I don't even like are not a substitute for a proper life! I fling the trowel across the grass, put my head in my hands and weep. It's hopeless. I'm never going to get away from here. Never. Perhaps I should kill myself. Being dead would be better than living a half-life like this.

I let myself cry and cry, sobbing so hard that I can barely breathe. Suddenly I am aware of a shadow falling over me. I look up and see Luca, the junior butler, standing there.

'My Lady? Are you all right? Are you unwell? Can I get you something?'

He looks at me with such kindness as he puts out his hand for me to hold to pull myself up. And in that instant I realize what I need.

An ally.

## 1988
The Nineteenth Lady of Creaglie

I allow Luca to pull me up from my seated position on the grass in the garden and deliberately stumble slightly once I am upright, pushing myself briefly against him before righting myself as if it was an accident.

He is a little older than me, though not as old as Alistair, and lives on site as all the staff do; they have to as we are so remote. I think he's Morag's brother, though I don't really know him at all, or even what he does here. He is quite good-looking in a forgettable way, although I am so lonely and starved of affection these days that pretty much any man looks good to me.

Most of all, he looks kind. I hope he will help me. But at the same time, I know that most of the staff are extremely loyal to Alistair and his family. Some of them have literally worked here for generations, like something out of *Brideshead Revisited*, so it will take more than me simply asking to get him to help me.

'Oh, I'm so embarrassed,' I lie, brushing away my

tears. 'You . . . won't tell Alistair that you saw me crying, will you?'

He frowns. 'If something is upsetting you, m'lady, I'm sure the laird would want to know,' he says. His open, guileless face almost makes my heart break. I need to take things slowly. Lay the groundwork.

'It's nothing,' I say. 'Just me being silly. But you will no doubt know that Alistair is very concerned with appearances, and he would be annoyed that I am crying where someone might see me. He'd think that reflects badly on him.'

His brow furrows again. 'But this is your home. Surely if you want to . . .'

A fresh wave of unexpected tears comes, and this time there's nothing I can do to stop them. This isn't my home. It doesn't feel like home. I don't have a home. I never have done, not really. What have I done?

Luca looks at me in horror. 'My Lady, please don't cry . . .' He touches my arm gently and I can't help but shuffle closer to him and put my head on his chest. I feel him glance around, no doubt to check that no one can see us, as he puts his arms around me and gently strokes my hair. 'Don't cry . . .' he says, 'Please don't cry. Whatever it is, I'm sure it can be sorted out.'

We stay like that for a few minutes as he lets me sob. And then I know what I want to do. What I need to do to get out of this situation. I press my hips closer to his, careful to make it seem like an accidental movement, my snuffles subsiding as I switch to planning mode rather than pathetic weeping wench, and I feel that he is growing hard. I pretend not to notice as he repositions himself, moving away and gently taking my arms in his hands.

'Come on. You'll be OK,' he says. 'Let's go inside and get you a cup of tea or something.'

After that, I know it's only a matter of time.

It's not like I'm used to doing anything like this. But I'm desperate, and I have nothing, except my own body. Back when I was a teenager I'd loved 'going out on the pull' as we'd called it then, and I was good at it. Could get anyone I wanted. It's years since I've done that. But I'm sure I can remember how.

For the next few months, even when Alistair is home, when he is out of sight I make sure to look extra sad whenever Luca is near. Whenever I have the opportunity to talk to Luca or ask him to do something, which I make sure is much more frequently than it used to be, I drop not-so-subtle hints about Alistair's controlling nature. I'm sure it's not my imagination that – at the same time – Luca is around me more often than he used to be.

And then when Alistair is away, I make sure to wear my skimpiest clothes at every opportunity around the castle even though most of the time it's freezing. I tell Luca that I love to feel the air on my skin, how much more comfortable I feel in a short skirt, but that Alistair thinks it is immodest, and how I can't wear the clothes that I want to when he is around.

I make a show of drinking more wine than I should

141

at dinner 'because it is so lonely eating alone night after night'. Afterwards, when Luca and I play chess, which he only agrees to when I manage to assure him that it's not improper, that Alistair wants his staff to make sure my every need and want is tended to, I'll leave my shirt more unbuttoned than I should to make sure he catches more than a glimpse of one of my favourite bras, bought from Liberty last time I was in London. Sometimes I don't wear a bra at all.

Our conversations gradually become less and less formal, and more and more personal. I take it slowly so as not to scare Luca away with his fear of behaving improperly in his role. Initially I tell him that I want to learn to play chess to help pass my lonely hours, and our conversations are purely around the game. Later, while we play, we start to make general chitchat about the garden, or the weather, or similar things of no consequence. But over the months our subjects of conversation become gradually less and less superficial and we move on to learning more about each other.

'So how long have you worked here?' I ask, opening with my usual move of king's pawn to E4.

'Just over five years,' he says, countering with his pawn to E5. Predictable.

'And before that?' Bishop to C4.

He pulls a face. 'You don't want to know.'

I laugh. 'I do.'

He looks straight at me. 'I was in prison.' Queen to G5.

I wasn't expecting that.

142

I try not to look shocked. 'Oh. I see,' I say. I look down at the board again and feel myself blush, I'm not sure why. I move my pawn to H4 – a stupid, pointless move, but I've lost all concentration now.

I look back up at him after I've made my move, but he is still looking at the board, not at me.

'Go on,' he says.

'It's your move,' I reply.

He smiles wryly. 'No, I mean, go on, ask. I know you want to. People always do.'

'Not sure what you mean,' I lie.

He laughs. 'Yes you do. People always want to know. I was in for robbery. But I was set up. I didn't do it.' He pauses. 'But your husband doesn't know about it. It was impossible for me to get a job anywhere with that kind of record, and I'm sure that would have included here if they'd known. Morag got me in. They prefer a personal recommendation to a CV here, as you probably know.' He pauses again. 'I think I can trust you not to tell. And, I hope, not to judge.'

I swallow. Suddenly I think I know where this is going. 'You can trust me,' I whisper.

He stands up from his chair and comes to sit on the sofa next to me. My heart starts beating faster. He puts one finger under my chin and tilts my face upwards towards his.

'Of course, it would be even better if we both had a secret,' he says. 'That way I could be sure that you would keep mine.'

He leans in closer and I hear an involuntary squeak which I think comes from me. 'You've been leading up to this for months,' he says softly. 'Don't think I haven't noticed.'

And then we are kissing.

## 1988–9
The Nineteenth Lady of Creaglie

It didn't take long from the first time I kissed Luca for it to progress to more. Alistair was away almost all of the time by now; even when he was back, he was becoming more and more distant. I had become quite afraid of him since he had hit me a few times, and I now tried to stay out of his way as much as possible. I was lonely and bored, and given that Luca was almost as incarcerated here as I was, I assumed it was almost the same for him.

While initially my fling with Luca was simply a means to an end, because I would need someone to help me leave, I quickly started to care for him more than I had expected to. We had much more in common than Alistair and I did, both being from humble backgrounds, used to working for other people.

When I think about it now, it's no wonder that Alistair and I have grown apart so quickly. We are from two very different worlds and want different things. I was dazzled by the perceived glamour of him at first, the life he could offer, the fact that he seemed to adore me, want only me. But now I see that he wanted someone he could control, to possess me, and all he is bothered about is keeping his precious family name alive and providing an heir. I don't matter, I could be anyone. All I am to him is chattel, a vessel, a prize cow whose only real purpose is to breed. Looking back, I can see that a large part of my appeal for him when we met was probably that I had no family, no friends, no one to run to, and no real life experience.

When Alistair is home, we still have that awful perfunctory sex every few days, have done for years now, but nothing has happened.

Until now. My period is late, my boobs hurt and I feel sick most of the time. I'm pretty sure I'm pregnant. There's no real way to check – Alistair will not allow me to go into the local town alone. He insists that a 'lady of my station' needs a chaperone – usually Morag – so I rarely bother. Morag has never warmed to me and I'm not going to ask her to buy a test for me – I don't want her knowing my business, plus she has always been much more loyal to Alistair than to me. I could ask Luca, but it would feel too weird. After all this time, with it happening now, I think it's much more likely that Luca is the father than Alistair.

I'm not sure what I was expecting when I tell Luca, but it wasn't the look of unabashed horror I receive.

'But we've always been so careful!' he says.

I shake my head. 'Not careful enough, it seems.' I feel tears come to my eyes.

'How do you know it's even mine?' he adds, sharply, in a tone he's never used with me before.

'Uh . . . I don't know one hundred per cent for sure. I just really think it is,' I say.

He clears his throat. 'I've never asked, because part of me doesn't want to know, but I assume you and he, the laird, that you still . . .'

'Yes!' I snap. 'Sometimes. But . . . please, believe me, I think the chances are this baby is yours.'

This is so humiliating. I don't want to talk to Luca about the awful sex life that I have with Alistair, but I guess if it comes to it, I'll have to. Perhaps I should have lied. Told Luca that Alistair and I never have sex. But it's too late now.

Luca's expression softens. He touches my hand lightly and then pulls it away. 'I'm sorry. It's just such a shock. I wasn't expecting . . . this. How are you feeling?'

I shrug. 'Not amazing, to be honest. I feel sick almost all the time. And I'm exhausted.' I smile weakly. 'So it's lucky I never have to do anything.'

'And have you told, um, your husband?'

Tears well again. 'Not yet. I guess part of me is thinking it's early days and . . . maybe the problem will go away on its own.'

He nods. 'I don't know what to say, to be honest.' He pauses. 'You really think it, the baby, is mine?'

'I do,' I reply. 'I don't want to go into too much detail but . . . Alistair and I weren't taking any precautions

147

for years but I never got pregnant and then with you, suddenly . . .' I feel myself go red and I can't meet Luca's eye.

'But he's away a lot?' Luca says, somewhat desperately. 'Might that not be the reason that it took a while?'

Fuck's sake. Do I have to spell it out? 'Luca. I really think it's yours. I don't know how far along I am exactly, but that's another issue. I'll probably have to pretend the baby arrived either early or late to fit in with . . . well. You know.'

He nods again. 'I see.' A few seconds pass in an uncomfortable and loaded silence. 'So I assume you're . . . not going to tell him the full story?' he continues. 'If it turns out that—'

'What? No! Of course not!' A bolt of fear lurches through me. 'I honestly think he'd kill me. You're not suggesting that I, that we, that you . . .' A wave of nausea rises and I stand up as, for a moment or two, I feel like I might throw up – it doesn't take much at the moment. My head spins – I shouldn't have stood up so quickly.

Luca puts his head in his hands momentarily and then looks up at me. 'I'm not suggesting anything. Please, sit down.'

I swallow the nausea back and retake my place on the sofa. Tears threaten again. I'm not sure how I imagined this would go but I'm pretty sure it wasn't like this.

'Look, I just meant . . . for both of us, all of us,' he continues, 'it's probably better that your husband remains none the wiser, isn't it? I'm in no position to look after a child, and while we . . . well, you and he are married and he's a powerful man, quite ruthless too, from what you say. Maybe there's a chance that it is his child anyway. Also . . . Morag said there was this stuff with his sister years back, where they said she brought shame on the family, and no one knows what happened to her. So perhaps, it's for the best all round, safer for everyone, including the little one, if . . .'

I pull my hand away, trying not to snatch, and tears start to fall. Of course he's right, I said almost as much myself. That while no man is likely to take his wife carrying someone else's child lightly, when it comes to Alistair, we could actually be putting ourselves in danger. I bury my face in my hands and sob.

I feel Luca's hand on my knee. 'Please don't cry. I'll help you all I can but . . . you understand this is for the best, don't you? Your . . . our child, won't want for anything if he or she stays with you and the laird here at Creaglie Castle. But if you – we – throw that all away, then who knows what he might do . . .'

I stand up and wipe my eyes. 'You've made your position very clear,' I say. 'I'm not sure there's any point in talking about it any more.' I turn on my heel and go to my room.

## 1989
### The Nineteenth Lady of Creaglie

I don't see Luca at all for the next few days. The castle is large and it is easy to avoid someone if you so choose, which I imagine is what he is doing. Though after the way he reacted, part of me wonders if he has gone entirely. He is not like Morag or Donald, weirdly loyal to their employer. He is a little cagey about his past but reading between the lines, I get the impression that being somewhat of a drifter and moving from one place to the next would not be a new thing for him. It isn't beyond the realm of possibility that he is too worried about the possible consequences of this baby and has simply made an excuse and left both me and his job. There's no reason anyone would think to tell me if he had. I wonder about asking Morag, but she's a nosy old bitch and I don't want to arouse suspicion. She would wonder why I was asking.

Might Luca have told her about us? No. No. Surely not.

I feel more trapped than ever. I don't want this baby. I'd never really thought beyond the awful, soulless sex Alistair and I were having as he tried to impregnate me because nothing ever came of it. But suddenly I see that having a baby, even if Alistair is not the father, is a disaster for me. It is vital that Alistair doesn't find out that I am pregnant by another man but, even aside from that, I don't want to be tied to him forever by a child.

I try drinking gin in a hot bath because I've a vague idea that it's meant to sort out the issue, but all it does is make me feel woozy and sick. I spend time in the library, scouring texts to see if I can find any other home 'remedies' for my problem. After finding an ancient book about natural poisons and medicines, I forage for plants which I think might be mugwort and pennyroyal in the garden, infuse them into a tea and drink it several times. It tastes foul and makes my stomach hurt but nothing else happens. My period still doesn't arrive and the baby continues to grow inside me.

Eventually the time comes when I feel I have to tell Alistair. My breasts are larger and tender – I will have to get some new bras – and were I to wear tight clothes, which I have not done for the past few weeks for this very reason, it would be clear that my belly is starting to swell.

'I think I'm pregnant,' I tell Alistair the next time he is back home and we are sitting together at one of our dismal, silent dinners.

He glances up at me and smiles, the first time I've seen him do so in months.

'That *is* good news,' he says. 'I was starting to think it would never happen.' He takes another forkful of his food. 'So when can we expect the happy event?'

'Um . . . I don't know exactly, but I think probably December? A little before Christmas maybe? It's difficult to be precise.'

If my theory that this is not his child is correct, and it arrives on time, it will either be the beginning or end of December. But as these things aren't an exact science, I'm pretty sure I can fudge this without Alistair noticing – he doesn't exactly pay attention or even want to know more than necessary when it comes to 'ladies' things', as he puts it. Eventually I will have to see a doctor or midwife, I imagine, but it will be easy enough to keep things vague – I will say that I have never had regular periods and don't keep a diary of when we have sex.

'Well, that will be nice,' he says. 'A little Christmas present for us both.' He raises his glass. 'Here's to the little one.' He pauses. 'And to you, of course,' he adds, clearly as an afterthought.

My pregnancy is uneventful, like the rest of my life. Alistair is a little nicer to me, slightly less dismissive, asks how I am feeling more often, makes a bit more effort with conversation perhaps. And thankfully we no longer have to have sex, so that's something.

It turns out Luca hasn't left the castle. But he is different with me – polite but distant – and tries to avoid me as much as he can, especially when I am alone. There is certainly no intimacy any more, physical or emotional.

I am as lonely as I have ever been. But unless I kill myself, which I have to admit, I do consider in my darkest moments, I can now see no escape.

The birth is like nothing I could imagine. I literally think I am going to die. No one can come through this kind of pain, surely? But then I do, and the baby is handed to me.

A daughter. She is beautiful.

I know Alistair will be disappointed that she is not a boy. But I don't care. As soon as I see her, I know that she is my everything.

The birth of my baby is not what I had expected at all, but Thalia gives me something to live for. She is the best thing that ever happened to me.

I am wracked with guilt over the thought that I tried to get rid of her before she was born, that I tried to poison her, putting myself at risk too, because I didn't want her. The thought that I might never have met her – that she might never have existed – sends shivers down my spine.

Alistair briefly goes through the motions of pretending to be pleased when she arrives, but it wears off pretty quickly, and he goes back to spending more and more time away. I hope he has a mistress in London, I don't care if he does. Whatever keeps him away from here is good news for me and Thalia as far as I'm concerned.

All thoughts of trying to escape have gone. My daughter is everything I need emotionally, and Alistair provides everything she and I need materially. He might be cold and uninteresting, but if I stay, she and I will always be safe and warm, and want for nothing. Thalia will have a better life here than I could ever provide for her by myself, or indeed with Luca.

I tell Alistair that Thalia doesn't need a nanny – I am happy to look after her myself. It is hard to persuade him; he is so stuck in his ways.

'But I had a nanny – and my father before me, and so on – it's the way we've always done things!' he protests, though thankfully he eventually relents when I promise that I will not be leaving the castle with Thalia without Morag as a chaperone. As usual it is the impression we might give that he is most worried about – he wouldn't want others to know that a Creaglie child is simply being brought up by her mother.

She will perhaps have a governess when she is older. We are too far away from any school for her to go every day, and I am not well educated enough to teach her myself. And there is no way I am sending her away to a horrible, sterile boarding school like Alistair went to, though I will no doubt have to have that battle with him too when the time comes. But that is a worry for another day. He has said himself his mother was weak, and never stood up for him, and I wondered if he blames his mother for allowing him to be sent away to school. Alistair clearly never felt he fitted in at school, and you'd hardly have to be Freud to work out that his upbringing, far away from his parents with apparently little to no warmth or love must have contributed to his coldness.

When we first met, he seemed to have a little awareness of this, but almost as soon as we got married, he became determined to do things as his parents had done. That is not what I want for Thalia. I am resolute – she will break the chain.

In the warmer months, Thalia and I spend most of our days in the garden, me nursing, reading as she naps, pottering around. And once Thalia can crawl, I put on my oldest clothes and we explore the grounds on our hands and knees together, pretending to be tigers, picking flowers, gathering petals and herbs to dry and make teas. Sometimes we take the little rowing boat out on the water and have a picnic on an islet a short distance away. It is covered in flowers and there are dozens of butterflies. When it is colder we sit by the fire, playing with wooden blocks and toys which once belonged to Alistair and generations of children before him too, or spend time in the kitchen, the only place that really stays warm here in winter, baking cakes in the Aga. Morag's little girl Sarah has taken a real shine to Thalia and often likes to hang out with us too. I am glad; Thalia should have a playmate.

I have found more contentment in our simple daily routines than I ever could have imagined.

To start with, Luca keeps his distance from Thalia, as he has continued to keep me at arm's length. But almost like a shy feral cat, over the months, he slinks closer.

Thalia is the spitting image of me – almost as if she's been cloned. But even so, I think I can see a hint of Luca in her eyes when she smiles, and around her mouth when she laughs.

Others might say that this is wishful thinking, of course. You could argue that her hair colour is more like Alistair's, for example. But I am convinced she is Luca's daughter and I get the impression that he thinks she is too.

I take things slowly with Luca, just as I did when I was originally trying to seduce him, which now feels like a lifetime ago. When I see that he is stacking wood one day in the garden, I sit nearby under a tree with Thalia. And then when I feel the time is right, I say:

'Luca? I need to go inside and use the bathroom. Could you please watch Thalia for me for a minute?'

He turns bright red and blusters, 'Oh no, I don't think so, m'lady,' looking around to see if anyone else is in earshot, though I have already made sure that they aren't. 'I don't know anything at all about babies, I wouldn't know what to do if . . .'

I wave my hand. 'Don't be silly. I didn't know anything about babies either before she arrived but,' I touch her nose gently and she giggles, 'somehow we muddle through, don't we, my darling?' I smile at Luca. 'Sit here on this blanket with her, tickle her tummy or something maybe, she likes that, and I'll be back in no time.'

He sits down uncertainly and looks at Thalia. I see his expression soften. 'OK,' he says. 'But don't be long. What do I do if she starts crying or anything?'

'Pick her up and give her a cuddle,' I say. 'But she won't, I promise.'

I walk away and, when I'm at a suitable distance, hide behind a tree. I watch as, for a couple of minutes, Luca simply looks at her. Then he gently touches one of her hands and smiles as she grasps his fingers. He tickles her tummy like I suggested and I hear her giggle. He eases himself down onto his elbow and tickles her again. Then he lies down flat on the rug by her and strokes her hair, gazing at her like she's the most amazing thing on the planet. Which, to me, she is.

I smile. I don't need the loo at all. I just want to get Luca used to spending time with her, to fall in love with her, in the same way I did, the second I met her.

It seems like sensible insurance for the future.

## 1990
## Sarah

I live in a castle. It should be like something from a fairy-tale. All the space I want, a forest as my playground, a lake as my swimming pool. Sliding down long banisters of massive staircases, playing hide and seek in all the enormous rooms, weaving through adults' legs as they hold glamorous parties or banquets like I read about in books.

But it isn't like that at all. It is boring living in a castle if you are all alone. I have no one to play with, and it is too far away from anywhere to go to school. Mama says that's OK because I am being 'home educated' by her and Uncle Luca, but they are always very busy so I don't have many proper lessons, though Uncle Luca is good at teaching me about plants in the garden and Mama at teaching me to cook. There are a lot of books here and I am very good at reading, so a lot of the time I do that because that way I am quiet

158

and not getting in anybody's way and because there is nothing else to do.

Servants' children are to be neither seen nor heard, like the children in the old stories. Mama says that if I make a nuisance of myself, she might lose her job, and then where would we be? On the streets, she warns, that's where. We're only here, warm and safe, thanks to the kindness of the man who owns the castle and who gave her a job, she says. He never seems very kind to me, but I don't say that to Mama as I know she would get cross. And actually it is not usually very warm, but I wouldn't want to be living on the streets because that would be even colder, and so I understand that it's important that I don't annoy anyone and I am good at doing what I am told.

I behave nicely, most of the time keeping to our little flat, which is tucked away on a high floor of a remote wing of the castle, or helping Mama in the kitchen. I like it in there, it's warm and cosy, unlike most of the rest of the place, and I am good at helping with weighing things, stirring bowls, licking the spoon. Collecting eggs from the chickens is also my job, and I have my own little basket to bring them in. I am not allowed to name them though, because once they stop laying they are ready for the pot; they are not to be treated like pets. I once asked if I could have a pet, a cat or even a hamster or a gerbil, but Mama says it would be extra work for her, and that the people she works for might not like it, so I am not allowed. Sometimes I feel like

I am never allowed to do anything at all, but we are safe and not on the streets and Mama says that is the most important thing.

And the man in charge of the castle, he scares me. Mama tells me to stay out of his way, and I always make sure that I do anyway, because being near him is not nice. He doesn't shout or anything like that, but it feels like there is an invisible black cloud around him which you might get sucked into if you are not careful.

And then the baby comes and everything is different. Better, so much better. Before the baby arrived, the man was always scary and the lady always sad. Mama had told me before that the lady wanted to have a baby but it wasn't arriving, and sometimes it happens like that and no one knows why, and that was what was making her sad. So before the baby came, I wasn't supposed to be where she could see me more than necessary because Mama said it would probably make her even more sad because I was a child and she couldn't have a child of her own.

But once the baby arrives everything is nicer. The man is away from the castle much more, and when he is away, it is always a much happier place. The lady smiles more and even laughs and sings. She doesn't do that when he is here.

And the little girl, she is so sweet. I adore her. She is like a doll, but real and alive. But Mama tells me that babies are very fragile, and the lady is very busy looking after her so it is now even more important that I mustn't make a nuisance of myself around them.

But then one day, when it is warm and sunny and I am on my way back from collecting the eggs, the lady and the baby are in the garden on a blanket under a tree. She sees me looking and beckons me over. At first I am scared because I think she is going to tell me off for looking at the baby when I shouldn't have been, but she smiles and says: 'Would you like to meet baby Thalia? I'm sure she'd like to meet you!'

She has never spoken to me before because I always try to keep out of her way and I'm not sure if Mama will think it's OK or not, but surely it would be very rude to ignore the lady or to say 'no', and I really want to see the baby properly anyway, so I go closer, half whisper, 'Yes please', and sit down on the blanket next to them.

'She's really small,' I say, because I can't think of anything else to say and she is really, really small.

The lady laughs. 'She is. Very small. But she'll get bigger. And then she might be fun for you to play with. Would you like that?'

I nod. I am so bored on my own at the castle and want a friend more than anything. 'I'm sure she'd love to play with you too,' the lady adds. She smiles at me. 'Would you like to hold her?'

I look around the garden – I don't think Mama would be pleased about me spending this much time with the lady. She'd say she would have better things to do than pay attention to someone like me.

But the lady is being so nice to me and I never have anyone to talk to, so I whisper, 'Yes please.'

She smiles at me again. 'Lovely. Why don't you sit with your legs crossed so you can sit up nice and straight . . .' I do what she says as she lifts the baby off the ground. 'See how I've got my hand under her head? That's important because her neck isn't very strong. So put your hand on top of your leg, palm up, yes that's right, and I'm going to place Thalia down in your lap so you can hold her. OK?'

I'm suddenly a bit scared and worried that I won't be doing it right and will somehow hurt the baby, but at the same time I really want to hold her. The lady gently places her down on my legs with the baby's little head in my hand. It is hotter and heavier than I thought it would be.

I am almost too frightened to move, in case I scare her or do anything wrong because I have never even touched a baby before. Her deep-brown eyes look up at mine and her little mouth, which has no teeth, breaks into a smile.

'Oh! There we are! Look, she likes you!' the lady cries.

I smile back at her. I touch her tiny little hand with my free hand, and she curls her miniature fingers around mine. 'She's holding my hand!' I squeak, excitedly. In that instant her face changes and she starts to cry.

'Oh . . . oh no . . . I'm sorry . . .' I say, and I feel like crying too. I have messed things up and I will never be allowed to hold the baby again. Maybe I will be in trouble for talking to the lady and Mama will lose her job and we'll have to live on the streets like she said. 'I didn't mean to . . .' I continue.

But the lady picks up the baby and holds her close to her chest. She stops crying almost straight away. 'It's OK,' she says. 'Don't worry at all. Babies cry all the time for no reason. You didn't do anything wrong, I promise. She's probably getting tired and hungry now – I'm going to take her inside for some milk and a nap.'

She stands up. 'Thalia likes you, I can tell. So if you'd like to play with her another time, you can do that. Would you like to?'

I nod. 'I would. But Mama says I'm not to bother you.'

She smiles again. 'Don't be silly. You're not bothering me at all. I will talk to your mama and tell her that.' Her voice softens. 'You must feel lonely sometimes here, with no one to play with?'

I shrug. I don't know what to say. I don't want to get Mama into trouble by saying the wrong thing. And I don't want the lady to think I'm ungrateful for them taking us in.

'Well, I'll look out for you when we're in the garden,' she says. 'Do you know where the nursery is?'

I nod. 'You can always come and play with us there,' she tells me. 'Whenever you like. Don't be shy. We'll always be happy to see you.'

## 1992
## The Nineteenth Lady of Creaglie

Sometimes I worry that a problem is looming. As Thalia gets bigger, starts to lose her baby fat and becomes more like a little person than a pudgy little ball of a baby, it becomes more and more obvious, to me at least, that she is Luca's child. She has his full, almost cupid's-bow lips, rather than Alistair's mean, narrow mouth, and now that her soft blonde baby hair is changing, it's clearer that it's actually much more like Luca's.

To start with I don't think about it too much. Alistair spends so much time in London, and that is when Thalia and I have the best time, pottering about the house and garden, sometimes even having Luca take us to the local town when the weather is good. Though Morag also has to come along for the sake of 'propriety', which puts somewhat of a damper on things. She often brings her little daughter who adores being with Thalia. If I mentally block Morag out of the picture, I can pretend to myself that Luca, the two girls and I are a normal,

164

happy family. Though I am careful not to impose myself upon Luca too much as I don't want to scare him off. He is my only friend, even though we can only be friends in a very limited way now, but that is better than nothing.

Things are still not as they were between us, far from it, but I think Luca still has feelings for me, as I do for him. We both know that continuing the way we were before is not an option, it's too dangerous. It couldn't go on for ever; on some level, we both always knew that. The castle can be a lonely place, he doesn't get much time off from it and, as far as I know, has no real home to go to. The only other woman here is his sister. So it's not especially surprising that nature took its course between us the way it did. It was fun while it lasted, a comfort to us both. And there's no denying that he is clearly becoming extremely fond of Thalia, so I try to arrange things so that he can spend as much time with her as possible.

We still play chess together. And we have spent the occasional night together since, though nowhere near as often as before. And each time, he swears it will be the last. He says it is too risky, there is too much at stake, especially for me. 'I can simply move on if need be,' he says. 'For you, and for Thalia, it would be much more complicated.'

He is right, of course. As the Lady of Creaglie, I should not be doing this, and as our employee, neither should Luca. But he is easily led, and we are both sexually frustrated.

I'm not sure if he believes that he is Thalia's father or not. We don't talk about it directly. But I am sure that he is.

Perhaps it doesn't matter who her father is, as long as no one ever finds out. I am never lonely now that Thalia is here. I dread Alistair coming home as much as I ever did. We are civil but distant, going about our days avoiding each other as much as possible and enduring silent dinners together. We still have sex every three days when he is home, as before. He has clearly not given up on a having a male heir. But we barely even look at each other while we do so, and he abandoned any attempt to make it even remotely enjoyable for me long ago.

And then, much to my surprise, I find myself pregnant again.

From the very start, this pregnancy is harder. I feel so sick I have to stay in bed most days, as even sitting up makes me feel worse. I can barely eat anything and keep it down. I am weak and tired, too tired to play with Thalia most of the time. As I am still resolutely refusing a nanny, she spends more and more time with Luca, which is good news, but it makes me sad that I am unable to give her the attention she deserves.

Before she goes to bed each night, she is brought to me by Morag or her sweet little daughter – I can't arouse suspicion by allowing Luca into my bedroom. I read to Thalia as she curls up against me in my bed, and it is by far the high point of each day. But being away from me so much is difficult for Thalia, and she tells me about the nightmares she has, which are so terrifying that they prevent me from sleeping myself, they are so vivid. She says a lady with wet hair and covered in pondweed stands by her bed and points at her. She says that sometimes she tries to lie next to her on her little bed, and it is then that Thalia's screams echo through the house, and even though her bedroom is far from mine, at Alistair's insistence while his precious child is growing, but I hear her even so. I swallow down my nausea, drag myself out of bed and calm her, rocking her to sleep and soothing her until her eyes close again. I often lie down next to her and spend the entire night there, creeping back before Morag brings my breakfast because I don't want her reporting back to Alistair that I am 'spoiling' my child. Or worse.

The next time Alistair comes home, he arrives with a doctor. 'I am worried about your health,' he says, bluntly. 'Morag tells me you're hardly eating and are growing weaker and weaker. That you barely get out of bed. You are carrying my heir and he needs to be born healthy. Dr Reece is going to take a blood sample to ascertain if everything is as it should be. He thinks we should check that your iron levels are high enough. See if there is anything which can be done to make you feel stronger.'

I am so sick of feeling so terrible that I simply proffer my arm. Anything that might make me feel more normal would be welcome. The doctor ties a tourniquet, jabs in the needle, and I turn my head away as the red viscous blood starts to rise up into the vial. I'm a little surprised he doesn't ask me any questions or feel my belly, but perhaps he feels that's the midwife's job.

It's only later when Thalia comes to visit me for her bedtime story and shows me a pinprick where 'the nasty man hurt my arm but Daddy said not to tell you' that I realize what Alistair was doing.

He has clearly started to have suspicions that Thalia is not his child – I can think of no other explanation as to why he would take her blood without telling me, the poor little mite. How dare he?

One of the only community-minded things that Alistair and I do, along with all the staff at the castle, is to give blood when the donation unit comes to the local town. Apparently there is some ancient Creaglie ancestor who had haemophilia or a related condition, and relied on blood donations, so it's always been a thing for the family. No idea why that means the staff have to do it too, but it's clearly expected of them.

Alistair and I are both O. Luca tells me he is A. And I'm no biology expert, but I remember from school that – with that combination – there's a good chance that Thalia's blood could show that there's no possibility Alistair could be her father.

I feel nausea rising yet again and reach for my bowl. Thalia starts to cry, and Morag arrives to take her away. She returns to fuss around me, cleaning me up, no doubt trying to hide her bemusement about why I have become so hysterical – I am so used to vomiting daily now, it doesn't upset me any more.

I don't know how long the results of the blood tests will take, but there is no time to lose. When Alistair discovers Thalia isn't his, what will he do?

He might pretend he doesn't know, for appearances' sake. But if he does that, he will be biding his time, I am sure of it.

He might throw me out on the streets, probably with Thalia too.

He might even kill me. He has been violent before when he believed I was being unfaithful to him, even though I wasn't. And his wife carrying a child who isn't his would surely be the ultimate slur on the family name, in his eyes.

I still suspect that his sister's 'shame' will have been something like that. And it wouldn't surprise me if she had met with a convenient 'accident'. Alistair has certainly never been forthcoming about what happened to her or where she is now, or indeed whether she is alive or dead.

But I am carrying his child. A child who could be his heir.

So he still has a use for me. At least until the baby is born. At least until he can find out if the child is his.

Either way, Thalia is the most important thing in my life. Alistair has never shown any interest in her, because she is a girl. And once Alistair knows she isn't even his . . . I think she could actually be in danger.

There is no time to lose. Sick and weak or not, I need to leave, taking Thalia and my unborn child with me.

## 1992
## The Nineteenth Lady of Creaglie

'You think your husband is arranging blood tests?' Luca whispers. 'Why?'

In spite of still feeling like death barely even warmed up, I have dragged myself downstairs to lie on the sofa while Thalia plays with wooden horses on the floor. It seems wise to talk to Luca here than to try to get him to come to my room in the middle of the day in case someone sees him doing so. He is now my only hope for keeping my daughter safe, and I need to persuade him to help me.

'I think Alistair suspects what happened with us,' I hiss. 'Otherwise why would he take Thalia's blood too?'

Luca is sitting on the floor with Thalia. He 'gallops' a horse over towards hers and makes a neighing sound as he mimes it rearing up on its hind legs. She squeals in delight.

He would be a great father. Is a great father. He's a

natural with Thalia. Whether he now feels anything for me beyond occasional lust is secondary. I think he does. However, that is neither here nor there. What matters is getting Thalia to safety.

'You can see how much she's starting to look like you,' I whisper. He smiles fondly at her.

'I suppose,' he says, hesitantly. 'Perhaps. From a certain angle. But the blood . . . that might not tell him anything, might it?'

'Alistair and I are both O,' I whisper. 'You are A. If she has A-type blood, Alistair can't be the father. I'm sure that's why he's taken the blood. It must be. He's not worried about my welfare. And he's certainly not worried about hers.'

Luca frowns. 'Will her blood definitely show that she is mine?' He pauses. 'Even if she is, I mean?'

I shake my head. 'Not definitely, I don't think. I'm not sure. I can't remember. But it might do, and I can't take that risk. *We* can't take the risk. And I think these days they can do other tests which are more specific than that, can't they? Who knows what kind of things Alistair has access to? When money is no object and you can afford to pay the right people, you can find out almost anything you want.'

I lean in closer. 'The family line and respectability are everything to him. If he finds out that I've been . . . well, you know, and that Thalia is what he'd call a –' I mouth the word 'bastard' – 'I honestly worry he might kill her. And me. And quite possibly you too.'

Tears come to my eyes. How did I get myself into this mess?

Thalia picks up her favourite horse, crawls into Luca's lap, leans her head against his chest and starts sucking her thumb. I feel a pang of jealousy. They have grown very close since I've been feeling unwell with my pregnancy, and I have spent much less time with her than usual.

But I push the feeling away. That's unimportant now. Luca feeling close to Thalia is a good thing. It works in my favour. Makes him more likely to agree to what I am planning to ask.

'Do you really think he'd do something like that?' he asks.

'I really do. Honestly, how his family appears to others is all he cares about. You know his mysterious sister? He's never actually said so, but I very much get the impression that she did something the family disapproved of, and one way or another they made sure she wasn't around to embarrass them, as they would have seen it. I'm not even sure if she's dead or alive.'

He looks at me uneasily, 'Yeah. I think Morag said something about that. But she wouldn't tell me any more. I'm not sure if she even knows. If anyone does. Whatever happened there, it happened a long time ago.'

'He would never tell me anything about her, even in our early days when we still actually liked each other,' I say.

I can't bring myself to say 'love'. Did I ever really love Alistair? I'm not sure now that I did.

172

Luca frowns. 'So what do you think we should do?' he asks, stroking Thalia's hair absent-mindedly. I see her eyelids drooping. She is adorable. I love her so much.

'We need to get her away from here,' I say. 'And I've come up with a plan. But you'll need to help us, and it's quite a big ask.'

## 1992
The Nineteenth Lady of Creaglie

Over the next few days I gather everything I own of value into a backpack, plus a few pieces of my non-costume jewellery. I choose only items which I rarely wear and don't think Alistair will notice are gone, should he think to check. Most of these are guilt-presents Alistair bought me after each violent incident so, beautiful as some of them are, I will not be sorry to see them go. I also pack a few personal things for myself and Thalia.

I will need to make my escape over the water; there is obviously no other way to leave the island. And the best way to do this without being seen or heard will be to take the little rowing boat.

The rowing boat is not designed for much more than pottering around on a sunny day. I feel like my heart might burst as I remember the happy times I've spent in it with Thalia, fishing for shrimp and crab with little nets, or rowing over to the little islet for a picnic. She adores being on or in the water, and I have grown to love it too. I love anything which makes her happy.

I still can't swim well, but it's shallow between here and the islet, and I've become more confident on the water the more I've used the boat. I put armbands on Thalia and she loves splashing about in the water with me nearby – she's like a little fish, or a mermaid. When we are settled in our new place, I'm going to take her to swimming lessons. I'm sure she'd love it.

I've never rowed all the way to the shore before – when I go, I'm taken in the tender. I don't know if you need a licence to pilot the boat – I've never asked. When I want to go to the mainland, Donald takes me. He is the only person who ever drives it, but obviously that can't happen this time. I don't know how it works or even where the keys are kept, and it's only now it occurs to me that perhaps this is deliberate on Alistair's part. But aside from all that, even if I *was* able to take it, someone might hear it start up. It is too risky.

But I have thought about my plan a lot these last few days, and know I need to do more than simply escape. I need to actually disappear, or Alistair will come after me. Especially as I am, or at least could be, carrying his child.

I will need Alistair to believe I am dead. That we are dead, Thalia and I. A sob rises in my throat at even the thought of harm coming to Thalia, but I will not let that happen. I am doing all this for her. So that she can be safe.

Late at night, the two of us will row out to the islet

175

where we usually have our picnic, so that we are not seen. We will then transfer ourselves over to a little inflatable dinghy, which I bought for a beach holiday about a thousand years ago when Alistair and I still did nice things together. It's in the same shed as the rowing boat, but I can't imagine Alistair would ever go in there so he won't even remember we have it, I'm sure. Then we'll tow the first boat out with us as we head to the mainland and, while we are still far from land, I'll turn it upside down and make it sink.

Then we'll continue on to the shore, where Luca will pick us up, help us to hide, and then go back to work. He will leave a few weeks later when it seems unlikely that anyone will link him leaving his post to my disappearance, especially given that I will be believed to be dead.

Even if Alistair *does* suspect that there has been something between us, and that Luca leaving his post is in any way connected to my disappearance, I don't think it matters. With me and Thalia dead, there's no way Alistair would want anyone else to know what happened between us, to bring shame on the family, as he would see it. I don't imagine he would expend any energy looking for Luca – he is a servant, and therefore a nobody in Alistair's eyes.

In the meantime, Thalia and I will hide out for a couple of weeks in an abandoned bothy that Luca has prepared for us. As we will be assumed to be dead, we'll need to stay well out of sight until any search is over.

When we feel the time is right, the three of us will drive down south and set up a new life somewhere where no one knows either of us, which won't be too hard as we've both been holed up here in this castle in the middle of nowhere for so long. I've got enough jewellery to sell to last us a month or two while we lie low; we will be OK.

With his background, no one will be surprised that Luca has disappeared again. And no one is likely to be that bothered, apart from possibly Morag, but I feel she is unlikely to spend much time or energy looking for him. They are not close and, given her weird loyalty to Alistair, I think she will feel that Luca has let her down by jumping ship at short or no notice – we haven't yet decided which way will be best. The impression Luca has always given me is that Morag is someone who feels bound by duty, and she helped him get the job at the castle for that reason alone. But even so, her overriding feeling towards him seems to be one of disapproval, and that she is deeply embarrassed and ashamed that he spent time in prison. We both think that she will see this as a betrayal too far.

We pick a night for me to make my escape having studied the weather forecast. It is due to be calm and clear – not very warm, but we can't wait until spring, it is too risky. I'm not sure exactly how long the blood results will take to come, but I fear it may not be very long. Once I give birth, I will no longer have the protection that this unborn baby gives me. Without his heir inside me, I am worth nothing to Alistair.

I have told Thalia that we are going on a picnic to have a midnight feast on our special island, and she must not tell anyone or it won't happen. She is very excited. I have put her to bed as usual so as not to alert the staff to anything unusual, and will go and collect her just before we leave.

It is hard because I still feel so very sick and weak, and I am scared of tonight's journey for so many reasons. I set a discreet alarm on my watch, not that I sleep at all, quietly dress and go to fetch Thalia.

'Come on, darling,' I whisper, touching her arm gently. 'It's time to go.'

Thalia has always loved her sleep and doesn't wake up properly, so taking her pyjamas off and dressing her in her warmest clothes is like dressing a rag doll.

I haul my backpack on and carry her down the stairs. The staff are up on the top floor in a different wing, so thankfully they are unlikely to hear us.

I open the shed and lie Thalia gently down in the boat, covering her with one of the blankets I stashed in here a few days ago. I add my backpack and the little rubber dinghy, which I took the risk of inflating a few days ago because no one goes in the shed at this time of year, put the oars in and push the boat out into the water, hopping in at the last minute as water sloshes into my wellies.

I am scared, but feel a lurch of excitement. We are going to be free.

It is peaceful on the lake, and surprisingly calming watching the oars glide through the water in the moonlight. Thalia stays fast asleep, sucking her thumb. She didn't wake up as I wrapped her into the life jacket – adult-sized, but the only one I have. It's never felt necessary before.

I think about the new life we are heading for – materially entirely uncertain, but definitely safer than the one we are leaving. I vow to make sure Thalia grows up knowing she must never fall into the trap that I did, allowing myself to become little more than chattel. No longer a person in my own right.

Luca will be a good father to her, and perhaps in time we can get back to being the couple we once were. But that is only of secondary importance. The main thing is that we get Thalia and my unborn child to safety. That is what matters here.

We reach the little islet and I row the boat onto the beach. Thalia stirs as I do so but doesn't wake. I tie the little dinghy on to the rowing boat with the rope I brought, transfer everything over, including Thalia, and push the bigger boat back into the water. I then carefully step into the smaller boat and start to row towards the shore.

Now that I am pulling the larger boat behind me as I row, it takes significantly more effort to move through the water and I soon find that I am sweating. So I decide sooner rather than later that I have gone far enough. I untie the rope and lean over to try to turn the rowing boat over to make it sink.

I had thought it would be easy to flip the boat, but it has a wide base and it seems impossible to make it turn over. I lean a little further to try to get a better hold of it, and try to lever it over with one of the oars, but that has no effect without firm ground to press on. Nothing works.

I feel tears of desperation rise. I need to get this boat to flip, it needs to look like we have fallen out. Alistair needs to believe we have drowned, or he will come looking for us. The lake is large and very deep once you get past the little islet; people have drowned here before and their bodies never recovered. It's something to do with its depth and freezing temperatures, I believe.

But the boat needs to be capsized, otherwise why would anyone think we have drowned? It could easily drift and if it is found near the shore, Alistair will know we have left, and come after me. I'll need to get back in and pull the drain plug.

Glancing at my sleeping angel, I pull the rope so that the boat is close and step one foot into the other boat. And that's when it happens. The two boats drift apart, and I fall into the water.

## Silas's voiceover

The year of death was 1814.

Isobel, the eldest daughter of the Twelfth Laird of Creaglie, was a quiet girl with a gift for playing the pianoforte. But she was timid and a little unusual, and preferred to play only for herself.

Her father was a vain and arrogant man and wanted to show off his daughter's talents. One night, when he was entertaining friends, after a little too much to drink, he summoned his daughter.

'Play for us! Play!' he insisted. Isobel tried to refuse, but her father and his friends would not let it go.

Isobel played a few bars of one of her favourite pieces, then dashed from the dining room and ran towards the sanctity of her bedroom.

But in her haste to get away, she tripped on her long dress and tumbled down the vast staircase, breaking her neck and dying instantly.

Her mother, the Twelfth Lady of Creaglie, unable to

cope with her grief, followed her beloved daughter into death weeks after, throwing herself from a gallery high above the same staircase.

The instrument was removed from the castle and, since then, no piano has ever been brought to Creaglie Castle.

Yet ever since, those sleeping in the East Wing report hearing the piano – soft scales, unfinished melodies – drifting through the walls after midnight.

Some say the sound is young Isobel, playing on for herself on another plane.

Others say it's simply the noise the wind makes as it winds through the trees and reverberates off the water.

We'll probably never know for sure.

## 1992
The Nineteenth Lady of Creaglie

I fall into the water and it closes over my head. It is so cold it feels like a slap.

I thrash my arms and manage to grab on to the bigger boat. Thalia. I need to make sure Thalia isn't tipped out of the dinghy. What was I thinking? Why did I even start this? I try to drag myself out again and again, and eventually manage to hook my elbows over the edge of the boat and then haul myself in.

I lie on the hard bottom of the wooden boat. I am so, so cold that I want to give up and go to sleep. But I need to do this for Thalia, who I see stir in her sleep and put her thumb in her mouth, gently sucking. She looks so alone in the little dinghy, so vulnerable. I feel a surge of love for her which gives me strength. I sit up, locate the drain plug and pull it out. The water starts coming in immediately, much more quickly than I imagined it would. I pull the dinghy close again, using the rope, and try to roll myself back in, back to Thalia, but it tips and then we are both in the water. I grab at the shoulder of Thalia's life jacket, but she falls through it and sinks down into the darkness below.

Soundlessly, she is gone. I flail and splash and try to make myself sink too to grab her, but I don't know how to do it and it is useless, she is already out of my sight. All I can see is blackness, and all I can feel is cold.

21 September 1992
*The Daily News*

The search has been called off for a mother and child believed to have drowned in Lake Creaglie in Dunbraekshire, Scotland.

The woman, 27, and girl, 2, who have not yet been named, left the castle late on Friday night. There are unconfirmed reports that the woman was pregnant and may have been suffering from depression.

A rowing boat belonging to the family was found semi-submerged close to a small islet where the mother and daughter would apparently often enjoy picnics together on sunny days.

A search of the lake, which covers 70 square miles and is up to 400 metres deep in places, was carried out by specialist divers, but no trace of the mother or child has been found.

The water temperature in the lake is currently around 4 degrees centigrade. Divers are unable to descend to the deepest parts of the vast lake.

DCS Callum Drummond, who coordinated the search, said: 'An ill-equipped person is unlikely to survive more than half an hour in the water in these conditions, so sadly we have to assume that the worst has happened.

'It is an extremely difficult lake to search because of its size. Its depth, along with the very cold nature of the water means that bodies, once submerged, do not typically come back to the surface. Very sadly, it's possible that the bodies may never be recovered.'

## 1992
Sarah

I wasn't sure if I should tell Mama about what the lady had said about being able to go and play with the baby whenever I wanted, so I didn't say anything. But from then on, whenever Mama didn't need me to help, I'd go and find the lady and Thalia. Mama never had a lot of time to talk to me because she was always busy with work, but the lady talked to me quite a lot, mostly about the baby. She explained to me that she didn't want Thalia to have a nanny because she wanted to look after her herself, but sometimes it was useful to have someone like me who could keep an eye on her for a bit if she needed a break.

She taught me lots of things – how to change a nappy (it was stinky and gross but I didn't mind), and then, as Thalia grew, how to feed her. Sometimes I'd play with her while the lady went to the toilet or, as time went on, while she went for a little rest. She showed me which things could be dangerous for Thalia – she wasn't allowed to put anything small in her mouth, or anything at all from the garden in case it made her sick, and when she started to stand up I was to watch her even more carefully in case she fell and bumped her head. I think the lady knew how much I liked to be with Thalia, who I pretended was my little sister . . . but only to myself; I never told anyone. I was never left alone with Thalia very long, and I was always really, really careful, and I think the lady trusted me to look after her well.

The bigger Thalia got, the more fun she was to be with, and the longer the lady seemed happy to leave me on my own with her. I read books to her and helped her learn to count. We built things out of wooden blocks together and I gave her horsey rides on my back. We paddled in the lake when it was warm enough and caught little fish in nets to put in buckets, but we always put them back again because we didn't want to be cruel. We picked flowers and made little posies, and she and I had our own little patch in the garden that Uncle Luca cleared for us, where we could plant seeds and grow things – beans, tomatoes, flowers, all sorts. Of course Mama noticed in time that I was spending a lot of time with Thalia, but the lady told Mama that I was a real help to her and that Thalia loved playing with me, so she was happy for me to carry on what I was doing.

And then when the lady of the house was growing a new baby in her tummy and was not very well, I spent even more time with Thalia. The lady had to spend a lot of time in bed, and Mama and Uncle Luca were already busy with all their other jobs, so sometimes they'd give me a few pennies or some sweets to play nicely with Thalia so they could get on with the other things they needed to be doing. But they didn't need to pay me at all. I loved Thalia so much. I always wanted to be with her, as much as I could.

I was so happy then. I finally had something to do, someone to play with and an actual purpose which made me feel important and useful, other than just collecting eggs. I would help Mama make Thalia's breakfast – she liked dippy eggs best – and then sit with her while she ate it, which also meant that I got to have two breakfasts because I'd have one with Mama too when we got up, so that was a double win. Then I'd take Thalia upstairs and we'd play together in her nursery. I was eight years older than her, so she looked up to me and would tell me that I was her best friend. She was like a little doll to me, the younger sister I'd always wanted.

When I heard the clock strike twelve noon, I would take her back downstairs, holding her hand all the way so she didn't fall, and we'd have lunch in the big dining room. Before, I had always eaten in our little apartment with Mama, but Thalia wanted me to stay with her and it helped Mama and Uncle Luca as I was there to look after her while they got on with their jobs. Thalia's food was nicer than what I would eat with Mama, too. Afterwards we would play some more and, if the weather was good, we might go out in the garden for hide and seek. Then it was tea in the dining room again,

I'd help with her bath, and then I'd take her to her mama's room before bedtime so she could read her a story.

And then one day I got up and Thalia wasn't there and there was a strange atmosphere in the house and two men wearing uniforms who I thought might be policemen. Mama told me to be quiet and not to ask questions, to go back to our apartment and stay out of the way. She would be especially busy that day, like everyone else in the castle, she'd said, so it was important that I was extra good.

'But where is Thalia?' I'd wailed. 'She'll want me. Why can't I see her?'

Her expression softened as she looked at me and touched me gently on the shoulder. 'Thalia and her mama have gone missing,' she told me. 'We're not sure yet, but they think they might have fallen in the lake.'

Part Three

# What the Nineteenth Lady
# of Creaglie Did Next

# 1992

## The Nineteenth Lady of Creaglie

After Thalia falls in the water, my first thought is that I don't want to go on. Perhaps I will stay in the lake too, for ever; allow myself to sink to the bottom, with my darling daughter, and we will be together always. We will never have to worry about Alistair catching up with us, we will be free. Perhaps we could become mermaids, living at the bottom of the lake in some kind of Atlantis.

But on autopilot, survival instinct kicks in, and I manage to drag myself into the rubber dinghy. I am so cold I can barely move my arms. Is staying alive really worth the effort? I left the castle, did all this, for Thalia, to protect her, and failed in the worst way possible. I deserve to be punished. I deserve to die. Perhaps this is karmic payback for when I wanted to kill the poor defenceless little girl before she was even born. Perhaps I was given her to love for a few short years as a punishment for that, and for my infidelity. All of this is my fault, and I will never forgive myself.

But then I remember the child inside me and the responsibility I have to him or her. I cannot let another innocent being die. I force my frozen arms to row me to the other side of the lake in my sodden clothes, and to Luca. I can barely get the words out to tell him what happened to Thalia, not even thinking of what will happen if he blames me, as he surely should. I may have walked away from Alistair, only to walk into more violence here with Luca – though I have never seen it myself, and for all I know there could be violence in his past too.

He sinks to his knees and screams but then he gets up and holds me and we both cry, and then he puts me in the van which he tells me is untraceable because he has done something with the plates – I don't understand these things but I don't need to – along with the little dinghy which we will dispose of far away somewhere. I take off my wet clothes and wrap myself in a blanket and we drive away, saying nothing as we both cry.

For the first couple of weeks, I hide in an abandoned bothy around an hour's drive from the lake, sufficiently out of the way that I can hunker down there and no one will notice. Everyone will think I drowned, so it seems very unlikely they will be looking for me. Luca has kitted it out with a mattress, heater, water and some non-perishable food, so I have everything I need to survive.

But there should be two of us here, and I simply cannot bear that there are not. It is tempting to simply stop eating and drinking, let myself waste away to nothing. Luca visits every few days to check on me and bring supplies, but we barely speak. There is nothing to say. But he ensures that I keep myself alive, and while I feel that I will be torn apart by my own grief, I have that obligation to my unborn child, and I am grateful to Luca for making me eat and drink, even though I don't want to. What happened was not the fault of this child. It was mine, all mine, and I cannot punish them because of it. So I make the effort to force down the bland and unappetizing tinned food, which is more than I deserve, and to keep myself hydrated.

One day bleeds into the next, but eventually Luca tells me that enough time has passed and that I should prepare to leave. I look at him for the first time in days. He has black rings under his eyes and looks like he has barely slept.

We drive the length of the UK and sleep in the back of the van in places where no one will notice or disturb us. We cling onto each other in our grief. As we travel, I sell the jewellery I brought with me at different places along the way, at outlets which look dodgy enough that they are unlikely to keep decent records, and where most transactions would be in cash. I receive well below the market value, but it is enough.

We rent a god-awful flat in an obscure mid-sized town on the south coast, large enough to be sufficiently anonymous and which neither of us has ever been to before. Luca takes on low-key cash-in-hand jobs on building sites. I cut and dye my hair to change my appearance just in case, and start wearing clear-lensed glasses, but there is probably no real need; no one is looking for me. As far as anyone is concerned, which is probably no one, I was a sad, kept wife, with no family or friends, who drowned in a lake a long way from here.

I spend my days reading to try to distract myself from thinking about Thalia, and wandering in graveyards because they are quiet and suit my low mood.

I become obsessed by the graves of babies, of the ones who were about the same age as Thalia when she died. What happened to them? Did they have neglectful mothers who allowed them to perish too?

My new hobbies become a path to my new identity – I find the grave of a baby who died in 1968, who would now be about the same age as me, had they lived. Then I take the train to London and go to Somerset House, find the listing in the giant red books and request their birth certificate. I hold my breath as I assume they will want to know why I'm asking for it, make me give a reason for wanting it, but no one questions me. A few hours later, it's ready for me to pick up and I can become Lauren Thompson.

I use my fake name to admit myself to hospital when the time comes for my child to be born. The flat where we are living is too grim to risk trying to give birth on my own, and even now I am almost a non-person, I don't want the same for my child. I want him or her to have the chances that Thalia never did. Perhaps they can live life for her too.

Luca comes with me to the hospital but I keep him at a distance as far as possible and put 'father unknown' on the forms in case anyone is looking for him, which I doubt. Neither of us wants to leave any clue or trace. So with no father and with Ms Thompson as a mother, this child has no links at all to Alistair. At least not in name. They will be safe.

Thalia was born in my bedroom in the castle, with just two midwives to help me, during a labour which took the best part of two days. My experience in the hospital is very different. After four short hours of contractions and a few pushes, the baby arrives. I feel none of the rush of love I felt when Thalia arrived. And I can see immediately who the father is, too. This poor, innocent little thing looks far too much like Alistair – my husband may as well have cloned himself. Even the way this tiny baby appears to scrutinize me with its almond-shaped, almost-black eyes freaks me out.

Tears start to stream down my face. I thought it would be OK once the baby was born, that love would overwhelm me like it did when Thalia arrived, but it doesn't. I wonder about simply getting up and walking away, the baby is in a hospital and will be safe and cared for in the short term. Then the child will go to someone who will make sure they will have a better life than they could possibly have with me and a man who no longer loves me, or on my own with barely two pennies to rub together.

But I have seen what happens when new mothers abandon their babies in hospital; their name and picture is in the papers, and the police put out appeals and create a fuss. I must not draw attention to myself. I certainly don't want my photo appearing in the media.

I have already told Luca to stay away, that he should get back to work, that I don't need him fussing around me.

I don't want to be near this baby any more. I feel like Alistair is radiating off it. I tell a passing nurse that I would like to have the child adopted. She says she will send someone to talk to me and perhaps I've got a case of the 'baby blues'.

But I don't want to talk to anyone about this. It might lead to awkward questions or checks which I am not equipped to answer. An hour or two later I tell her I have changed my mind, that she is probably right, that I am extremely tired and feeling over-emotional. That it will all be OK if only I can get some sleep. That I'd like to go home and try to bond with my baby after all, and that I will be fine in time.

I know even then that it's a lie.

**1992**

The Nineteenth Lady of Creaglie

Mine and Luca's relationship cannot possibly last long. While we initially cling to each other in the immediate aftermath of Thalia's drowning, her death casts too long a shadow over both of us. And though Luca claims not to, I'm sure there is a large part of him which blames me. How could he not? I certainly blame myself. I should have taken more care. Found a different way to leave. Not had the affair with Luca in the first place. This is all my fault.

I think of Thalia every day. Even during my second pregnancy as the child within me grew and my body distorted, I became more and more repulsed, both by myself and, though I tried hard not to be, by my unborn child. I always knew this baby could never replace Thalia.

Luca thinks the child is his, because I have let him think that. It is obvious to me that this is not the case, but he doesn't seem to see it. He was there at the birth because I didn't want to go through that alone, and it was clear that, raw from Thalia's death, he reacted in the exact opposite way to me. He has fallen in love with this tiny thing who, of course, deserves to be loved like any child.

I'm relieved he feels this way because I feel nothing for it, and every baby should be loved. What happened to Thalia is obviously not this child's fault, and they should not be punished for it.

'Look at those lovely long eyelashes!' he'll coo. 'And their little nose! Miniature lips! Mostly like you. But with my eyes, I think? Don't you?'

I paint on a fake smile and agree yes, just like me, just like you. But I only think of Thalia, and I only see Alistair in this new baby's eyes. I guess poor Luca is simply blinded by love. The baby is a new start for him, a new lease of life.

Luca is a good man. He rescued me, brought me here, looked after me when I needed him most. But it is clear to me that he no longer cares for me; I am not the person I was before. With Thalia gone, I am nothing, I am no one. I'm a mere shell, going through the motions. There is no joy left anywhere for me.

I look after the baby while Luca is at work. I keep it alive, but I do the bare minimum. It's not fair to it. This baby would be better off without me. So a few months after I left my previous family, I do it again.

200

*Dear Luca,*
*I am sorry. I cannot do this any more. I know you*
*will look after our child well. Please do not try to*
*find me. It will not be possible.*
*x*

I pack a small bag and take the birth certificate with
my fake name which Luca doesn't know I have.

Luca works on the black, so I help myself to a small
pile of cash we keep in a drawer but I leave most of it
where it is – he will need it for the baby.

He will be a good father. He will work it out. And
I know he'll do his best for the child, which is a lot
more than I am capable of.

He will be home in an hour. The baby is asleep in
the cot and will be fine. I am not breastfeeding – I
couldn't bear to after I had enjoyed breastfeeding Thalia
so much. It would have felt like a betrayal. So all the
supplies they need are already here.

I take a final look before I leave. Perhaps I am a
monster, but I feel nothing but relief as I step out of
the front door and close it gently behind me so as not
to wake the sleeping child.

## 1992–8
Sarah

Nothing is ever the same again now that Thalia is no longer here. The castle goes back to being a horrible, cold, lonely place, where I have no one to play with and there is nothing for me to do but be quiet and behave myself.

But not long after that, Mama finally decides that the castle isn't a healthy place for a girl like me to grow up. She sends me to stay with some distant relative so that I can go to school in the normal way. But Great-Aunt Agnes clearly doesn't want me there, and I've missed out on a lot of things I should have learned at school and never did when I was growing up in the castle with no formal lessons, so I never do well at school and never fit in with the rest of the kids either. I'm not used to being with children of my own age as I've only ever had Thalia to play with. In theory I was being home-schooled, but I was basically left to my own devices and I'm pretty sure no-one official ever checked up on me. We were so remote. I don't remember ever seeing anyone like a doctor as a child and, for all I know, before I went to school, the various authorities may not have even known that I existed.

Because I am so miserable at school, I rarely attend, so I leave with no qualifications at all. I have never stopped thinking about Thalia, the little sister I was gifted for such a short time, who was then taken away from me.

Mama is still working at the castle and keeps me up to date with what is happening.

The Laird of Creaglie has remarried, and there is a new baby too, or rather, a toddler now – a boy. The new Lady of Creaglie is apparently a little older than the first; beautiful, yes, but mean, apparently, and, according to Mama, quite neurotic and unstable. 'She's obsessed with the nineteenth Lady of Creaglie,' she tells me, 'to a completely unhealthy degree. Always asking me questions about her. He has forbidden anyone in the castle to speak of her at all, but even so, she is convinced the laird is still pining for her, which I know for a fact he is not.'

I don't know how she knows this 'for a fact' but, equally, I don't care.

The little boy is apparently looked after by a nanny/governess, one of those old-fashioned ones who wears a uniform and is trained at some exclusive college in England. He is signed up to go to the same boarding school as his father, grandfather, and generations before him, and will start at the age of eight.

Mama is by now much more bitter about life than she used to be. I sometimes ask her about Uncle Luca, who left the castle not long after Thalia drowned, because we never see him any more. She tells me that she doesn't want to talk about him; she doesn't know where he is and feels that he has abandoned us. 'He always was an ungrateful wretch,' she says. 'I bent over backwards to get him a job at Creaglie Castle when no one else would take him on, and this is how he repays me. That's the last time I do him any kind of favour. He's dead to me.'

She doesn't seem to like working at the castle any more; she says she is too old and tired to be a 'glorified skivvy'. I tell her she should go elsewhere, get another job, she has plenty of experience now. 'Why not go and work somewhere warm and sunny?' I suggest. 'Or with a family who travels, see the world a bit?'

But she refuses, weirdly loyal to the Laird of Creaglie in a way which I've never been able to understand.

'He took me in when I had nowhere to go,' she says. 'And he did the same for Luca too, when I asked him to, not that I should have done that for him, but that's all very well in retrospect. The laird is a good employer in his own way. I'll always have a roof over my head while I'm working here, and you never wanted for anything growing up. I have no one else, I couldn't have done that on my own. He deserves my loyalty. If I was to leave, he wouldn't find anyone who knows his ways and the household as I do. It's not the easiest place to work, and nor would it be the easiest place to find staff for. I will stay until I am ready to retire. Better the devil you know, I always say.'

**1992**
The Nineteenth Lady of Creaglie

Leaving Luca and the child is my very lowest point since losing Thalia. I don't want to be with Luca and he clearly doesn't want to be with me, and nor can I bear to be in the presence of the baby I feel absolutely nothing for. So leaving had to be done, but for the first time in my life, I find myself completely alone, and it is very much harder than I had imagined.

For the first few days, I live literally on the streets, after hitching a lift to a random and anonymous small town which the truck driver happens to be passing through. I feel it is far enough from Luca that I won't be found, either accidentally or deliberately. Though I am fairly confident that Luca will not search for me, which is something.

I don't deserve anything better than a cold pavement anyway, and I now have very limited funds which I don't want to squander. In the same way I felt as when I dragged myself from the lake, for a while I am not even convinced that I even want to carry on living. I leave it to chance – if I simply drift away during the night, perhaps down to the cold, never to wake up, then that is the way things are meant to be. I don't care. Everything I felt I had to live for – Thalia – is gone. I gave birth to the child and it is safe. Whether I personally live or die no longer matters.

I am not worried about dying, because once I am gone, the pain will be over and that will be that, simply a welcome relief. But I do not want to be attacked or raped, and when I am robbed I quickly realize it is too unsafe to carry on the way I am going. Thankfully the attacker doesn't hurt me and is interrupted before he can do anything worse.

But that gives me the wake-up call that I need to take better care of myself. It also makes me realize that I *don't* actually want to die. I have things I want to stay alive for, things I want to do. Thalia's death shouldn't go unnoticed. I have disappeared and am now a non-person, and I don't care if anyone remembers me, but Thalia deserves better. She should be remembered.

And avenged. I owe her that.

I need to stay alive to do that for her, because there is no one else who will.

Suddenly I am determined to live. Before I met Alistair, I grew up in care and had to learn to fend for myself. I was resilient and determined, even if unworldly, but ballsy enough to make my way to Scotland to take on a job I knew nothing about and where I knew no one. But then Alistair sucked dry all the life I had in me; any self-confidence I had, he took it away. I'm sure I can get back to the way I was again, if I try. The girl I used to be must still be there inside me somewhere.

I go to the library, ignoring the looks of people around me who are no doubt shocked by the state of my appearance, my hair, my clothes and – if I'm honest – the way I smell. I find a number and ring a free helpline for victims of domestic violence and tell the woman who answers the phone that I have left my abusive partner and have nowhere to go. Which is all true if I'm talking about Alistair rather than Luca. I give her my new, false name. She asks me if I want to press charges, because they can put me in touch with people who can help me with that if I do, and of course I say 'no'. That I want to put the past behind me. Which I do.

I tell her I have nowhere to live, no friends or family to go to, and she gives me the address of a refuge, where she says I will be safe, as well as some brief directions of how to get there. She tells me that they will be expecting me and recommends I tell no one where I am going. I look it up on one of the library's maps and head over immediately.

I am expecting some kind of municipal building, but I arrive at a house which looks like any of the other large Victorian houses on this street. I wonder if I have come to the wrong place, but when I knock on the door the woman who answers says, 'Lauren. We've been expecting you. I'm Sylvie. Come in!' with such kindness that I feel like crying.

She shows me to a room – a very basic room with a single bed, small window, chest of drawers and a little desk, but it's clean and has walls and a roof. That's all I want or need, and right now it looks like a palace.

Perhaps she notices tears come to my eyes because she touches my arm gently and says, 'You're safe now.'

I swallow back the tears and whisper, 'Thank you.'

She smiles at me. 'I'll leave you to get settled in. There are towels in the top drawer there,' she indicates a small wooden piece of furniture, 'and there's a bathroom down the hallway.' She pauses. 'Do you have some other clothes to change into, or do you want me to see if I can find you some?'

I'm about to say that I'm OK as I did bring a few things with me, but then I realize that because I've been sleeping outside, most of my stuff has got quite wet. She seems to misunderstand my pause as she says: 'There's no charge. We're given donations by well-wishers. I can't promise they'll be your style but I'm sure we can find something which fits and is clean and warm.' She looks me up and down. 'About a size twelve, maybe?'

'Yes, about that,' I agree. Usually I'd be smaller, but I haven't quite lost my pregnancy weight yet. I hope the bathroom is reasonably private and not something akin to the after-PE showers at school, because I don't want anyone noticing my stretched stomach and wondering where my baby is.

'That's so kind,' I croak.

'It's what we're here for. I'll leave you to have a

shower and bring you a few things while you're doing that. Do you need a toothbrush? Toiletries? Anything like that?'

My eyes fill with tears again. The bag that was snatched had my washbag in it. 'Actually . . .' I say.

She touches my arm again. 'It's fine. Many of our women come here with nothing but the clothes on their backs. And folk are very generous with their gifts. Give me a minute and I'll bring you a starter pack.' She smiles again and leaves the room.

I sit down on the chair by the little desk because I don't want to risk making the lovely clean bed dirty with my filthy clothes. I ease my shoes and socks off – the first time in days, and almost cry with relief. My feet are almost black and I smell appalling, but Sylvie didn't bat an eyelid. I guess she's used to it. Maybe some women turn up here in an even worse state than me. Though that's hard to imagine.

There's a gentle knock on the door and Sylvie hands me a large – if somewhat worn and faded – towel, and a proper little toilet bag. 'Here you go. Should have everything you need and a few treats that you probably don't, but that are always nice to have. It's a travel set which someone donated, so everything is miniature, but nice. We've got the more day-to-day stuff downstairs too, so we'll have a look at what else you need when you're ready.'

She closes the door again. I take off the rest of my clothes and wrap myself in the towel. Picking up the bag, I go to the bathroom she indicated and am relieved

210

to see that the showers are in cubicles, and there are also a couple of loos and a wall of sinks. No one else is here. I choose a cubicle, hang my towel on the hook on the door, and take the little bottles out of the bag. I switch on the water and enjoy the best shower of my life.

Drying myself off, I notice I smell amazing. The shower gel, shampoo and conditioner are Penhaligon's, the same as I used to use back when I was lady of the manor at Creaglie Castle.

I feel a flash of anger. I wonder what Alistair is doing now? Whether he ever grieved for me or Thalia? I doubt it. He'll probably simply be embarrassed that his wife was deemed 'unstable', as it said in one of the newspaper reports I saw after I left, in which he'd hinted that I'd killed myself and Thalia because I was mentally unwell.

I don't think he would ever actually have believed that that is what happened. He must have known that – however ill or desperate I might be – I would never, ever have harmed Thalia. He must have known that we were escaping from him. So he didn't care if we died.

Unless it's what he told himself to absolve himself of all blame. But either way, he will have put it behind him and carried on. Probably gone to the woman I always suspected he had in London. Maybe she can even become his wife now – who knows? Good luck to her, as far as I'm concerned.

And as for Thalia – she wasn't a boy, so he was never interested in her. He will have pretended to grieve, of

211

course. But it will just have been for propriety's sake. He never paid her any attention when she was alive; why should he care about her now that she's dead?

I wonder about the blood test. With us gone, would he even have bothered to get the results? I was always so certain that Thalia was Luca's child. But since the second child was born, doubt has crept into my mind. The baby was so like Alistair. He was clearly capable of fathering a child, so was not infertile as I had imagined. Perhaps Thalia had been his after all? In which case, we could have stayed. I would have been trapped in a loveless marriage, but Thalia would be alive and with me. She could have grown up and had a normal life. So perhaps all this, Thalia's death, might have been for nothing.

I push the thought away. It's too horrifying to deal with.

I go back into the little bag to pull out the hotel-style slippers and smear on some of the body lotion. It is months since I've done anything like that. Wrapping myself in my towel again, I open the door cautiously and am relieved to see that the bathroom is still empty. I wonder if anyone is staying here apart from me?

Back in my room, Sylvie has laid out some unflattering sweatpants and a battered, unfashionable, oversized sweatshirt on my bed. The freshly laundered smell is heavenly and putting them on feels like a hug.

## 2002
Sarah

As I get older, I start to wonder if Mama and the laird had had an affair, or at least had sex at some point. Maybe that would explain the weird loyalty she has to him? I try to think back to when we lived at the castle – did I ever notice anything unusual between them? Nothing comes to mind, but I was very young and extremely unworldly – even if there had been anything going on, chances are I wouldn't have noticed.

Could the Laird of Creaglie even be my father? Mama has always claimed she can't remember exactly when she started working at the castle. In spite of me asking many times over the years, she has resolutely refused to ever tell me who my father is, saying only that he wants nothing to do with me.

I stare at myself in the mirror. Do I look anything like him? Perhaps my eyes are a similar colour? I turn my head to the side. Is my jawline a little like his?

My breath catches in my throat. Could little Thalia

have even been my *half-sister*? Is that why I felt such a connection to her, why she is the only person who has ever felt like real family to me?

Perhaps Mama even *blackmailed* the laird at some point? Would she have it in her? She seems meek and mild, but I know she has a hard edge too. Perhaps she told him that she would reveal I was his child if he didn't take us in. Maybe that's why she was also able to persuade him to take Uncle Luca on, in spite of his criminal past? The Laird of Creaglie has always been obsessed with his family's reputation. The way Mama talks, you'd think she was as good as on the streets before she came to the castle. I don't know if that's true, but maybe he took advantage of her in some way? Perhaps she threatened to tell someone what he'd done? Or perhaps something happened between them after she arrived?

There must be a reason for her blind loyalty to him. Sometimes I have been tempted to ask directly. But even if what I suspect is true, I know she would deny it.

One day I will find out in my own way.

# Part Four

# Creaglie Castle

## 10 November 2025, 2.00 a.m.
Ben

The person I've dragged from the smoke-filled room is Kayla, dressed in silk pyjamas, her face grey, clearly not breathing. Somehow she doesn't look like someone who is just asleep. There's an absence. Something that was there before and no longer is.

My hand flies to my mouth and tears come to my eyes. Bile rises and I swallow it down.

I am again standing there uselessly, doing nothing, as Josh pushes past me and leaps into action, doing the mouth-to-mouth and CPR and all that, just as Kayla did for his father earlier this evening. But you can tell even from the colour of Kayla's skin, there is no way of getting her back. I think Josh knows this too, because he gives up pretty quickly. He rearranges Kayla's limbs a little, steps back, and he, Donald and I stare at Kayla lying on the ground for what seems like minutes but is probably only a few seconds.

'I'll go and fetch Mrs Laroche,' Josh says, quietly.

'I think, for now, it's best that we, um, put her back in her room. But there should be a woman here to help us, to chaperone while we . . . lay her out, it feels more proper. I'll find Mrs Laroche and send her up, and then I'll go and tell the rest of the group what has happened. I think it's only right that they should know.' He gives a brief nod and walks away.

I take a deep breath and let it out slowly. Christ. Another person dead. What the fuck is going on here?

'What do you think happened?' I ask, lamely.

Donald frowns. 'With the amount of smoke there was in there, it looked to me like the chimney became blocked. Though I don't understand why; they've all been recently swept.'

'Why didn't the smoke wake her?'

'It doesn't work like that,' he says. 'The carbon monoxide from the smoke would have suffocated her so she wouldn't have woken up.'

A few moments pass as we stand there in horrified silence.

'But we have smoke alarms in every room,' Donald says. 'That should have gone off. They were newly installed and checked ahead of the launch.'

He goes back into the room from where the smoke has now largely cleared, pulls a chair over to stand on and unscrews the plastic alarm from the ceiling. He turns the base towards us. 'No battery.'

What the fuck? 'So you mean . . .' I tail off. Is he really saying what I think he is?

Stepping down, he heads over to the fireplace and

peers down at the still glowing embers. He picks up a poker and prods them, frowning. 'And you see that?' he says.

As far as I can see he's pointing at some blackened twigs and leaves in the grate. 'Um, not sure what we're looking at?' I say.

'Oleander,' he says. 'It's very poisonous – including the fumes.' He looks at the chimney. 'It's too hot to examine now, but my betting is the flue has been deliberately blocked too.'

I look at him in horror. 'You mean someone did all this on purpose?' I ask. 'That someone wanted to harm Kayla? But why?'

He shakes his head. 'I don't know why. Perhaps I'm wrong. I hope I am. But it casts a different light on the death of the Laird of Creaglie, wouldn't you say? I'm wondering now if that wasn't an accident at all.'

Once Mrs Laroche arrives, the three of us move Kayla back into her room with as much dignity as we can. We place her back into bed and pull the covers up over her. The room still smells smoky but she looks as if she is sleeping. Poor Kayla. How can someone like her, who was so beautiful and alive a couple of hours ago, now be dead?

And her little son. Oh God. I hope he has someone to look after him.

## 2002–25
## Sarah

'Working in service' might sound like something from *Downton Abbey* or a Jane Austen novel – a life of living in attic rooms and toiling 'below stairs' in fusty old piles and wearing starched black and white uniforms as you scurry around after the lord and lady of the manor. In truth, that's pretty much what it was like for Mama, working at Creaglie Castle.

But not for me. After school I got a job in the US as a housekeeper with a rich family who were impressed that I'd grown up in a castle and worked for British 'nobility'. I'm pretty sure they'd tell their friends I worked for the Queen at Balmoral or similar, rather than for some obscure laird who no one outside of his own circle is ever likely to have heard of. Service was the only world I knew as a child, and it felt natural that I should go into it as an adult. It turned out that largely being left to my own devices with Mama, cooking with her, being quiet and deferential at all times and spending so much time helping to look after Thalia had made me perfectly suited for this role.

In my first post in America, I had my own apartment within the giant Beverly Hills house which belonged to the family I worked for. My main duties were taking the children to school and to their activities, keeping the house tidy and well-stocked with everything they might need, and cooking dinner some evenings. The family also had a cleaner so I didn't have to trouble myself with that. They went on lavish holidays three or four times a year and always took me with them so that I could look after the children while they went out to dinner or lounged on the beach, making myself scarce when they wanted 'family time' which, as it turned out, wasn't usually very often.

I stayed with that first family for ten years, and it was towards the end of my time there that I met my husband Brad, who was their gardener and also 'lived in' like me. They were very generous to us and threw us a lavish wedding in the grounds of their summer home in the Hamptons. Brad and I continued to work for them for a couple more years and then spent the next few years working for a series of different families in increasingly exotic locations around the world.

Almost as soon as we were married, we started trying to have a baby. I had always looked back on the time I spent with Thalia as the happiest in my life, even though by then it was a long time ago. I was sure that motherhood was my destiny. If I could have a little girl of my own like her, everything would be OK. I would finally feel fulfilled.

I was still reasonably young then; I had assumed it would happen quickly and easily. After a year of nothing happening, we both had tests, and nothing was found to be wrong. 'Carry on what you're doing,' the doctor had said. 'Have regular sex, eat healthily, get some exercise, take folic acid.'

We did all that. But nothing happened. By now the carefree early years' sex had gone and it was all thermometers, ovulation predictors and baby-making to order on pre-planned days.

Because we moved around so much it was difficult, but I managed to persuade Brad that we should try a couple of rounds of IVF, which only added to the stress and discomfort of the situation, plus it ate up all our savings.

I withdrew into myself and Brad tried to be understanding, at least to start with, but I pushed him further and further away until eventually he told me he was leaving. And because we'd split up and we had taken our job and in-house accommodation as a couple, we both had to find new employment too.

So by now I was on my own and fast reaching an age where having a baby was becoming more and more unlikely, I knew that. But I scrimped and saved and bought myself two more rounds of IVF using donor sperm. I didn't need a father for my baby. As long as I could have a child, they would be everything I would need and I could be everything to them, I was sure. I gave up work so I could fully devote myself to the task, in case work was causing me any stress I wasn't aware of that was preventing me from conceiving. I rented a little house and spent my time meditating, walking and trying to live as healthily as possible.

My work had always kept me very busy, and suddenly having time on my hands meant that I had too much time to think. I thought about Thalia a lot. But I also thought more and more about my father who I had never known.

The IVF didn't work. I was by now broke, unemployed and thoroughly depressed. The older I got, the less likely I was to become pregnant, and I had no more money for IVF anyway. It was simply not going to happen for me.

I wept for Thalia, once my surrogate little sister and now, in my mind, just how my own daughter would have been.

By now my mother had Alzheimer's and was in a care home. When I was still working and could afford it, I would go and see her when I could, but I didn't get much time off, and I didn't go as often as I should have done.

Back in the past when she had been able to think more clearly, she had always shut me down whenever I'd asked about my father. She'd tell me simply that he wanted nothing to do with us and I shouldn't meddle in things which didn't concern me.

The last time I visited, it was clear I had left it too

late. Very little of what she said made sense, and sometimes she didn't even know who I was. But in amongst the ramblings, there was the occasional phrase which made me wonder if I might have been on the right track when I had idly wondered if her employer might be my father.

'The Laird of Creaglie was a kind man,' she'd said. 'Very kind. He didn't have to take me in, but he did. I was pretty in those days, of course. When I was young.'

'Mama,' I'd said, taking her hand, 'Did you and he ever . . . have relations?'

She looked at me in horror and snatched her hand away. 'Lady Creaglie! How dare you suggest such a thing? I have no designs on your husband. I would never dream of such a thing. The very thought!'

'Mama, it's me. Sarah. I'm not the Lady of Creaglie. I'm your daughter. But I wondered if the laird might be my father?'

She snorted. 'You're getting ideas above your station, young lady. He is a kind man. Kind. From a good family. Mustn't sully the good name. I promised him that. I promised. But he was always kind to me. So kind.'

And round and round in circles like that. I wasn't going to get anything coherent from Mama, and I suspected that she'd probably told no one who my father was, whether it was the Laird of Creaglie or not.

The only way to find out for sure was a DNA test.

I wrote him a letter, but received no reply. I wasn't surprised. I knew from what Mama had told me about him that if I *was* his child, illegitimate and born to a mere housekeeper, he would want me brushed under the carpet like dust that no one wants to know exists.

But I needed to know. I needed to find a way.

And then, a few months later, I spot an advert, and come up with a plan.

**1992**

The Nineteenth Lady of Creaglie

There are three other women staying at the refuge and I meet them that evening over a simple dinner of spaghetti bolognese. Two are around my age and one is older, and they all seem to have been literally in fear for their lives when they left their partners. Each of them has a child staying here with them, apart from the older lady, whose children are now apparently grown up and have left home.

'I've only just found the courage to leave him after twenty years,' she says, sadly. 'I should have left ages ago, but I was worried for the children. I wouldn't have been able to provide for them on my own, and, for all his many faults, he gave them a good life. At least materially. And he never touched them, took all his anger out on me. If he'd ever touched a hair on their heads, I'd have been out of that door immediately.'

It strikes me that her story is a little like mine. Kind of. I wonder how many other women are living that way? In fear of their husbands, staying for the children because they can't afford to leave.

'You were very brave,' says Sylvie. 'It takes a lot of courage to make that decision after all that time. You did the right thing.'

She smiles gratefully and goes back to her pasta, surreptitiously wiping a tear from her eye. The two younger women then share their stories without being asked – one left after her partner invited his mates around after a night out at the pub to hold her down and take their turns to rape her, and the other finally left when he smashed her head so hard against the wall she passed out and woke up to find her toddler crying by her side because he thought she was dead.

Their stories give me pause for thought. I have no regrets at all about leaving Alistair, who I entirely believe may have killed me if he'd found out about my affair. But while Luca clearly no longer loved me, if indeed he ever did, I don't think he would have ever deliberately hurt me, physically or emotionally. I don't think he had it in him. I feel a pang of regret as I wonder if I've done the right thing.

But then again, another part of me very much thinks I have. My child is certainly better off without me. I failed to protect my darling daughter the way I should have and, however I try to frame it, she died in my care. And then I tried to love the new baby, but I couldn't. And while I hope to stay under the radar for ever, if Luca and my child are with me, there is always a higher chance that Alistair could find us. If I was ever to be discovered and was still with the child, then it stands to reason that they would be discovered too. And I could never risk that.

Alistair, like everyone else, believes that the unborn child died with me and Thalia in the lake. I hope and pray he has no inkling that this child exists. They are surely safer without me. They can have a good life with Luca. I don't want any child of mine to grow up closeted in that awful castle under Alistair's coldness and tyranny. I couldn't save Thalia, but I can do this for them. Surely that's something?

'And what about you?' one of them asks, snapping me out of my thoughts. 'What brought you here?'

'Oh I . . .' I start, my voice quickly tailing off as I realize I don't want to share any of the details of my coming here. I need to stay as anonymous as I can.

'There's no need to tell us if you don't want,' Sylvie says.

'No, that's OK,' I say. I will eventually have to come up with a convincing back story, so it may as well be now. 'My story isn't as dramatic as any of yours. My husband kept me as a virtual prisoner. He's rich, very rich, but I didn't have any access to money and was never allowed out on my own. He was only occasionally violent, but I worried that he might become more so. And especially now that I have left him, if he ever found me, I'm quite convinced he would kill me. He would say that I have brought shame on him and his family. He's something big in business and reputation is everything to him. Compared to that, I am nothing, as far as he is concerned.'

I read somewhere once that the best way to lie is to stay as close to the truth as possible. Almost nothing I have actually said is untrue, but obviously I have left a lot out which they don't need to know. I made up the businessman bit on the off chance they saw my story in the papers, though that seems unlikely. For all his grandeur and posturing, Alistair is an obscure laird from the middle of nowhere, and I his depressed, nobody wife with no family to advocate for me, so my story wasn't big in the press. Thankfully I can tell by their faces they think my story isn't as terrible as theirs and, as I've told it, it isn't. But as far as I know, none of them has lost a child as they made their escapes from their partners.

'No one has to justify their reasons for being here,' Sylvie says softly, giving my arm a gentle squeeze. 'And coercive control of the type you describe is absolutely a form of abuse. If you feel in danger, we are here to help. And tomorrow, we'll get on with helping you build your new life.'

I tell Sylvie that I have never worked, which is almost true, at least as far as official records go. I was paid cash in hand when I was working in the lodge in Scotland and haven't worked since. Getting the birth certificate means that I can do everything in my new name, so Sylvie helps set me up to receive various benefits using my fake ID while I look for work. I can't believe how simple it is.

Sylvie buys some local papers and we take them to the refuge for me to trawl through the job adverts. I have no skills, but I've always liked cooking, and did OK at the lodge during the brief time I was there, so I start by looking at anything in catering. Sylvie says that while having no references can sometimes make things tricky, and I will need to start with something very basic, she can vouch for my reasons for never having worked before and is well known in the area. 'There are some good people here, willing to give my ladies a chance to get back on their feet without asking too many questions – as long as they're happy to work hard,' she says. 'I'm sure we'll find you something in no time as long as you're happy to be flexible.'

And we do. Later that morning I go for an interview at a picture-perfect pub with low ceilings, an inglenook fireplace and a resident large ginger cat. They are looking for someone to help out in the kitchen, which suits me fine.

'It's not very glamorous I'm afraid,' the landlord says apologetically, 'but one of our current waitresses is heading off to university in a couple of months so, if things work out on both sides, we could look at moving you to something more front of house then, if you'd like?'

'I don't mind,' I say. 'I'm just grateful to have the work and the chance to start getting back on my feet. Thank you.' It is the truth, I'm very happy to work in a kitchen. Even though I have cut and dyed my hair, am now wearing glasses with clear lenses which I found in a charity shop, and have also entirely changed the way I dress, I still live in fear of someone recognizing me. But because Alistair never allowed me to go anywhere, few people have met me that are likely to remember me, especially here, in a town I have no connections with and have never been to before.

But always better to be safe than sorry.

# Part Five

# The Twenty-First Lady
of Creaglie

## 2023
Tabitha, the Twenty-First Lady of Creaglie

I never meant it to turn out like this.

When I first met Alistair in London, I had recently split up with the latest in a series of terrible boyfriends who had treated me like shit. I had never been very good at choosing the right man. The last one I had actually caught in bed with my former best friend, like something from the beginning of a third-rate cheesy romcom.

I hated my job as a receptionist at a firm of account-ants, which was about as unexciting as it sounds. I'd fallen into it after being made redundant from my previous, equally low-paid but marginally more inter-esting, job in marketing, which I'd taken once I realized that my dreams of being an actress were never going to pay the rent. I was getting behind on my rent payments, I was sick of living in a crappy house share, my credit card bills were stacking up and it felt like nothing was going to change any time soon.

And then Alistair appeared in my life. It would be an exaggeration to say that I fancied him as such. I didn't; he was far too old for me to think of him in that kind of way. But when he came into the office he was always charming and polite, especially when you compared him to most of the rich wankers I had to deal with day to day. He started by simply making conversation when he came for his appointments, basic things like asking me about my day; nothing out of the ordinary or particularly memorable. And then, one morning, when he asked me how I was when I was just back from a particularly awful Tinder date the night before, I probably overshared more than would be considered professional. He gently enquired whether a good lunch might help me feel better, but only if I had the time and the inclination, of course. I was feeling so sorry for myself, it was the end of the month and I had no money. The thought of eating the soggy sandwiches on slightly stale bread which I'd brought in with me from home because I couldn't even afford to go to Pret made me feel so depressed that I said yes.

We left the building and he hailed a black cab. We went to a three-Michelin-star restaurant at one of London's most old-school hotels. He didn't ask whether that suited me, and normally that would have annoyed me. But I'd never been there before, would never realistically be able to afford to go even if I wanted to, and it somehow felt quite nice having a decision taken out of my hands, the mood I was in, so I went along with it.

He was the perfect gentleman, which was exactly as I'd expected he would be, asking me about myself and not talking about himself too much. I asked polite questions about him even though, being pretty familiar with his file, I knew the answer to most of them. But we also talked about film, music, politics, all sorts, and I enjoyed myself much more than I had expected to. And after lunch as he put me back in a taxi to work, handing a twenty pound note to the driver for the fare, he turned to me and said: 'I hope I succeeded in brightening your day.'

I smiled. 'You did.'

'Delighted to hear it. A good lunch can work wonders, I find. I wouldn't flatter myself to assume that my company had too much to do with it, but if you would permit me to take you for lunch again, or even for dinner, I would be honoured.'

This was so far removed from the usual end-of-date attempt to get me into bed, sometimes successful and sometimes not, largely depending on how lonely I was feeling that day and how much I'd had to drink, that I found myself saying 'yes'.

After that, I think the term is he 'love-bombed' me. Flowers, muffin baskets, wine, hampers, jewellery and other gifts appeared both on my desk and at my manky house share almost every day, much to the bewilderment of both my colleagues and my housemates. Lunches progressed to dinners, which morphed into surprise weekends away in Paris, Milan and Rome, always travelling first class or even by private plane, eating in the finest restaurants and staying in the best hotels. And eventually a trip to his incredible castle in Scotland.

I felt looked after. I felt loved. And I felt wanted. He made life easy for me. I never had to do anything I didn't want to any more. And when he took me flying in a hot-air balloon over Provençal lavender fields, and pointed down to show the words, 'Will You Marry Me?' cut in huge letters into one of the scented purple fields, it felt like the most natural thing in the world to say yes.

Everything would be simple and easy for me from then on, I was sure.

## 2024
Tabitha, the Twenty-First Lady of Creaglie

As Alistair had already been married twice, we both felt that something discreet was in order for our wedding. We headed off to St Lucia and got married on the beach with a couple of waiters as witnesses.

I knew that everyone looking at us, with our age gap of more than forty years, would be thinking that I was marrying Alistair for his money. And, if I'm honest, there *was* a large element of that. The idea of no longer having to do a job I hated to scrape together the rent to live in a house I loathed with people I detested was extremely appealing. As well as not having to navigate the quagmire of online dating. It felt like it could all stop.

And Alistair was kind, clearly adored me, seemingly couldn't believe his luck. And while I perhaps couldn't say I truly loved him, I didn't dislike him in the slightest. Though there was a part of me which knew that he very much enjoyed that I, a young, not unattractive woman, was by his side as a status symbol. And, with the help of a little blue pill, he also enjoyed that side of things now and again too with me, though thankfully not too often. And at the start at least, he was fun to be with. Well-educated, well-travelled, interesting to spend time with, treated me like a princess and lavished me with gifts. Really, what's not to like?

He told me quite early on, though not in so many words, that any future wife of his would not be inheriting the bulk of his estate. 'The Creaglies are a traditional family,' he said, 'And I have my son and heir, Joshua. He will be inheriting Creaglie Castle and the lion's share of my other assets to protect the family name. Joshua has already proved himself to be pretty innovative and has come up with some ideas about how to help the castle pay for itself. It needs a lot of repairs, and sadly my investments no longer cover everything that is needed. I will not allow the Creaglie fortune to diminish, so it is important that the castle, or any marriage, is not a drain on our resources.'

I have already seen all this on his file, having had a bit of a deeper nose through after our first lunch, seeing exactly how much money he had and what his set-up was, so it doesn't come as a surprise. Though obviously I don't tell him that.

'I wasn't hugely keen on Joshua's idea at first,' he continues. 'Inviting paying guests into the ancestral home seems somehow a little . . . gauche – but both Joshua and my accountants – your employers – have persuaded me that the castle costs so much to upkeep that this is now the best way ahead. Work is beginning on the new spa annexe very soon. It has been quite an outlay, but Joshua assures me it will be an asset.' He pauses. 'I only hope I don't live to regret agreeing to it.'

I had always been somewhat intrigued by Joshua, as I'd heard quite a lot about him; a little from Alistair, but more in a work context because of him needing money from the family estate for the renovations and new spa. Alistair is an incredibly traditional man, and I got the impression that he saw Joshua primarily as someone who should secure the Creaglie family's future, rather than as a son to love or be proud of. Or at least he never talked about him in those terms. 'Innovative' was about as complimentary as he ever got, and even that word was used with a somewhat sneering tone, as if it should be followed up with 'with his new-fangled ideas'.

I didn't meet Joshua until after our wedding and because of this, I had always assumed he disapproved of his father remarrying or, more specifically, probably him remarrying someone of my age. Though Alistair assured me that he was fine with the idea of our marriage, that he accepted that his mother was gone, and a very long time ago at that, and that his father was ready to move on. I didn't know if that was the truth, and it seemed a little unlikely to me. I didn't know much about Alistair's second wife, Joshua's mother, other than that she had died of a brain aneurysm when Joshua was still quite young.

And while I felt sorry for him for this reason, it also

led to me imagining him as an overgrown little boy, scowling and sulking at the idea of his father's attention being taken by a woman he had never met and whom he had already decided he despised. He had been due to come to our wedding as the sole guest but at the last minute decided he was unable to, citing some work emergency or other, which only served to heighten my conviction that he was going to hate me.

But I didn't care either way. It wasn't as if we were going to have to spend much time together, I didn't imagine. He was a grown man, and I had no intention of playing the part of a stepmother, wicked or not.

After our honeymoon, Alistair and I moved to Creaglie Castle. I had already given up my room in the house share, and since then we had been spending most of our time in Alistair's lavish pied-à-terre in Knightsbridge. I was excited to leave London and be somewhere different, and looking forward to helping prepare the castle for its new life as a high-end hotel. I'd worked in hospitality in the distant past, in between my few-and-far-between acting jobs. I was looking forward to giving it a go again, but this time in the elevated position of lady of the manor, rather than simply as a lowly receptionist. The castle was remote, sure, but I'd always loved my visits there, cosying up by the many open fires, pottering around and reading, a bit of hiking when the weather was OK. And it wasn't as if I could never leave; we'd still have the London place, so I could come for shopping, bars, restaurants and to see friends whenever

I liked. But I'd already spent so much time doing that kind of thing it felt somewhat empty by now. Some peace and quiet in the lap of luxury with servants (imagine!) on hand would suit me fine.

In the end, the first time I met Joshua was shortly after our arrival in Scotland, when he came to spend some time at Creaglie Castle while he was preparing for its launch as a hotel retreat. He wasn't what I had expected at all. Fresh from an MBA at MIT in the States, he was an unusual mix of privileged yet under-confident British public schoolboy and brash American entrepreneur with big business ideas. Absolutely nothing like his father.

The spa he had commissioned was beautiful – a glass cube at the back of the castle, invisible from the front and seamlessly blending into the surrounding trees almost like magic. Inside was a large, ultra-heated pool with waterfall jets, plus a glass tunnel leading to an outdoor pool where, as long as you kept your shoulders under the water, you could be outside even on the coldest of nights, looking at the stars as steam rose from the water. Not having spent much time in the countryside and certainly not in the Highlands, I found it pretty magical and unlike anything I had seen before. The idea was that staff would bring hot toddies out for guests to enjoy while they were relaxing in the water.

I hadn't expected to, but I liked Joshua a lot. He was clearly bright and business-minded, eager to make a go of things and run Creaglie Castle as a successful enter- prise. His years in the US seemed to have knocked the stuffy pomposity (which so many of the ex-public schoolboys I used to meet in my accountancy job seemed to have) out of him, and he was generally great company and fun to be around.

He was confident that people would come flocking once we launched the castle hotel with its 'live like a lord' concept. The idea was that people would pay an all-inclusive price and come here to simply be, drift about, order drinks to be brought by butler Donald, eat lavish meals in the dining room, dress up in period clothing should they so desire, and spend the rest of their time reading in the library, playing billiards, or hiking, boating on the lake, perhaps hunting and shooting if the weather and season allowed. 'People love all that!' he'd enthused. 'Getting a taste of what it's like to live as the British nobility! Americans can't get enough of that kind of thing!'

But we had very few enquiries, and eventually the grand opening had to be put back.

The bills continued to rack up. And suddenly Alistair, never entirely comfortable about allowing the castle to be rented out to 'oiks', as he put it, became a lot less supportive of Joshua's ideas.

## 10 November 2025, 3.00 a.m.
Amelia

'I think it's best that we all stay together from now on,' Silas is saying. Everyone is grey-skinned and exhausted looking, no doubt not only because of the lateness of the hour, but also because of the shocking news Joshua has imparted about Kayla. I feel quite devastated. That beautiful young woman, snuffed out, just like that. A terrible thing.

'In light of what's befallen poor Kayla, after what happened to the Laird of Creaglie,' he continues, 'and the fact that Tabitha also appears to have been taken ill, I don't think we can entirely discount the possibility that there has been . . . some foul play.'

There is a collective intake of breath. Joshua rubs his face with his right hand and looks around the room.

'Silas,' he says in a measured voice. 'I realize tonight's events are . . . extremely shocking and unfortunate, but I would very much hope that they are not more than horrible and coincidental accidents. My father, God rest his soul, was not as young as he used to be, and his health had sadly deteriorated recently. I tried to get him to see a doctor, but he was stubborn about these things, as many men of his generation are. It's most likely that his tragic fall was caused by a medical issue, perhaps a heart attack or a stroke, something of that nature.'

God. It seems a bit of a stretch to imagine all three incidents are sheer bad luck, but I can see why he'd want to frame it that way. It's not exactly the best look for your opening weekend, is it?

'However,' Joshua continues, 'if everyone would feel more at ease if we stay together, then I am of course happy to agree to that. Whatever you all think is for the best. Given the circumstances, my first concern is to make you feel as safe and comfortable as humanly possible.'

'I'm happy to go along with that,' Ben says, and a general murmur of agreement goes around the room.

'I warned that there was an evil spirit,' Elvira intones. 'If you had listened, and perhaps allowed me to carry out a cleansing ceremony, then it's possible that . . .'

'Oh stop this!' Rosemary snaps. Good for her. This psychic woman is awful. 'No more of your nonsense, please!' she adds. 'These terrible events were either accidents that happened to occur close in time to each other, or, God forbid, someone killed these poor souls. Tabitha is ill, we can all see that, but we don't know why. What I *do* know, though, is that none of this was anything to do with spirits, and you bleating on about them is far from helpful.'

Elvira pulls a pantomime affronted expression and bursts out: 'Well! Never in my life have I been spoken to in such a way! I can only hope that—'

'I've had some time to think about your séance while I've been sitting here with Tabitha,' Rosemary continues, unabashed. 'If my Dave was going to come back to me, he wouldn't do it like that.' Tears start to fall and she swipes them away. 'He was a gentle man who loved me. He wouldn't want to scare or upset me. I'm sorry to say it, Elvira, but I don't believe he was speaking through you. And I think it was very wrong of you to try to make me believe that he was.'

Elvira looks like she's readying herself for another outburst but then slumps in her seat and shrugs. 'Well, that's up to you, dear. I am but a conduit. I'm neither here to explain myself nor the spirits, and I do not feel the need to justify myself to you. You are, of course, entitled to believe what you will.'

'Ladies,' Joshua intervenes. 'I realize this is all extremely upsetting, and we are all very tired, but hurling insults around isn't going to help, and is only going to make the situation more stressful. Please. This will get us nowhere. Let's all calm down and . . . try to get through the rest of the night without shouting at each other.'

'I hope she's going to apologize,' Elvira mutters. Everyone ignores her.

'Look, why don't I go and organize some drinks and snacks for us all,' Joshua suggests, 'and then we can hunker down here in the library and try and remain civil towards each other until the storm calms down and we can get in touch with the authorities.'

'You agreed that no one should go anywhere alone,' Rosemary pipes up, 'and that should include you, surely?'

Joshua nods. 'Of course. Mrs Laroche, perhaps you'll accompany me to help rustle up a few things in the kitchen?'

I'm not sure if I'm imagining things, but she appears to give him somewhat of a dirty look; it's the first time I've seen her polite and willing demeanour slip all evening. But she must be exhausted and desperate to get to bed or, even better, to get away from this island.

'Very good, Mr Joshua,' she says curtly, and the two head off towards the kitchen.

The room is almost silent as we wait. I'm not sure providing snacks and drinks is likely to improve anyone's mood very much, but I suppose it's worth a go.

Around ten minutes later, Joshua, Mrs Laroche and Donald return with trays laden with a pile of cheese on toast and a huge tea pot and mugs. They set things down on the coffee table and start fussing around, handing out plates and cups of tea.

'And finally we have some good news,' says Joshua. 'It looks as if the storm is starting to abate. It is still too wild for anyone to risk leaving now, but once it gets light, if it is a little calmer, hopefully we will be able to get the boat out and go for help.'

**2024**
Tabitha, the Twenty-First Lady of Creaglie

It was around the time it became clear that Joshua's big launch of the castle was doomed to failure that I started to see another side to Alistair.

He had never pretended he was happy to see the castle 'pimped out to all and sundry', as he put it, but he had, at first, accepted it as a necessity to pay for the upkeep of what was his and, by extension, the Creaglie family's pride and joy.

But when the bookings failed to materialize in the way predicted on the spreadsheets and graphs of Joshua's assiduously mapped-out business plan, Alistair took on a sneering, 'I told you so' attitude towards poor Joshua that I had never seen in him previously.

'I'm going to London for a week,' he announced, 'and I suggest that while I'm away, you come up with a better business plan. One which might actually work. Otherwise,' he looked his son up and down derisively, 'I may have to seriously reconsider whether you are the right person to be managing the estate once I am gone. I wouldn't want you to fritter away the value it still has in it, or to sully its name. It might be better off in the hands of trustees and advisers for a generation while we see if you can create a more capable heir.'

I breathed in sharply, shocked, as I'd never heard Alistair speak like that to anyone, let alone his own son. I waited for Joshua to bite back and stand up for himself, as I certainly would if I was spoken to like that, but he simply went bright red and stared at the floor.

'Tabitha can help you,' Alistair continued. 'She's got a good head on her shoulders and,' he turned to me, 'you worked in a hotel at some point too, didn't you, back in the day? And I think you said you had some kind of marketing role before too?'

'I did, yes,' I agreed. 'But please don't patronize me in that way. I don't wish to be spoken about like I'm a thing.'

He waved his hand and tutted dismissively. 'I said you had a good head on your shoulders. It was a compliment – take it as one. You're a clever girl. You can help my boy here come up with something good, I'm sure of it. Now, I'll see you both in a week and we'll go from there.'

## 2024
Tabitha, the Twenty-First Lady of Creaglie

I am enraged at Alistair pronouncing that I am to stay and help Joshua with his business plan without even thinking to check with me that I'm happy with the idea. It is the first time he's ever spoken to me like that and I can't help but think he's throwing his weight around to assert himself not only over me, but also over Joshua. Make sure he knows who's boss. And given Joshua's meek reaction to him, I'm guessing that's not untypical of the way Alistair treats him.

However, on the other hand, neither Alistair nor I has left the castle for ages, and he has been getting on my nerves more and more lately. I am looking forward to some time alone without him, watching what I want on TV, not bothering to dress for dinner, or taking part in various other old-fashioned rituals he still insists upon, which I could do without now that the novelty has worn off. I mean, surely Creaglie Castle must be the only place in the world where a gong is still sounded for dinner, seemingly without irony.

It turns out that marrying someone a couple of generations older than you isn't always the best idea. Who knew?

Joshua takes a very business-like approach to his task, sitting at the one computer in the house which has internet (no WiFi here, Alistair thinks it fries your brain) and poring over spreadsheets full of lines of numbers, I don't even know what.

At first I leave him to it while I drift through my day, doing my usual not very much at all. The way Alistair spoke to me before he left riled me, and I had no intention of helping out initially. I had nothing against Joshua, but I was sure he would be fine without my input. I certainly didn't want to get involved just because Alistair told me to.

And yet. When I met Alistair, or when he rescued me, as I had seen it at the time, I had thought I was desperate to leave work in favour of spending my days reading and pottering around the castle and gardens playing lady of the manor.

But it turns out it's actually quite boring having nothing to do when you're stuck on an island up a mountain and can't even meet a friend for lunch. Alistair won't even turn the heating on in the spa until we have our first guests here, so I can't even use that.

So once I got over the ignominy of Alistair basically ordering me to help, I decided it would be quite nice to actually have a project for a change. Joshua and I start to chat about his ideas over lunch prepared by Irina, the new skivvy/chef who has arrived from Estonia. At the moment she is our only member of staff apart from Donald, who has by all accounts been here pretty much since time began – he was certainly here when Joshua was a child. We have tried to employ more, but it is difficult to find people who want to be, I hesitate to say 'stuck' here, but that's what it is, living so remotely.

'Given the nature of the setting, and the fact that there are plenty of luxury hotels which are easier to access, I think we need to think about what Creaglie Castle's true USP is,' I say to Joshua. 'The spa is lovely, of course, but there are many beautiful spas. What can you find here which you can't find anywhere else? Or at least, something which is harder to come across in other places?'

'The fact that we are a proper castle, one which has been in the same family since the sixteenth century, none of this *nouveau riche* stuff. Here, guests can live like a lord,' says Joshua. 'Literally.'

I frown. 'Yeah. But you already tried offering that, and it didn't work,' I say, trying not to sound too unkind. I don't want to be like his father. 'No one booked. They weren't interested. It wasn't enough.'

We both fall silent, chewing thoughtfully. There is a sudden loud crash upstairs.

'What's that?' I ask, leaping out of my chair.

Joshua shrugs. 'Dunno. One of the ghosts probably.'

'Ha, ha,' I say. 'Seriously, what was it? It sounded like something fell. Do you think we should check?'

'Check what?' he says. 'It won't be anything.' He pauses. 'Are you really telling me you haven't noticed the ghosts yet?'

Oh. He's serious. I laugh. 'I don't believe in ghosts,' I say.

He looks at me incredulously. 'Really? If you'd never been here I could maybe understand that but . . . well. Creaglie Castle is believed to be one of the most haunted places in Europe. People are always getting in touch asking if they can investigate, but my father always says "no".' He pauses. 'He thinks it's undignified, the idea of the public crawling about the place, poking into our business, as he sees it. But given that he seems to have accepted that we have to make the place at least semi-public to hang onto it without digging into the family fortune, maybe I can see if I can get him to reconsider.'

I smile. 'I think that could well be your answer.'

## 10 November 2025 5 a.m.
Ben

It feels like this night is never going to end. We are all in the library, slumped at various angles, still listening to the grandfather clock ticking. Perhaps it's simply my lack of sleep, but it's starting to sound like some kind of toll of doom – funereal, even.

We agreed between us (very democratically, it was put to a vote) that Donald could continue to sit with Alistair's body as he wished to, as long as Josh or someone else sat with him at all times. No one is to go anywhere except in pairs. We are all in the library now, glancing at each other, wondering who did what.

Why did Alistair fall from the landing? And what happened to poor Kayla?

Is someone here a killer?

I can't see it, somehow. The old laird was exactly that, old, and clearly not that well. Chimneys get blocked – perhaps something fell down the chimney in Kayla's room in the storm? The batteries and the smoke alarm are harder to explain, but everyone would have had a lot of setting up to do to get the place ready for the opening – things can get overlooked, surely? They don't seem to have many staff so it wouldn't be that surprising. And Tabitha . . . well, her husband has just died. I'm no medic, but it hardly seems beyond the realms of possibility that her mind would feel it best to shut off for a while, does it?

Perhaps I simply don't want to believe there is a killer – it's too frightening. Until the storm calms down, I'm stuck here with these people, like it or not. It will be OK. We've agreed that no one is to go anywhere alone, so surely nothing else can happen?

I feel sad for Kayla, all alone, dead in her room, but given that none of us actually knew her, sitting with a corpse would somehow feel weird. I resolve to find out where her funeral is and make sure I go to it. It's the least I can do.

Poor woman. Whether it was an accident or not, her death is a tragedy. And God, her poor son, losing his mother like that. I hope he has other family. She didn't say, but I know his father wasn't on the scene.

Periodically Mrs Laroche, still straight-backed and immaculate in her uniform, asks if she can get anyone anything. You have to admire her professionalism; she hasn't had any sleep all night either, and yet is still determined to look after her guests.

Rosemary appears to have now set an alarm on her watch which beeps every hour to wake her up if she dozes off so that she can check and note Tabitha's pulse.

256

I look out of the window. Josh is right, the storm does seem to be dying down a little. Thank fuck. Hopefully we can get out of here soon and get home.

I can't wait for this night to be over.

## 2024
Tabitha, the Twenty-First Lady of Creaglie

I have never believed in ghosts and never will, so while I may have already been vaguely aware of the castle's reputation as one of the most haunted places in the UK, if not the entirety of Europe, I hadn't paid too much attention to it. But now that Joshua mentions it, it rings a bell.

Given that he, one of the most well-educated and seemingly down-to-earth people I have ever met, genuinely seems to think that ghosts are the culprits making some of the strange bangs, crashes and creaks in the castle, this could indeed be the big business idea that Alistair was demanding. A ghostly reputation is something which Creaglie Castle has in spades. And that could easily be big business – especially as people have already been asking to come and investigate.

A quick internet search confirms that there are whole swathes of society who are obsessed with ghosts, including some people who seem entirely sensible and rational who genuinely nonetheless believe in them.

'And you really think this place is haunted?' I ask. Joshua nods solemnly.

'Yep. Absolutely no doubt about it.'

'OK. Give me some examples then.'

He places his hands on the table, looks up at the ceiling and then back at me. 'Well, where to start? There's this grey lady. She pops up in loads of the family diaries, going way back. Apparently she walks down the stairs, not the stairs as they are now but where they used to be back when she was alive, and then she—'

A grey lady! For fuck's sake. Not even very original. I hold up my hand. 'Hang on. I'm not interested in ghosts that you've heard about or read about. Anyone can tell stories like that. I want to hear about things that you've actually experienced yourself.'

'Fair enough,' he says. 'Pictures falling off walls when no one is standing near. Windows flying open when there's no wind. Unexplained voices, bangs like that one we heard earlier which happen from nowhere and for which there is never an explanation. Stuff like that happens all the time.'

He shrugs. 'There are loads of things. I was absolutely obsessed by it all, the supernatural, as a child. This one is difficult to explain, but when I was little there was a ghost who would come to my room and play. I couldn't see or hear him or her, but I knew when they were there. It wasn't even scary. It's always been a thing here. But over time you get so used to it that you end up not paying it that much attention.' He pauses. 'How long have you been here now? About a year? I'm kind of surprised you haven't noticed anything like that, to be honest.'

I smile at him. 'As I said, I don't believe in ghosts,' I say. 'Of course I hear bumps and crashes sometimes. But it's a big old castle in the middle of a lake which sees some serious weather. All those things are normal noises you'd fully expect to hear in a place like this as far as I'm concerned.'

He looks genuinely surprised. 'But there are other things too – not just noises – that happen all the time. Things have gone on through the centuries here and been experienced by countless different people. There's definitely something in it. All those people experiencing the same things at different times, sometimes decades or even centuries apart, can't all have been mistaken or making things up.' He pauses before adding, 'Don't get me wrong, I'm not *scared* of them or anything. The ghosts. They don't bother me at all. But they're definitely there.'

I nod. 'As far as I'm concerned, it doesn't matter if they are real or if they are not,' I say. 'What *matters* here is that the castle has the reputation for being haunted and,' I wave my arm around vaguely, 'its location, appearance and atmosphere, even the weather on most days, will contribute to that. From what you say, and from what I've seen during my quick search, people will come here and pay good money to stay here and find out.'

'You think?'

'I do. However,' I pause. 'I think it would be better for the business going forward if we do a bit more than simply let people explore the place by themselves, hoping for the best. If the ghosts can be "encouraged" to show themselves, let's say, and people tell their friends, or even better, write about it or post on social media, then that'll help keep the punters coming in. Creaglie Castle already has a reputation for being haunted. We just need to push the message out a bit more widely and more strongly to the right people.'

## 1993
## The Nineteenth Lady of Creaglie

I enjoy working at the pub much more than I had expected to. I stay at the refuge for a few more months while Sylvie and the other women help me find my feet and, as far as they believe, help me regain my confidence after leaving my abusive husband. I feel a little bad lying to them as they are so kind, but needs must; it's vital that no one discovers that I am still alive. And it's not merely lack of confidence I have to overcome, even though Alistair knocked every last vestige of that out of me. I am truly struggling to get over my grief for Thalia. I think about her every minute of every day, and I blame myself almost entirely for what happened. She should be getting excited about starting school by now, becoming her own little person in her own right, but instead she is dead at the bottom of a freezing lake.

I know that the grief will never fully go away. But keeping busy, instead of sitting around doing nothing, is helping a little. My work is mindless and easy, but the others who work there are friendly and Tom the landlord is impressed by me because I work hard and I'm always happy to do overtime. Both because the less time I have to think about other things, the better, and also because the more money I can earn, the quicker I will be able to do what I need to do.

Tom stays true to his word and, after a few months moves me to a waitressing job. By now I have become less worried about being traced – I am a long way from home, and I'm pretty sure neither Alistair nor Luca will be looking for me. Alistair believes I am dead, and even Luca probably doesn't know for sure that I'm alive. I deliberately implied in my note that I was not intending to live – when I left at least, that was very much the way I felt. And I'm sure he understands that the child is better off without me.

The refuge is a nice place to stay and Sylvie helps me a lot – I will be forever grateful to her. But the other women here all ask too many questions and, apart from anything else, now that things are more stable for me, I should move out and let someone else move in. So when Tom offers me a room at the pub, I jump at the chance. It is small, simple, and nothing special, but it's ideal for me.

One or two of the regulars start to flirt with me and ask me out on dates, but I smile sweetly and say 'no'. I'm only twenty-eight years old, but I've had enough of relationships to last me a lifetime. I'm not going to make that kind of mistake again.

Even though I'm pretty sure no one is looking for

me, staying in one place too long feels too risky, and being part of a couple would certainly tie me down too much, and mean that I would be asked too many questions. I don't want to get close enough to anyone to have to involve them in my lies. I need to be my own person now. I have plans. And it wouldn't be fair to tangle someone else in them. My plans are all about me. And Thalia. Honouring her in the way she deserves.

Now that I am living in the pub and don't have to pay rent for a flat or bills or even buy much food (Tom is happy for me to eat my meals with the staff at the beginning or end of service), I have more than enough money. And I know exactly what I'm going to do with it.

Once I have bought what I need, I keep a little cash aside for my own expenses and put the rest in an envelope, which I will deliver to the refuge anonymously. They helped me get back on my feet, and to find the courage for what I need to do next.

## 2024
Tabitha, the Twenty-First Lady of Creaglie

Who would have guessed that there was so much to know about ghosts? I have barely given anything supernatural a second thought before now – it doesn't interest me at all. But it turns out that Joshua is a bit of an expert on the subject on the quiet. I guess that's what comes from growing up in a house you believe to be haunted and your parents probably being absent or emotionally distant for most of your childhood, from what I have been able to garner. I guess you look for your comfort elsewhere.

But amazingly, to me at least, it turns out there is also some 'science' of a sort around ghost hunting. There are people who devote almost their entire lives to hanging out in 'haunted' buildings, testing temperatures, trying to record ghostly sounds, to capture images on film. There are online channels, even TV programmes, documentaries and films devoted to it. Perhaps 'science' isn't quite the right word. But there are certainly people who spend a lot of their time exploring and researching this kind of thing, and who I imagine would pay handsomely to do so at a place like Creaglie Castle, reputed to be so crammed full of ghosts you can barely move without bumping into one, according to Joshua and his ancestors, at least.

We spend all day researching, watching videos online where allegedly ghosts have been seen or heard, but I remain unconvinced. Ghostly 'grey ladies' like the one Joshua mentioned before look like a fault in the film processing, a trick of the light or even one image super-imposed on another to me. 'Voices of the dead' who breathless presenters swear are communicating with them sound like simple radio static. I can only hear any specific words if the presenter tells me what I'm meant to be listening to. Confirmation bias, I think it's called.

'It's definitely interesting,' I say, 'and this kind of stuff might be enough for those who already believe at a push. But I think we need a bit more theatre if people are going to come all this way, to ensure that there are things actually happening, activities people can take part in. And ideally some things which will make even hardened sceptics like me think there might be something out there after all.'

'Got you. How about a séance? Hang on . . .' He types in a name and brings up an image of a woman who encompasses every cliché of a medium there is, turning the screen towards me. 'Elvira. She's world-famous and people pay through the nose to see her.' He clears his throat and adds quietly: 'In fact, I have

266

to admit that when I was in the States, I travelled quite some distance and paid quite a lot of money to have a private session with her.'

I laugh. 'Seriously? And what did she tell you?'

The tips of his ears go pink. 'I can't tell you.'

I snort. 'Some kind of psychic's code? A bit like the Hippocratic oath, only for . . .' I am about to say 'shysters' or 'lunatics' but it's clear that he really believes in this rubbish. I don't want to be rude to him so I settle for simply 'mediums'.

He shakes his head. 'No. Nothing like that. I just . . . can't tell you.'

Fuck's sake. Is this like not telling people what you wish for when you blow out your birthday candles otherwise it won't come true?

Whatever. It doesn't matter. 'OK,' I concede. 'Fair enough. So you think if we got this psychic woman to come here and do a séance for guests – people would pay to come? Question is, would *she* come?'

He nods. 'I think there's a good chance she would. She'd definitely be interested in this place – we talked about it a bit after our session. She knows its reputation.' He pauses. 'We'd still have to pay her though, I'm sure, and she doesn't come cheap.'

'Hmm. We're already looking at charging punters quite a lot – I'm not sure we can put the price up any more.'

Joshua turns to look back at the screen. 'I know what we could do,' he says. 'We could get one of the better ghost hunters, a famous one, one with a big following, to come here at the same time to do some filming. Or maybe even press too if we can manage it. She'd love that; it would be free advertising for her. Elvira pretends not to, but she loves publicity. If we can promise her some decent coverage, I think we could probably get her to drop her fee, at least a bit.'

'Brilliant! If she's as big a name as you say she is, then it'll probably be good publicity for us too. I'll get on to some press and some of the online ghost-hunter people with a bigger reach, you get in touch with the psychic woman. Let's see what we can do.' I power down the computer. 'I think that's enough for today though. Let's go and have a drink and hope Irina's preparing us something good for dinner.'

## 2024
Tabitha, the Twenty-First Lady of Creaglie

I didn't mean it to happen with Josh. I don't think either of us did. But we drank a lot of wine that night and then one thing led to another and – well.

Afterwards we lie in bed together (his bed of course, I do have some standards) and stare at the ceiling. 'I've been wanting to do that since I met you,' he says softly.

He doesn't meet my eye. And I don't know what to say.

I turn my head to look at him. 'It's pretty terrible that we did this though, you know?'

He turns his head to me and then away again, his face back towards the ceiling. I think I see tears in his eyes.

'Is it?' he sighs. 'I don't think it's *that* awful, given the circumstances.' He pauses. 'You shouldn't be with him. With my father. The whole thing is ridiculous. You must see that, surely? He's too old. You're too beautiful.' He turns towards me again and props himself up on his elbow. 'You're nothing but a status symbol to him, you know that, don't you?'

I feel a stab of hurt, even though I know what he says is true. No one wants to be called a status symbol, after all, do they? 'I . . . um, I think he likes me quite a lot, actually,' I protest.

He rolls his eyes. 'Of course he likes you. Who wouldn't like you? But what he likes most is how you make *him* look. Like the hotshot, virile laird who can still get whoever he wants in spite of his age. It's gross. And I'm sorry to say this, but he doesn't love you. I honestly think he is incapable of love. At least, he's certainly never shown any to me.'

He flops back down on the pillows. 'Believe me,' he continues, 'you'll see. I can already see the cracks appearing between the two of you, and I think if you're honest with yourself, you can too. He's rude and snippy with you because now that you're married, you've signed on the dotted line, he no longer has to be nice to win you over. I've seen him do it before with other women, notably my poor mother.'

He turns to face me again. 'It's none of my business exactly why you married him, and I know it can't entirely be for his money, as I also know, as do you, I hope and would assume, that he's taken care of that side of things in his will. That you won't be inheriting – his money will go to me, and then to my children, assuming I have them, which eventually, I hope to. But whatever your reasons, I can tell you now, you marrying him was not a good idea. You know how he tells everyone my mother died of a brain aneurysm?'

'Um . . . yes,' I say. Oh God. Where is this going?

'Not true.' He pauses. 'She killed herself. He drove her to it. She was deeply unhappy but he wouldn't let her leave. He deliberately targets women with nothing, no family, no means of their own, so they can't leave and "bring shame on the family" as he sees it. Reels them in with generosity and fake shows of affection and then treats them how he likes, which is as disposable playthings with no lives of their own.'

I feel a lurch of alarm. That was a pretty accurate description of my situation when I met Alistair.

'She saw no way out,' he continues, 'so she took a whole load of pills while I was away at school to ensure it wasn't me who found her body. He paid off whoever needed paying to fake the death certificate, and that was that.' He sniffs and swipes at his eyes.

I touch his arm gently. 'That's horrific,' I say softly. 'But how do you know this?'

'I don't for absolute certain,' he says tersely. 'As in I don't have any proof. But it's the only thing which makes sense. She was young and healthy and he slowly ground her down just because he could. His first wife too, the one who drowned along with their daughter. I've done some digging and it sounds very much to me like that was probably also suicide too.' He pauses. 'I can't bear the thought that he could eventually drive you to do the same,' he adds quietly, his voice catching in his throat. 'That you could meet a similar end. He's toxic when it comes to women, believe me.'

A few beats pass in silence before I ask:

'So why . . . why are you here? If you hate him so much?' I ask.

He sniffs again and sits up in bed, rubbing his face. 'Because I am due my inheritance, eventually,' he says, his voice now stronger and more resolute. 'So it is in my interest to make this castle viable as an asset. I'm not having him ruin my life as well as my mother's. I'm going to make a go of this place. Set it up as a hotel, make it pay for itself, I'm sure I can make it work, whatever he thinks. In a decade or two he will eventually die, and then all this will be mine and I can run it as I want. But in the meantime,' he adds, 'You should be extremely careful. He's ruthless – believe me.'

## 10 November 2025, 5.30 a.m.
Amelia

I've been sitting with Rosemary, Tabitha and the others in the library for what feels like hours now. I've started to quite admire Rosemary, in spite of her seeming like an insipid nervous Nellie earlier in the evening. Since Tabitha's been taken ill, she's really come into her own. She hasn't left her side. I've been watching and she checks her pulse on the hour, every hour, and then writes something down, I'm assuming the reading, in a little notebook.

Since Silas's insistence that we all now stay together, this whole situation has felt a lot more tense.

That silly psychic woman is dozing periodically and snoring when she does. Right now she is awake, staring glumly into space. I don't like her. She's clearly a fraud. Silas is wearing headphones and fiddling with his various instruments, frowning and making notes occasionally. Ben is staring at the floor and periodically nodding off. Mrs Laroche is sitting with her back rod-straight and asking if anyone wants anything every half an hour or so – professional to the last. Joshua and Donald are in the other room, sitting with Alistair, not that he deserves anything respectful like that, as far as I'm concerned.

Tabitha hasn't woken up at all. I should say I hope she's OK, but actually, I don't care. It doesn't make any difference to me either way, though I bear her no ill will. She may or may not be a gold-digger, but either way, it doesn't matter to me now.

Her and Alistair's age gap of at least forty years is wildly inappropriate though, as far as I'm concerned. He was always very good at playing the affable toff, the charming posho with immaculate manners, but underneath it all, there was a heart of stone, and now I can see that he was also a dirty old man to boot. Gross.

I hear footsteps and then a low murmuring in the hall before Joshua and Donald reappear in the room, staying together as instructed, I see.

'How's Lady Tabitha doing?' Donald asks. 'Any change?'

Rosemary looks up at him. 'No. But that's probably a good thing. She's breathing fine, her pulse is strong, her colour is good, perhaps a little better than it was earlier, I think. Maybe it was the shock of it all that has somehow made her shut down. Though I have not seen anything like that before.'

'I warned you that there was an evil spirit present,' Elvira intones. 'That is why the lady is unwell. It is still here. I can sense it. We need to leave!' she adds, standing up, her voice becoming shrill. 'All of us! Now! We mustn't delay! Evil is close! I can feel it! I insist that you . . . start the boat! Arrange a helicopter! Whatever it takes! I demand it!'

Her face has gone bright red – I hope she isn't going to give herself a heart attack. That would be the last thing we need. She slumps back in her chair, closes her eyes briefly and then opens them again. 'Well?' she snaps, addressing poor Joshua, who can hardly magic a helicopter out of the middle of nowhere. 'What are you going to do about it?'

Joshua rubs his forehead. 'Elvira. This isn't helpful. We don't want to cause any unnecessary alarm here. No one is in any danger from . . . an evil spirit or indeed from anything else. As I said before, my father's death and that of Kayla are simply two unrelated and unfortunate accidents which have occurred and—'

'In one night?' Rosemary asks, her voice at a higher pitch than usual too. 'With respect Joshua, I think that seems unlikely, don't you? Especially with Tabitha being taken ill too.' She pauses. 'I would have put it more politely,' she shoots a glance at the mad psychic, 'but I agree with Elvira. We need to get out of here as soon as possible, before something else happens and before Tabitha can take a turn for the worse again. I am only a nurse, and retired at that; she needs to be seen by a doctor. Surely there is something you can do?'

As if on cue, there is an extra loud howl of wind and a window blows open, letting in an icy blast of air along with a few scattered leaves. Donald rushes over to the window to close it.

'As you can see, the weather is still not sufficiently calm, Miss Rosemary,' Donald says pointedly, 'and anyone leaving would be putting themselves in quite serious danger. I will check the conditions again, but while things do appear to be calming down a little, the safest thing for everyone is that we sit out the storm here a little longer. At the very least we should wait until it is light, and then we can seek help from the appropriate authorities.'

'I agree,' I say. Donald has barely changed in all the years he's worked here. I always liked him a lot. I'd trust him with my life.

If I was still alive, that is.

## November 1993
Amelia, the Nineteenth Lady of Creaglie

I treat myself to a plane ticket rather than travelling the full length of the UK by coach like I did when I went to Scotland for the first time to take up my post in the hunting lodge. Back then, I'd thought I'd be there simply for a few months, but ended up not leaving again for years, bar holidays with Alistair in our early days.

I rent a room in a cheap hotel while I work out how I'm going to get across the lake to Creaglie Castle. I decide it feels almost poetic to cross back the way I left – by rowing a small boat. And it's not as if there is any other real option anyway – this isn't the kind of place which has anything like a water taxi. I buy the supplies I need for cash, along with a rubber dinghy and oars, at a town a little way away as a precaution, even though I look entirely different from when I lived here. It's highly unlikely anyone would remember me anyway – I barely left the castle during my time here. Thankfully I am much stronger and in better health now than when I left, heavily pregnant and really quite sick, so if I managed to row a boat across before, I can do it again.

I will have to go at night to protect against being spotted. There is no real security at the castle: being in the middle of a lake is quite reasonably considered enough protection by its occupants.

Just as I did before, I pick a clear night to launch my boat, carrying a small backpack of things I will need. My heart is heavy as I think of Thalia and the last journey she ever took, which was across this same lake. The last time she drew breath.

She always loved the lake. I hope she is at peace in death. But she was such a vivacious, happy child, she would have obviously preferred to live.

For a long time I blamed solely myself for her death. But that is no longer the case. I blame Alistair. His cruelty drove us away, along with the fear of how he would react to a child which wasn't his. His coldness and the way he kept me as a virtual prisoner also led to me becoming so desperate as to have an affair in the first place. So when you think about it, all roads lead back to him when it comes to blame.

The boat feels empty without Thalia in it. My life has felt empty since she went. I think somewhere in me, I have always known what I needed to do since the moment I lost her. I needed to return here. I needed to complete the circle.

In the same way that I managed to appreciate the stillness of the night and the clear sky when we left,

I do the same today. I feel closer to Thalia here than I have for months, and that is a blessing.

I land the boat close to the castle in the same place from where I left. I take my bag and walk quietly up to the house. I open the door to the kitchen with the key that I kept more by accident than design. I take out the petrol and spread it liberally over the floor, switch on the gas oven and open the door. Back outside the kitchen, I set a rag on fire using a cigarette lighter, throw it in through the door and run back down to the boat. I have barely taken more than about ten oar strokes on the lake when there is an almighty explosion, and the kitchen, with Alistair's bedroom above it, goes up in flames.

The staff sleep in a separate wing. They should be OK. But hopefully Alistair will not be.

I get back into the boat and row away, watching the flames envelop the castle where I was both at my happiest, after Thalia was born, and most miserable, most of the rest of the time I was there. I see lights flick on in the windows and some figures appear in the darkness outside the house, running backwards and forwards. I am glad; I do not want to hurt the staff. They will not be able to see me in the darkness from where they are, but really, it doesn't matter either way now.

When I get to the deepest part of the lake, the part where I lost my darling Thalia, I stop rowing and watch the flames for a while. And then I hear sirens in the distance.

It is time for me to do what I need to do.

I take a rope and tie my ankles together. I fill my pockets with large stones I brought from the shore before launching myself over. The water closes over my head as it did before but this time, I do not try to resurface. There is no need.

Finally, I am going to be with Thalia.

# Part Six

# The Creaglie Family Tree

## May 2025
Kayla

We never had much when I was a child, but I always felt loved. Dad worked hard and did his best for me.

I don't remember my mother at all. When I was old enough to realize that almost everyone at school apart from me had a mother, and started to ask my dad where she was, he told me she had died when I was very young. 'Life just got a bit too much for her,' he'd said. When I was a little bit older, he told me that I'd also had an older sister who had drowned before I was born, and Mum had blamed herself which had contributed to the poor mental health she had suffered from. He never gave any more details other than the child, Thalia, had drowned in a lake. He made it clear he found it upsetting to discuss, so I never probed too closely. I had pictured a happy, sunny family holiday which had ended in tragedy. It turns out it was nothing like that.

As a child I had felt sad for both my mother and my dead sister but also, a little, for myself. I would have loved to have had a brother or sister. It had always been just Dad and me at home, and often it had felt lonely. I envied my friends with busy, noisy houses full of siblings and sometimes even cousins and grandparents. Dad had never even seemed interested in having a girlfriend – not as far as I was aware, at least.

My childhood and early adulthood were happy but pretty uneventful. I grew up, left home, but didn't move too far away, took a job as teaching assistant in a local school, got pregnant by a man I barely knew and had a child, a son, Ezra. Dad was a doting grandparent, helped out with childcare and I was happy in my own little unexceptional life.

But then something happened. When Ezra was five, he became quite poorly, having one infection after another. He started to wet the bed at night, something he hadn't done for years. He didn't want to eat; his hands and feet started to swell.

Eventually he was diagnosed with kidney disease. He started treatment, took drugs, which helped for a while, but soon he needed dialysis three times a week. He was rarely well enough to go to school. The doctors told me his best chance at a normal life was a transplant.

'I'll donate one of mine,' I told them, without hesitation. But I was incompatible.

'What about Ezra's father?' they'd asked. I spent weeks online trying to track him down, but got nowhere. I had barely known him when I got pregnant; he was long gone even by the time Ezra was born, and he was never exactly the stable type anyway. He could have even been dead for all I knew.

'Are there any other family members who might be willing?' the doctors had asked. 'Ezra is on the donor register, but there are many waiting and it could take years to find a suitable match. If we have a living donor with the right blood type, the operation can usually be carried out within a few months.' Unspoken was the risk that he might die waiting. I couldn't even think about it.

I wrestled with my conscience for days before asking Dad. I knew he'd do anything for Ezra but at the same time, it was a huge ask, massive.

I didn't get the response I expected.

He burst into tears. I touched his arm. 'Dad! Don't cry! If you don't feel you can do it, it's fine. I should never have asked. Forget I said anything.'

He shakes his head. 'I've been wondering how to tell you . . .'

'Tell me what?' I demand. Fuck! 'You're not ill too, are you? Is this a hereditary thing or something?'

I feel my breathing quicken and my face grow hot. 'Dad, if there's something I need to know, you need to tell me. Please!'

He rubs his forehead again. 'Yeah. I'm sorry. I should have told you before but . . . I couldn't bear to.'

'What is it?' Tears spring to my eyes. What hasn't he told me?

'I'd love nothing more than to donate my kidney to Ezra. But I can't.'

I touch his arm again. 'Dad. That's fine. I get it. Honestly. An operation like that is a big deal. I shouldn't have asked. Don't give it a second thought.'

He shakes his head. 'No. You don't understand. I'm the wrong blood type. I should have told you this a long time ago but . . .' He takes a deep breath. 'I'm not your father. Or Ezra's grandfather.'

I breathe in sharply. That was absolutely not what I was expecting. 'What?' I snap.

He wipes his nose as more tears come. 'I know. I'm sorry. I've always tried to ignore the possibility that you weren't mine but . . . when I saw your medical notes, when you were finding out if you could donate your kidney, your blood type . . . You can't be mine. I always knew it was a possibility but . . .'

He gulps in some air and steadies his breathing a little. 'I probably should have found out earlier. But it always felt like you were my daughter and, if you weren't, well, I didn't want to know about it.'

The tears that were threatening a minute ago start to roll down my cheeks. Dad envelops me in a hug. 'Please. Don't cry,' he says, his voice choked. 'I've done this all wrong. I should have told you as soon as I found out. And I should have done that years ago, but instead I buried my head in the sand. I shouldn't have waited until something like this came and forced my hand. I've always loved you so much.' He lets go of me as he breaks down into sobs again and it is a minute or two before he can even speak coherently.

286

'I was so convinced that you were mine and I didn't want to even entertain the thought that you might not be,' he continues eventually. 'I couldn't imagine a stronger bond with anyone, so I always thought that you must be my daughter, that it wouldn't be the same if you weren't. But it turns out I was wrong. You are everything to me but . . . we're not actually related.'

I stare at him in horror. I don't know what to say.

'But . . . if you're not my father, then who is?'

He wipes his face, grabs a tissue and blows his nose. 'It's a long story. Let me put the kettle on, and I'll tell you everything.'

Two hours later, we are both calmer and I finally know the whole story.

'So, let me get this straight,' I say. 'You and my mother were having an affair. Her husband, some rich laird in Scotland, kept her as a virtual prisoner. You, a butler, tried to help her and her daughter, Thalia, who you thought was also your daughter but you never knew for sure, to escape and fake her own death, but Thalia drowned. Then I was born. You believed you were my father, and my mother gave you no reason to think you weren't. But she couldn't get over the death of her first daughter, so she disappeared shortly after my birth and you believe she is no longer alive. Or at least doesn't want to be found.'

'Yep. That's pretty much it.'

'It's quite a lot to take in,' I say. Understatement of the year.

'I know. But you need to know that I am always here for you. As far as I'm concerned, you are still my daughter, who I love as much as I always did.'

I hug him. 'I know you do, Dad, and I love you too.'

The next day, I tell Dad I've decided I'm going to contact the old laird. 'Wouldn't he want to know me?' I ask. 'And obviously it's not something I would ask at the outset but . . . I might have a half-sibling who could be a match for Ezra, even if the laird himself is too old to donate. And when he or she hears about the situation . . .' I realize it is a long shot, asking someone to donate a kidney to a half-brother they've never met, but I will try anything. I have to follow every avenue possible.

Dad's face clouds. 'I think contacting him is a really bad idea. From what I remember of him, and from the way he treated your mother, he was not a good man. There isn't an ounce of benevolence in him. The Creaglies are like a family from another era, and it's hard to imagine that any offspring of his would be likely to leap into action to save Ezra, a boy he's never met.'

I feel tears spring to my eyes. Dad puts his hand on my shoulder. 'I'm sorry, I know it's not what you want to hear. But getting in touch could be kicking a hornet's nest. Family appearance was always everything to him, and I can't imagine that it would be any different now.

'You appearing on the scene . . . he wouldn't take it well. He'd see you as . . . it's an awful thing to say, but

I think he'd see you – as your mother's daughter, who left because she had an affair with me – as bringing shame on the family name. Back when I worked at the castle, there were stories about a sister who had done something they viewed as shameful and was totally cast out from the family.' He pauses. 'There were even rumours that he had her killed.'

'Oh, for God's sake Dad!' I exclaim. 'If it was simply rumours then—'

He holds up his hand to interrupt me. 'The whole reason for your mother's initial flight was because she was worried he was about to find out that Thalia, your half-sister who died, was my child. That he would kill her, and possibly your mother too.' He pauses. 'I realize it all sounds a bit medieval, but they are an extremely old-fashioned family, and your mother was genuinely in fear for her life, as well as her daughter's.'

'But that's nothing but supposition!' I explode. 'We can't just sit here and do nothing!'

'I think it's safer that way,' he says evenly.

I don't respond, but I'm not going to lie down and take things that easily.

The laird should at least know me, surely? Be given the chance to know I exist? After all, I am his child, if what Dad says is true. He will be old, he might have mellowed. He'll want to know me, I'm sure. He might have changed. And their family is the only blood family I have. They could be Ezra's best chance.

Or at the very least, I could make claim to my inheritance. Set Ezra up for the future. Help Dad out too.

He's looked after me all his life, he deserves it. I could take him on holiday, buy him a new car. Pay back in a very small way a little of what he's done for me over the years.

I start to research. And to come up with a plan.

**20 November 1993, 11 p.m.**
*Newswire* report

A fire has broken out at Creaglie Castle in Dunbraekshire, a remote area of the Scottish Highlands.

No members of the Creaglie family are believed to have been in residence at the time.

The alarm was raised by a staff member and all occupants of the castle, which was extensively damaged, are now safe and accounted for.

An investigation into the cause of the fire has been launched.

*More follows . . .*

## 2024–25
Tabitha, the Twenty-First Lady of Creaglie

Josh is holding my hand and staring into my eyes for longer than feels comfortable to me as we lie in bed. I'm not used to that kind of thing.

'You're not doing this to get back at your father are you?' I ask, voicing the thought I'd had since this started a few months back and, admittedly, somewhat spoiling the moment. 'For that thing he said about you perhaps not being the right person to inherit the castle? Or for how he treated your mother?'

He lets go of my hand, strokes my cheek and smiles. 'No. Of course not. I've wanted to be with you since the moment we met.' He pauses. 'In fact, you know I didn't want to tell you what Elvira told me? She predicted this. Obviously I couldn't tell you that. But she knew this was going to happen. Or at least, her spirit guide did.'

For a second or two I think this must be a joke, but

then I remember how earnestly he had talked about the stupid psychic woman before.

'She really said that?' I ask. 'That we'd . . . get together?'

'Well, not in so many words but . . . yeah. When I met you, I realized what she'd meant when she talked about my relationship with my father and how things would soon change in my favour. I thought initially that she meant he'd finally start to respect me and my ideas about how to develop the castle, but now I can see that she obviously meant that you would come into my life.'

Hmm. That seems like quite a stretched reading of what she said, but from what I understand, this is how psychics work. They speak in broad strokes so that the listener can interpret things how they want. That's if they haven't researched them first. Either way, I've learnt quite a lot about psychics lately, and it hasn't made me any more convinced that they can actually talk to spirits – if anything, I've gone more the other way. Though I do now have a grudging admiration for their cunning, if not their art.

But if that's what Josh wants to believe, that our relationship was written in the stars or the runes or whatever psychics claim to take their readings from, of course I'm going to let him. Initially it was drunken sex. I was bored and horny and, well, why not? But I've started to quite like him. He's certainly a better man than his father in every way.

Not forgetting that one day he's going to be very rich.

'So . . . what happens next?' I ask.

He takes my hand again. 'That has to be up to you. But I know what I want. I want to be with you.'

**Silas's voiceover**

The year of death was 1702.

The Eighth Laird of Creaglie, like most of the Creaglie family throughout the generations, was a stickler for form and politeness. But this particular laird took his love of following the rules of polite society to extremes, and would do almost anything at all to avoid behaving in a way he viewed as incorrect.

One evening, he was holding a banquet for dignitaries he wished to impress, and felt nature calling, as it does, after several flagons of mead. But unwilling to leave the table and abandon his guests, he ignored the call, and stayed in his seat, growing increasingly uncomfortable. Even after his guests had left, he found himself unable to relieve himself. And a week later, he was found dead in his chamber.

Some say he died of a burst bladder. Others say that it was likely he was poisoned.

But if an unexpected puddle of water appears in the

castle, some say it's the Eighth Laird of Creaglie, finally able to make himself comfortable.

Of course, it could be a spillage by a careless maid, or a leaking pipe.

We'll probably never know for sure.

**August 2025**
Tabitha, the Twenty-First Lady of Creaglie

Along with all the secret sex, which I have to say, has put a spring in both our steps, things are going very well with the planning of the inaugural ghost weekend at Creaglie Castle.

Elvira the psychic has agreed to come, thanks to a lot of smooth talking by Josh and also, as he predicted, a fascination she has with the castle and its reputation for hauntings. I've managed to get one of the most eminent online ghost hunters along, Silas, who has more than half a million followers and is famous enough to be known by his first name. He practically bit my arm off when I got in touch. He's been into ghosts all his life and even had a TV show of his own back in the day. Rather sweetly, I think he's a bit of a childhood hero of Josh's.

'I've been talking to one of the main streaming platforms,' Silas said, 'about doing something with them. Reviving the show I did all those years ago for the modern viewer. This could be the idea they actually go for, I'm sure.'

That may or may not be total bullshit, but I use his suggestion that something like that could be in the pipeline in order to get Elvira on board for little more than the price of her travel. Turns out that Elvira is a cheaper date than Josh imagined. She has insisted on flying business class from America, though, so she's still not exactly a bargain.

We've got ten paying guests signed up now, which will give us a healthy profit for this weekend. If we can replicate this perhaps once a month throughout the year, that will go a long way towards getting the castle to cover its own costs, which was the original aim. But with all these people coming, it's urgent that we recruit some more staff. So I place an advert and the replies trickle in – given our very remote location, which is cold for much of the year, staff recruitment has apparently always been tricky.

As we are aiming to offer a high-end experience, any front-of-house members of staff (which is realistically all of them) need to have enough experience to know what they are doing and speak good English. And applications which fit the bill are few and far between. Until:

'This woman,' says Josh, holding up a CV, 'I think I know her.'

## September 2025
Sarah

'You have a very impressive CV, Mrs Laroche,' says
Tabitha, the new Creaglie wife, who is unfeasibly young
and pretty. She looks even younger than the son who
was born shortly after Mama and I left must be by
now. He is not present at the interview as I was hoping
he would be – I wanted to see if we looked similar in
any way as I couldn't find any decent pictures of him
on the internet. 'We really need some extra staff here,
now that we're planning on inviting paying guests, but
finding a suitable housekeeper has been nigh on impossible,' she continues. 'It's a total nightmare.'

Well, count yourself lucky if that's the worst thing
that's ever happened to you, I think to myself.

'I'm sorry to hear that,' I say, 'and thank you for
your kind words about my CV. I hope you won't think
me immodest to say that I sincerely believe my experience is ideal for the post you describe in your advert.'

I have applied for the job in my married name even

though Brad and I are no longer together, in case the Creaglie family recognize my maiden name from Mama's time here. But it looks like it probably wasn't necessary – Tabitha seems to be very much taking the lead in the project, or in the recruitment of staff at least, and she obviously never knew my mother nor would she have any reason to know her name. Alistair is nowhere to be seen and the son would have been a mere child when Mama was here, and no doubt at boarding school the vast majority of the time anyway. He would probably barely remember her.

'As you can see, I've worked all over the world for some very important families, including some celebrities who I am sadly unable to name, due to the NDAs I signed,' I add.

This is not true but neatly covers the gap in my employment when I was trying to get pregnant, and also means that anyone she is likely to approach for a reference will know me under my married name.

'I am used to all sorts of duties – cooking, cleaning, childcare, receiving guests,' I continue. 'I'm very happy to turn my hand to anything. I'm aware that in a residence like this, especially one which is hosting paying as well as personal guests, it is important to be utterly flexible and hands-on at all times. I am excellent at managing and delegating, should you ever have a larger team as your business grows, but also very happy to take on the actual physical toil myself.'

Tabitha nods and casts her eye over my CV again. 'Very good. And what makes you want to work here?

As you will have noticed, we are extremely remote, so it's not a job for everyone. It's not easy to get back to see family, for example, or even to have a proper night out on your day off.'

'That's exactly what attracts me,' I say. 'I've travelled around the world for years, working in different posts in some very exotic locations, and now I want a job where I can have some peace and quiet. My mother has recently died, and I have no other family.' This is as good as true. Mama is not actually dead, but she is so incapacitated now that she may as well be. And I have entirely lost touch with Uncle Luca; I have no idea if he is alive or dead. 'I don't need nights out. I am happiest reading when I have time off, or walking, enjoying nature. And you are ideally situated for that.'

She nods again. 'I'm sorry to hear about your mother,' she says crisply. 'From what you say, I think you could fit in very well here. If you're interested in the post, I'll ask Donald to show you the quarters we can offer and give you a bit of a tour of the castle. Then if you're happy you can come back to me afterwards to discuss terms and conditions and salary. That sound OK?'

'Wonderful,' I agree. 'Thank you.'

Donald is called to lead me on a tour of the castle and I ask the kind of questions someone would ask who has never been before. Donald hasn't changed much – obviously he has aged, but he seems still to be the quietly spoken, polite and diligent man I recall from my childhood. If I remember rightly, his father was in service here before him too.

'Most of these paintings are reproductions,' Donald tells me as we ascend the enormous, imposing staircase I used to slide down in sleeping bags with Thalia when she was big enough, both of us laughing our heads off. I feel a pang of sadness. I still miss her terribly. 'Sadly, there was a fire in the early 1990s,' he continues, 'and while a few paintings were saved, most weren't. Still, I think whoever created the reproductions did a pretty good job – don't you? I think anyone apart from a fine art expert would struggle to tell the originals from the fakes. I don't even remember which are which myself, in all honesty.'

'Were you working here back then?' I ask, disingenuously, as of course I know he was. He must be due to retire by now, surely? Perhaps he has nowhere to go. Has he really been here all this time? I find it hard to imagine. Although Mama spent most of her career here too.

I will not be staying long. I only plan to work here long enough to do what I need to do.

If I told Donald who I was, I imagine he might remember me, but I was a child when I left, so he's hardly going to recognize me as my former self from all those years ago. I'm struck by the sudden thought that while I've lately become obsessed by the Laird of Creaglie being my father, it could be someone else.

It could even be this man in front of me now. Might that make more sense? Be more likely?

I wish I'd pressed Mama for more information while she was still lucid.

'Yes, I was here at the time of the fire,' he says. 'The family were away, and thankfully all the staff members escaped unscathed.

'I've worked here since 1975, and my mother and father before me too, God rest their souls. The laird took me on when I was still a teenager when both my parents, who worked here at the time, were killed in a boating accident.'

'Gosh. I'm sorry for your loss,' I say.

'Thank you. Long time ago now. But if it hadn't been for the laird, who was little more than a boy himself back then, taking me in, I don't know what would have happened to me.'

'Do they know what caused the fire?' I ask, even though I know the answer. Mama kept me updated about it all.

He sighs. 'It was investigated, and they came to the conclusion it was probably arson. An accelerant of some kind was found in the kitchen. But no one was ever arrested and, as you can see, given that we are very remote, their initial supposition was that it was an inside job. Even once they accepted it probably wasn't, neither we nor they ever worked out how whoever started the fire got to the island or made their escape.

'I believe the laird had an extremely stressful time with the insurers for some years. As I understand it, the delay in the insurance payout caused some financial issues too, as that was when most of the staff we had back then were laid off. Pared back to just me, a cook, and the housekeeper, Morag.'

Mama. It's weird hearing her name said out loud like that by someone who has no idea that she is related to me.

'But eventually the powers that be came to their senses,' Donald continues, 'and the castle was able to be renovated to its former glory, which was a huge relief all round.'

He stops walking. 'Now then, were you to accept the post, these would be your quarters,' he says, opening the door to the same apartment where Mama and I lived all those years ago.

I concentrate on keeping my expression neutral as a wave of almost every emotion imaginable washes over me. Nostalgia, love, regret, grief, loneliness, warmth and joy. I felt them all at some point while I was here. The more positive ones though, were not when I was actually in this apartment, but when I was with Thalia.

The rooms have changed, as of course they would have done over the period of thirty or so years. In some ways it is almost the same as I remember it, while in others, it is entirely different. The 1980s wallpaper has gone and been replaced by safe and inoffensive magnolia paint. The bathroom no longer has its avocado bath and instead offers a walk-in shower. The little kitchen is much the same bar some new cupboard doors and the bedroom, which Mama and I used to share, sleeping in little twin beds, now has one double and the same magnolia walls as the rest of the flat.

The apartment is cold and a little dusty; the place looks like it hasn't been lived in for a while. But something about the smell of it takes me right back, remembering how I'd hop out of bed, get dressed and race off to find Thalia. I feel that rush of love for her again which somehow never went away.

'This would be yours,' Donald says. 'Obviously it would be cleaned and heated before your arrival. It's difficult to find staff for somewhere like this, so it's been empty for a while, as you can probably tell.'

I wonder momentarily if there's been no one here since me and Mama, but of course that would be ridiculous.

'Is there anything else you'd like to look at up here, or to ask me? Or shall I take you back to the library so you can finalize things with the Lady of Creaglie, if you're happy?'

'It all looks perfect to me,' I say, and it does; all this suits my needs entirely. 'But I do have one question for you, if you don't mind. You said you'd been here a long time. Do you enjoy working here?'

His eyes cloud. 'Well. That is a question. If I'm honest, I suppose I've never known any other life, so I have nothing to compare it to. But as I mentioned before, the laird took me in when I had no one, and I will always be grateful to him. He's a fair employer, his demands are reasonable, and he provides us all with decent accommodation.'

He pauses. 'The only downside is the remoteness of the location. Sometimes I wonder what my life would have been had I married, had children maybe. But stuck away here . . .' he waves his hand in a dismissive motion.

'Anyway. That's neither here nor there. I made my bed and had to lie in it; no one forced me to stay.'

As Donald and I walk back through the long corridors, I tune out as he talks about the castle and its history. I think back to when I lived here as a child. I feel a wave of sadness as I once again think about Thalia, and her tragic end. Had she lived, she would be in her mid-thirties. I wonder what her life would have been like. Would she have got married? Had a family? Would she be living here and trying to run it as a business instead of it being operated by the son, Joshua, and the laird's new young wife?

Would she and I still be friends? I like to think that we would, in spite of our differing ages and stations in life. Though, as things turned out for her, she never got to know a station at all.

I feel yet another pang of sadness for the life she missed out on and the person she could have become.

Tabitha – she will never be the Lady of Creaglie to me, though of course I will have to call her that – doesn't only offer me the job, she practically bites my arm off. 'You are an absolute lifesaver,' she coos. 'With all these guests arriving, I've no idea what we would have done if I hadn't found you.'

I smile politely. Heaven forbid that she'd actually have to sully her hands and do some work. 'It's perfect for me,' I say. 'Exactly what I'm looking for.'

The salary is lower than I am used to but more than I was expecting, and I am not here for the money so it doesn't matter. We agree a start date of a week later, and I get ready to leave to collect my things. She shakes my hand warmly. 'I'm so pleased we found you,' she says. 'I'm sure you're going to fit in perfectly.'

## September 2025
Tabitha, the Twenty-First Lady of Creaglie

'What do you mean, you know her?' I ask Josh, who is staring at the photo on the CV. 'Who is she?'

'I recognize her face,' he says, 'but she's using a different name here. She wrote to Dad a while back saying she thought she could be his child and asking if they could get a DNA test to check.'

'Oh my God. Really? And what did he say?'

'He ignored it. He said it was a ridiculous idea. Her mother was apparently a maid here back in the day, I think her name began with M . . . Morag? Yes, that was it. But this woman who wrote to us never knew who her dad was, and she got it into her head that it might be my father for some reason.'

What the fuck? 'And is it possible that he could be?' I ask in a measured tone. 'And how do you know what this woman who wrote to him looks like anyway? Did she send a photo? That seems a bit odd.'

He smiles. 'No. She didn't send a photo. But she

included her address for a reply, so I got someone to tail her and steal a glass she'd been drinking from in a café so we could test the DNA ourselves privately.'

The shock I feel at sweet, gentle Josh doing something like that must show on my face as he says: 'Oh, don't look at me like that! The PI was very discreet. I found a female one as I thought that would be better all round, in case she got wind of being followed. I didn't want to cause her any unnecessary alarm. This woman,' he glances again at the CV, 'Sarah Laroche, wouldn't have known anything about us checking her out.'

'OK. So if you went to all that trouble, you thought she might be telling the truth?'

He shakes his head. 'No. Not really, not deep down. Even before I heard back from the private detective, I believed my father when he said it was nonsense. Basically, because there's no way he'd shag a maid. He's too much of a snob and would see it as beneath him. And even *if* he did, there's absolutely no way he would then keep her on staff, and no chance at all he'd have anything to do with a child she might bear.'

He pauses. 'But on the other hand, I felt that *if* there was any chance at all that I had a secret sister out there with a claim on my fortune, however unlikely, I wanted to know about it first. So I thought I'd get her looked into just in case – belt and braces and all that. The detective took pictures too, and this is definitely her. Same first name too. Sarah. Just a different surname.

'Anyway, I got her DNA compared to mine and was relieved and extremely unsurprised to find that we are absolutely definitely not related. Whoever her father is, it isn't my dad.'

'OK. Well that's . . . good I guess? Did you let her know?'

He shakes his head. 'No. Thought it was better to leave it as she sounded pretty unhinged in her letter. And she wrote several times too. Plus, I think legally you're probably not actually supposed to have people tailed or steal their DNA, so it was probably wiser not to flag up that I'd done that either.'

I laugh. 'You think? So why is she applying for a job here now? And without mentioning that she lived here as a child?'

He shrugs. 'Well, there are three options really. First is she just wants a job and didn't feel that having lived here was relevant which, you could argue, it isn't, she was a child. She does seem to have a background in service; I think her CV is probably legit apart from her using a different surname. And she could easily have been married and divorced or something – it's not that unusual for people to use more than one name, is it?

'Second option is that she's some kind of lunatic who is fixated on me or my father, which is possible, especially given how good-looking I am . . .' he jokes, 'but I think perhaps that isn't the reason.'

'So why do you think she's applying for a job then? It seems weird. Creepy, even,' I say.

'I imagine the most likely option is that she's trying to get access to us, the Creaglie family, to persuade us that we should take her seriously.' He pauses. 'Or even

310

that she's decided to do something similar to what I did – steal some DNA from me or Dad and get it checked out for herself. See if she should be putting in a claim for my fortune, such as it is. Or will be.'

I put the CV down. 'Right. Whichever of those it is, sounds like we definitely don't want her here.'

He picks the CV up and scans it again. 'On the contrary. If she *thinks* she's a Creaglie, and I have the correspondence to prove that she does, I think she could actually be extremely useful to us.'

## 2025
Tabitha, the Twenty-First Lady of Creaglie

Of course, we didn't decide that we needed to kill Alistair in an instant. But over the next months, Josh and I became closer as Alistair started being more and more mean to both of us. I am sure he never suspected that there was anything between us – he was far too arrogant for it to occur to him that either of us might cross him in any way, let alone in such an, admittedly, extreme one. And what started out as light joking between Josh and me about what a pain in the arse Alistair was and how much easier our lives would be without him in it, all the amazing things we could eventually do together, it slowly morphed into an actual plan.

Obviously we had to be very careful that no one knew what was happening between us. But given that usually it was just the two of us here, along with Donald, and Irina who doesn't speak much English or appear to have much interest in any of us, that wasn't too

312

difficult. We never went out together in public, that would have been too risky.

Alistair was by now in his early seventies, and the kind of man who doesn't go to the doctor unless something is pretty much hanging off him.

That said, the Creaglie clan are a robust bunch. He could easily live to be ninety or more, judging by his ancestors, and Josh and I didn't fancy waiting fifteen or twenty years for nature to take its course.

After some research, Josh and I finalized our plans and began to execute our scheme. When Alistair was home, I started to poison his morning smoothie with a high dosage of vitamin A, as well as persuading him to take a multivitamin, which contained more of the same. I told him it might alleviate his tiredness, he had no idea that the overdose of the vitamin I was giving him was actually the cause of it.

From what we had discovered, we knew that what I was doing should weaken but not kill him, which is exactly what we want. The symptoms that the excess Vitamin A induce are ideal, including tiredness, headaches, aching joints; all things which someone like Alistair would simply put down to getting older. As I predicted, it is not enough to bother a doctor with, as far as he's concerned.

We decide it will be best to finally finish him off in plain sight, with plenty of people in the castle to witness his death. If something were to happen while Alistair was alone with Josh and me in this remote venue, it would put us firmly in the frame. Whereas no one would imagine we would do anything to him under the noses of a random group of ghost hunters, surely?

Especially as we had a plan for an extra twist in the tale too.

## 2025
Kayla

I thought it would be tricky to track down my biological father given that he's old and, according to Dad, very private, usually only going between his remote Scottish castle and his pied-à-terre or gentlemen's club in London. I assumed someone like that would have no internet presence at all and I'd have to spend ages researching him in the old-fashioned ways – I'm not sure I would even know where to start. I totally drew a blank when searching for Ezra's father, so this kind of thing is clearly not my forte and there's no way I could afford anything like a private detective.

I imagined that even when I did find him – there was to be no 'if' as far as I was concerned – it would be even harder to engineer a visit. I could hardly launch in with, 'Hi, I'm your long-lost daughter. Do you have any children who might be willing to donate a kidney?' Could I?

And although I had a suspicion that Dad was somewhat overplaying it, there was also the possibility that the laird could be dangerous. Dad claims my mother thought he would kill her if he found out about her infidelity. But she could have been wrong. She could have been suffering from post-natal depression, anxiety, or anything. From what I can make out, Dad and she didn't even know each other for that long, and had to keep their relationship, such as it was, a secret. Would he really have known that much about her mental state? It's entirely possible that my mother's fear for her safety was in her mind, and that my biological father would never have done anything as terrible as she was imagining.

But as it turns out, it is as good as laid out for me on a plate. Creaglie Castle will soon be opening its doors to the public, and it has a flashy website showing off its facilities and giving you the chance to book online.

*As well as a state-of-the-art spa, and gourmet meals prepared by a chef who has worked in some of the best kitchens in the world, you'll be hosted by the Laird of Creaglie himself, with his wife Lady Tabitha and son Joshua, who can't wait to welcome you into their home.*

*A stay at Creaglie Castle has a house party atmosphere, with guests paying one all-inclusive cost with no hidden extras, so you can simply sit back, relax, and live like a member of the aristocracy during your stay. Apart from the family's private apartment, nowhere in the castle is off-limits.*

Rage floods through me when I read the next paragraph.

*Creaglie Castle dates back to the sixteenth century, and is believed to be haunted by many ghosts from several eras. Join us for our inaugural ghost-hunting weekend this winter, when you can help uncover some of the castle's best-kept secrets of the past.*

Reading on, the site lists various alleged ghosts, a 'grey lady' from the nineteenth century, the seventeenth century maid who died in penury, and the child who suffocated after becoming trapped in a heavy-lidded chest.

Of course there is nothing about my dead mother or half-sister, who would surely haunt the castle if ghosts exist, given the way they died.

As far as I'm concerned, ghosts don't exist.

But if they're inviting people to uncover secrets, I need to be there. I'm their biggest secret of all.

# Part Seven

# Joshua, the Twentieth
# Laird of Creaglie

## 2025
Joshua, the Twentieth Laird of Creaglie

My mother had always been obsessed with my father's first wife Amelia, and her poor child who drowned. I had been aware of this from quite a young age – whenever Dad was away on one of his many trips, she was always digging through old records, or asking the housekeeper of the time, Morag, not-so-subtle questions. What was Amelia like? Was she prettier than her? Did Alistair love Amelia better than her?

It was only as I got a little older that I realized how inappropriate this line of questioning was for poor Morag who, as far as I could see, always answered with the utmost tact. Basically she told my mother that she didn't know, that it wasn't the business of someone in her position to know anything like that; that they were both very beautiful women, no doubt the envy of anyone who met them. If pushed, she would reply that she was quite sure that he loved them equally and, as the former Lady of Creaglie was no longer alive, God rest her soul, it was of no real consequence anyway.

My father clearly had a type: thin and willowy with auburn hair, pale skin and dark eyes. I hadn't seen many photos of his first wife as they were always hidden away, but from the few I had caught a glimpse of, I could see that she and Mum had a lot in common in the way they looked. Tabitha is similar too, though I try not to think about that too much as it gets too weird, for obvious reasons.

But Amelia had been younger than my mother and – more to the point – was dead. So in Mum's mind at least, she had become a Platonic-ideal version of a wife, the perfect prototype who could never be equalled or surpassed.

Sometimes she would try to ask Dad about her directly, but he would never be drawn. 'The poor woman was extremely unwell,' he would say. 'Her pregnancy clearly caused her mind to become unbalanced. A terrible thing.'

But he didn't like to discuss it further and would quickly shut her down, as was his way when he was asked about anything he didn't want to talk about. But this simply led to my mother becoming increasingly obsessed.

I had known from quite a young age, thanks to my mother's obsession, that I had had an older half-sister who had drowned before I was born. I also knew that my father's first wife had been pregnant with what would have been another older sibling when she died, though my father never discussed it with me, and I somehow instinctively knew never to ask. Plus, in that selfish way in which children are the centre of their own world, the lives and loss of this woman and her children felt somewhat irrelevant to me. It had all happened long before I had existed.

But as I got older, it occurred to me that if my father's first wife Amelia *hadn't* drowned along with her child, that child would now be the heir to Creaglie Castle. And to take it further, if Amelia hadn't drowned, my father would probably never have married my mother, as he views divorce as shameful for a family like the Creaglies, and would never allow any wife of his to leave him. So the chances were that I'd never have existed at all.

Therefore I think it was possibly my acute awareness of these dead children which ignited my initial interest in the supernatural. Did my deceased half-siblings still exist somewhere on another plane? Would they know about me, be jealous of my position, feel that I had usurped theirs? Or might they be benign presences, still here on some level, watching over me, wanting to be my friend? Keeping me company as I played as a child?

I had always very much had the feeling that it was the latter. As a child, I had often felt a presence, though I didn't know of exactly what, and imagined it as a warm and welcoming being. I can't remember a time when I didn't, which is perhaps why I had always viewed it as normal and never been frightened by it.

And this is why I initially started visiting psychics.

I know full well there are a lot of charlatans out there of course, so I usually visited under a false name so that I couldn't be Googled before my arrival, which would give them an advantage in terms of what they communicated to me, and I was always careful about what information I gave them.

Because I am reasonably young in the psychic-visiting world at least, most of the spirits I was 'connected' with were old men and women who I assumed the mediums wanted me to believe were elderly family members who had passed. Some of them were more convincing than others, but I had never known any of my grandparents, and so had little interest in hearing from them, nor from my mysterious aunt who had allegedly 'shamed' the family. Similarly, I imagined that these spirits would not be particularly interested in coming back from the dead to talk to a random grand-child or nephew they had never met. I don't know much about the afterlife, but I would hope that the spirits have better things to do.

I can entirely understand why Tabitha and many others are sceptical. Because I have seen so many psy-chics, I get used to spotting the ones who are making guesses out of nowhere, who are being deliberately vague, saying things which could apply to absolutely anyone who sits in front of them. The ones who have no real powers, whether they believe they do or not. Which is many. Most.

But very occasionally, something happened in a session when the medium seemed to come up with something surprisingly specific that I felt they couldn't possibly know about me any other way, other than by communicating with the dead. And that was what happened with Elvira.

'There is a small girl,' she said. 'A pretty little thing. She says that you never met in this life. But she lived in your family home, and sometimes when you were a child, she would return from the spirit world and play with you. She felt you were lonely, with no playmates of your own, and she wanted to comfort you. She would make the wooden horse in your nursery rock to let you know she was there. She says it has green eyes and a red mane and you called it Naynay.'

I didn't mean to, as I try not to give the psychics any clues or feedback at all, but I actually gasped out loud. The rocking horse is still here, in the castle. It is exactly as she described, and my name for it was indeed Naynay. And when I was a child, sometimes it would rock of its own accord. But it never frightened me. Whenever the horse started rocking, there would be a sense of warmth and fun, things which I didn't feel very often growing up under the froideur of my father and the intensity and neuroticism of my mum. So I would climb onto the horse and rock, until I felt the warmth leave the room, and then I would know that whoever or whatever had been there had gone and I'd go back to my lonely solitary play.

So while my mother was obsessed with Amelia, I was perhaps more interested than would be usual for a child in my dead half-sister, who I eventually learned – by digging through some family records and finding some old press cuttings – was called Thalia. But there were no pictures of her or Amelia anywhere on display at home. It was as if they had been erased. Perhaps it was in deference to my mother, her weird paranoia and jealousy towards Amelia, but I got the feeling that it was more likely that my father preferred to pretend they had never existed.

And then the psychic said something else. 'The little girl – she is telling me that she was not your only sibling. That there is another who remains on this mortal plane.'

I kept my gaze impassive as I felt a stab of disappointment at her mistake – I don't have another brother or sister.

'Can you tell me more about that?' I asked, even so, to see what she would come up with. She resumed the low humming she'd been doing on and off during our session before proclaiming:

'She lives far away, and she has a different name to you. She doesn't yet know who she really is. But the spirits indicate that one day soon she will work it out, and then the two of you will meet.'

Initially I didn't pay much attention to what she had said. But then, once I had returned home, I thought about it more. Elvira had got one thing absolutely right, something which no one knew about me, that I had never told anyone. She was the first psychic, and I had seen many, who had done so.

What was to say that she wasn't correct about this

too? Obviously it's not something you want to contemplate for too long when you're thinking about your own father, but surely it was possible that Dad had an illegitimate child? However much he had protested before? I had already ascertained that Sarah Laroche was not related to us, but it didn't mean there might not be *another* out there somewhere who was.

He had probably had other girlfriends before he'd married, and possibly between his marriages too. He could have got a woman pregnant without even knowing about it. It wouldn't necessarily mean he had had an affair, though equally, he may well have done – he has always spent a lot of time away from the castle in London, as far as I understand. For all I know, he could even have been in the habit of visiting prostitutes. I have never been close to my father, never truly known what kind of man he is. Who knows what he could have done?

I got a private detective onto it – it cost a fortune as I had so little to go on. She turned up nothing and I was almost on the point of giving up, deciding that the psychic was a fraud after all. That she had somehow found out the name of my rocking horse and simply made up the extra sibling to add another layer of mystery.

And then my long-lost sister decided to come to me.

2025

Dear Laird of Creaglie,

My name is Kayla Thompson. I live in Southampton. This might come as a shock to you, but I believe I may be your daughter.

My dad has told me that my mother was once married to you and escaped from Creaglie Castle when she was pregnant with me, faking her own death, though she is believed to have died soon after, not long after I was born.

I realize it sounds like an unusual story, and I would welcome the chance to meet and discuss it with you.

Look forward to hearing from you,
With my very best wishes,
Kayla

## Silas's voiceover

The year of death was 1798.

The Eleventh Laird of Creaglie liked to throw lavish parties and, considering himself a very modern man, always liked to show off the latest drinks, dishes and even inventions to his guests.

Thrilled by the invention of the hot-air balloon in the late 1700s, he decided that at midnight, one of his more adventurous and biddable servants would be sent into the air high above the castle in this new contraption to release fireworks above his guests' heads.

Initially all went well, and the guests oohed and ahhed as they watched the display above them, bright lights fizzing against the night sky.

That is, until a stray spark from a firework ignited the gas in the balloon, it exploded and the servant fell to his death.

Today, if a light flickers in the castle, some say that

it is the ghost of this same servant making his presence known.

Then again, it could be a fault in the electrical circuit, or a power surge.

We'll probably never know for sure.

## 2025
Kayla

For the next few weeks, I keep an eye on the post and am disappointed every day when nothing arrives. Obviously I could have sent an email through the form on the website but for something like this, it felt somehow too informal, too casual. And I never trust those forms anyway – how do you know if it's actually sent?

Given that the castle is so remote, it seems possible that the letter won't have got there. So I send a second a month or so later. And then another. And another.

There is still no reply. I start to concede that maybe Dad was right. That the laird wants nothing to do with me.

I will have to cross my fingers and hope that a donor comes up for Ezra from the register. I always feel terrible wishing for that, because it doesn't escape me that in effect, I am wishing for someone else's death so that my child can live, and that never sits well with me.

Maybe the laird thinks I'm a scammer, simply

someone after his fortune. Which I very much am not. Well, I guess it would be nice, a bonus, but mainly, apart from the possibility of a kidney for Ezra, I want to know where I came from. So perhaps that is his reason for not replying. It is, after all, quite a fantastic story, and I'm not sure if I'd believe it if I received a letter like that out of the blue. If he knew I *was* actually his daughter, he might feel differently.

Also, I'm not sure if Dad hasn't thought of this option, or if he simply hasn't said it to me, but just because I am not Dad's daughter, that doesn't mean the laird must necessarily be my father. If my mum had an affair with my dad, who's to say there weren't others she had affairs with too?

My head starts to hurt. There are a lot of possibilities. Perhaps Dad was right and I should leave well alone. I was perfectly happy with my life before, wasn't I? What would be the point of shaking things up in this way, unless it's going to help Ezra, which admittedly seems like a long shot, given that they probably don't know that I exist, let alone him.

But if there is a chance, any chance, that one of their family might help him, I need to try.

And then, three months after the first letter, I finally receive a reply.

Dear Miss Thompson,
    Thank you for your letter and many apologies for the delay in replying. The Creaglie family have sadly been exposed to quite a few attempted

hoaxes and scams in the past, and I'm afraid my father simply discarded your letters believing yours to be of the same type.

However, I have recently taken over handling my father's correspondence and have also been researching family history, and your account tallies to a certain degree with records I have found here.

As you may know, we are opening the castle to the public soon and intend to hold a ghost-hunting weekend – perhaps you would like to attend as our guest? It might be a nice informal way to introduce you to the family. I will of course prepare my father for your visit, but I thought perhaps it might be more festive and relaxed all round that way? I for one am certainly looking forward to meeting my long-lost sister!

What do you think? Our post is slow and not very reliable so please feel free to email me on joshua@creagliecastle.co.uk rather than sending a letter.

I very much look forward to meeting you!

Best wishes,

Joshua Creaglie

## 2025
Joshua, the Twentieth Laird of Creaglie

Once I had opened up correspondence with Kayla and she'd agreed to come along to our opening weekend, I told her that her presence would be the icing on the cake for the video which Silas would be making. The reveal of her being a long-lost member of the family, an extra strand for viewers who might not believe in ghosts. A story of a family reunited which anyone could enjoy.

I asked her not to let on to the other guests who she was for this reason and also told her that my father was on board and couldn't wait to meet her. It was easy enough to ensure that they were never left alone so they couldn't discuss it privately.

I did not tell my father about her. There was no way he would have sanctioned her coming to Creaglie Castle, but he would be long dead before he learned her identity. Undoubtedly for the best – he wouldn't have dealt well with the 'shame' of a secret daughter, brought up by another man. Bless Kayla for thinking he would want to know her. Quite clearly she has no idea what he's like at all.

In her correspondence, Kayla told me that the man she has always called her father had had reservations about her getting in touch with the evil Creaglies (she didn't put it quite like that, but that was clearly what he had meant), but felt better about it now that he knew that she was being welcomed into the family with open arms at what amounted to a public event. He felt it would be safer that way.

Poor Kayla. I almost felt sorry for her. Like a lamb to the slaughter.

# Part Eight

# Creaglie Castle

## 8 November 2025, 9 p.m.
Sarah

I had thought Kayla looked familiar as soon as she walked in, but servants like me aren't expected to comment on anything like that, or indeed converse with the guests in a normal manner unless invited to do so. We are subservient, deemed less worthy, and must remember that at all times. So I did all the stuff I was meant to do like taking her coat and ferrying her bags up to her room, unpacking them, stoking her fire and making sure everything was set out just so in her room, the way I am meant to, without making conversation. But whenever I had the chance, I couldn't help but stare at her because I knew she strongly reminded me of somebody, and I couldn't quite work out who.

And then the next day when I was tidying her room, I had more of a snoop around than a trusted employee like me should do. I opened a file I'd packed away in the desk for her and found some press cuttings from around the time Thalia and her mama drowned.

I squinted at the faded old picture and stroked Thalia's little smiling face. I remembered the same picture of her being on the mantelpiece in the living room when I was a child. But all the photos of her have gone from the castle now.

I put the cutting back in the drawer, wondering if perhaps Kayla had it because she's interested in the history of the place and the ghosts, but it seems unlikely because – as far as I'd seen so far, she didn't seem particularly interested in the ghostly stuff.

I opened the file to look at the picture again.

My hand flew to my mouth as I realized who Kayla reminded me of.

She looks just like Thalia's mum.

Could Kayla actually be Thalia? They would be about the same age, had Thalia lived.

But no, that's surely not possible. Thalia drowned many years ago along with her pregnant mama, the Nineteenth Lady of Creaglie. The lady who was always so kind to me when I was a child and let me play with her daughter who I loved so much.

They are both long dead.

Aren't they?

## 9 November 2025, 11 p.m.
Tabitha, the Twenty-First Lady of Creaglie

The upstairs banisters were riddled with woodworm and badly needed replacing. They had escaped the fire in the 1990s, but had been left in a state of disrepair, Josh sensibly prioritizing for renovation the areas of the castle in which the guests would be staying. The upper floor, which houses the apartment that Alistair and I were to share when we have paying guests here (with two bedrooms, thankfully), was way down a very long 'to do' list of things which still needed to be attended to. The old upper-floor banisters are probably also too low to meet safety regulations for guests, but Josh and I decided that would be OK for now as there are no guest rooms on this level.

We took the precaution of loosening some of the upright spines a little more ahead of the arrivals but decided against actually damaging the rails. We figured something like that could be spotted, either by Alistair himself or if there was any investigation afterwards.

After the séance which, as we predicted it might, freaked everyone out so much that they wanted to take a minute or two to themselves, the guests scattered to different parts of the castle and Alistair said: 'I'm just popping upstairs for an instant to use the facilities, but in the meantime, Mrs Laroche, could you organize some drinks?'

This was the moment, and I was going to grab it.

I said, 'Have we got any amaretto? I fancy something like that,' to Josh, which included our agree code word 'amaretto' to indicate that this was our moment.

'And perhaps some of our house cocktails? Why don't we all reconvene in the library in about ten minutes?' Josh added, before beginning a deliberately protracted conversation with Donald about the best way to proceed once the storm has abated, in order to ensure a solid alibi for himself, as we had discussed he should.

I quietly followed Alistair up the stairs, waited for him inside an empty room by the pre-loosened banisters, and then slipped out to shove him over as he passed on his way back. It didn't take much – he was already weakened from the vitamin A overdose I have been subtly feeding him over the past few weeks.

He didn't even see me do it. The only sound he made was a vague noise of surprise which was somewhere between a squeak and a groan, before there was the horrible but muted dull thud of his body hitting the flagstones below.

I immediately raced down the stairs to stand by Alistair's body and started screaming blue murder.

Everyone ran in, everything was suddenly very hectic and busy – it would have been almost impossible to remember who came from where. But most importantly, I was there first, seemingly hysterical at the discovery of my husband's body. We are husband and wife so, if it came to it, there would be nothing unusual about finding my DNA on his body. Josh had already disabled the internet by dropping a branch onto the cable outside to delay any emergency services arriving – no one would be remotely surprised at it failing during a storm. The storm was a gift, but we would have managed even so – we could always have scuppered the boat and communications anyway. Neither event is especially rare when you live as remotely as we do.

The sweet old lady guest, who was apparently a nurse in her younger days, led me away to the kitchen, and I sobbed and wailed as she plied me with sweet tea, at which point I pretended to start calming down a little and allowed myself to be led back to the library and laid down on the sofa.

Without any fuss, and without drawing any more attention to myself, I eventually closed my eyes, after another of our admittedly excellent cocktails, not planning to wake up until the morning. I had taken a triple dose of my sleeping pills when I nipped back upstairs – enough to make me sleepy and to show up in the blood tests I would be given later when I made the claims I was planning to make, but not enough to do any damage. I was already feeling drowsy, and feigned sleep in the meantime.

Even though I was not to benefit from Alistair's will, as those who didn't already know would soon find out, Josh and I felt that – as the young trophy wife and probable prime suspect should anything be deemed suspicious about his death – it was better that we err on the side of caution. And if I was incapacitated after the sad demise of my husband, I couldn't possibly be blamed for what was to happen to Kayla next, could I?

That would be down to someone else.

## 10 November 2025, 1.15 a.m.
Joshua, the Twentieth Laird of Creaglie

Stupidly I left the door to the tower open when I went up to drop the branch on the internet line to make sure it wasn't working, and then one of the guests, Ben, who clearly isn't the sharpest tool in the box, got himself stuck in there. Well, I say got himself stuck, actually I noticed him heading into the tower and closed the door behind him while I did what I needed to do in Kayla's room along the corridor. Everyone else was downstairs; there's no way they'd hear him calling out from all the way up here, however much of a noise he made.

Which as it turned out, was quite a lot. He was making a terrible din, banging and shouting as I was on my way back from putting the oleander leaves in Kayla's fireplace and half-blocking it with a large log I wedged there. I wasn't worried that she would wake while I did this – I heard her saying she was planning to take a sleeping pill, so I was fairly sure she'd be out for the count. And if she had woken, I'd have said I

345

was checking she was OK after she'd bolted from the room. Like a good host would, of course.

I opened the door to the tower and Ben practically collapsed on the floor in his hurry to get out. 'What's all the shouting about?' I asked.

He sat up and rubbed his arm.

'I was looking for you,' he said, a somewhat plaintive, almost whining tone to his voice. He looked almost like he might cry. For fuck's sake, it's just a tower! What a wet blanket.

'I went up to the top of the tower, because I thought that's where you might be trying to find some phone signal, and then someone locked me in,' he added.

Oh yes. The excuse I gave of looking for phone signal – I suppose it made sense that I'd be going up high. Truth is, there's never been any mobile phone signal here in the castle ever, but of course the guests aren't going to know that.

'Really? I'm sure no one would have deliberately locked you in,' I lied. 'The door must have shut behind you. Or maybe someone closed it without knowing you were there to keep the draught out,' I added, to cover all bases, 'which I'm going to do now because it's fucking freezing.'

'So did you find any phone signal?' he persisted.

*For God's sake, have you not seen where we are?* I thought to myself. *How would there be phone signal? Do you see a mast? Get over it!* But I didn't say that, of course. I was nice. It is my job here as genial host.

I offered him my hand and he took it to haul himself up to his feet. He brushed himself down.

'I didn't find any signal,' I confirmed. 'On a good day you can get a signal in the old nursery sometimes, but obviously today isn't a good day.' Lies. All lies. We rely on the landline, which in turn relies on the internet, which obviously I have ensured is currently not working.

'So you weren't up the tower?' he asked. 'I thought – as it's so high – that might be where you went.'

'No.' *Fuck's sake. How many times? Just leave it.* 'And now you mention it, I don't even know why this door was open,' I continued. 'No one should be up there, it's not safe, especially on a day like this.' I pretended to examine the door. 'I'll make sure we get a lock put on this before we have any more guests staying here – I don't want anyone else going up there.'

'So what now?' Ben continued. 'Is there anywhere else we can try to get a phone signal? Rosemary seems quite worried about your, um, stepmother.'

'Don't call her my stepmother,' I snapped, because Tabitha and I had agreed to show a low-key mutual dislike in public for obvious reasons. We actually both quite enjoy it – it feels a bit like slightly kinky role play, and it certainly adds an extra frisson when we do get to spend time together alone. I don't like to think of her as my stepmother anyway as that's weird on several levels. 'My mother was worth twenty of her, God rest her soul,' I added.

He held his hands up in a gesture of surrender. 'Sorry, I didn't mean . . .'

I clapped him on the shoulder. 'Sorry, mate. Don't mind me. I'm a bit overwrought after . . . well, you know. Tabitha'll be fine I'm sure – probably just looking for attention. I'm not worried about her at all. But my father deserves better than lying on a cold, hard floor draped in a sheet. I want to get the right people here so that he can be dealt with in a way befitting a man of his station.

'So, mark my words, I'm doing my best to sort this out. I want to get in touch with the mainland just as much as you do, believe me.'

Again, more lies. We are not finished yet. Far from it.

## 10 November 2025, 6.00 a.m.
Joshua, the Twentieth Laird of Creaglie

Sarah Laroche applying to work as a housekeeper for us was a godsend.

I still had the letters she'd written to my father, claiming she was his daughter.

I put a half-empty packet of sleeping pills in her bathroom cupboard, the ones Tabitha sometimes takes, and some small pieces of oleander leaves in the pocket of her apron – small enough that she wouldn't notice, but large enough that forensics could find them.

And I will, of course, be telling the police about her secretive behaviour since she arrived at Creaglie Castle, and about the strange questions she'd been asking. And how I had only made the link between Sarah Laroche and the deranged woman who had repeatedly written to my father after his death.

The things we have done may or may not be enough to convict her. It doesn't matter. As far as I know, no one suspects me or Tabitha of a thing.

That's what really matters.

Once all this has blown over, we can be together.

It was decreed by the spirits, and is all I've wanted since the moment I met her.

I can't wait.

The storm is abating now. I'll go and wake Tabitha up. I think it's time, and the pills she took, which we will claim Sarah Laroche must have put in her drink or food, should be wearing off by now. For all I know, she's still feigning sleep. She's such a clever woman. So many talents.

My father never deserved her, just as he never deserved my poor mother.

He won't be taking advantage of any more unsuspecting and vulnerable women now.

We have done the world a favour.

And I can be with the woman who was always destined for me, with my inheritance intact, and Creaglie Castle a viable asset from which she and I can run our growing business. Perhaps one day we can even have a family, break the awful Creaglie chain and bring up our children as decent human beings.

I smile to myself. It's all gone exactly to plan.

And then there is a scream.

'Tabitha's not breathing!' someone shouts.

I leap up and rush down the stairs.

**November 2025**
Sarah

My first day at work was two months before the paying guests arrived. Back when I lived here before, there was quite a team of staff, Mama, a housemaid, Donald, Uncle Luca, a cook and assistant, a gardener, and I think possibly another butler or two.

My job was to be much like Mama's had been, head of housekeeping, though there were now way less staff than in the castle's heyday, so I would be doing a lot of cleaning and bed-changing too. But that would be fine – in fact, it's exactly what I had wanted.

When I was small, the entire castle was for the family's exclusive use, except for the staff quarters. Now that it is basically becoming a glorified hotel, an apartment has been created for Tabitha and Alistair, where they can relax away from the guests who are given the run of the hotel for that authentic 'live like a lord' experience.

It's pretty nice as apartments go, much nicer than

my quarters of course, with two bedrooms and two bathrooms (I noticed that Tabitha and Alistair sleep apart – interesting, but not altogether surprising), a decent living room, kitchen, study and a private terrace which isn't overlooked by any of the guest areas.

I told Irina that I would make cleaning their apartment each day my job. I gave the reason that this is because I have years of experience and want to make sure that our employers are happy with our work, and the best way to do that is to ensure that their own living area in particular is clean and tidy.

But gross as it might sound, what I needed was access to the laird's nail clippings.

After a little internet search before I started my job, I realized that the usual way to collect someone's DNA was a cheek swab, but clearly that wasn't something I could do discreetly.

Apparently you could now do it with a toothbrush, which seemed like a possibility. Although while my new duties were quite wide ranging, and I always tried to anticipate my employers' every need, I thought he might notice a replaced toothbrush and find it odd.

But the same thing can also be done with nail clippings. I got the collection kit sent before I arrived and checked the laird's bathroom bin every day when I emptied it. Eventually, I found what I needed, collected the clippings and as soon as I get the chance to go back to the mainland, will send them off to be tested, along with my own. With so much to get ready for the guest arrivals I haven't had a day off for weeks, plus I also need to arrange a PO Box for the return – I can't risk the results coming here.

I want to know if the laird is my father and with Mama being the way she is now, I'm never going to find out through her.

I kind of hope he isn't. I'm not interested in an inheritance – I live a simple life and don't need money or the stress of money – and I'm quite sure the smarmy son would fight me all the way anyway. I certainly don't have the stomach for that.

I just want to know the truth.

December 2026
*The Daily News*

The trial of a housekeeper accused of carrying out three murders at a remote castle in Scotland began today at the High Court of the Justiciary in Inverness.

Sarah Laroche, 45, took a job as housekeeper at Creaglie Castle in the Scottish Highlands in September last year, shortly before the castle opened to paying guests for its inaugural ghost-hunting weekend.

Alistair, the Nineteenth Laird of Creaglie, 73, Tabitha, the Twenty-First Lady of Creaglie, 29, and Kayla Thompson, 33, were each killed by Laroche on the night of 9 November and in the early hours of 10 November, the prosecution alleges.

Unbeknown to her employers when she took the job, Mrs Laroche had lived at Creaglie Castle as a child for several years while her mother was employed as a house-keeper by the Creaglie family in the 1970s, 1980s and 1990s. According to reports, Sarah Laroche had become obsessed by the unfounded notion that Alistair Creaglie could be her father. She had written to the laird before his death, asking that he take a DNA test so that her parentage could be confirmed. It is believed that she became frustrated at receiving no reply, and infiltrated the household by applying for a job there.

Lady Tabitha of Creaglie was unaware of the claim when she offered Laroche the job.

Laird Alistair of Creaglie fell from a third-floor gallery late at night on 9 November, and was initially believed to have suffered a dizzy spell or heart attack following a recent spate of poor health. It is the prosecution's case that he was pushed by Laroche, having been fed an overdose of Vitamin A in drinks prepared by the house-keeper since her arrival to cause weakness.

Meanwhile Kayla Thompson had recently learned that she was related to the Creaglie family and had been invited by Joshua, the Twentieth Laird of Creaglie, to attend the event. She was later discovered dead in her room due to smoke inhalation. Lady Tabitha of Creaglie fell unconscious shortly after her husband's death and stopped breathing in the early hours of the morning. An autopsy found that she had consumed a lethal dose of sleeping pills.

'The phone and internet were down because of the storm, and it was too dangerous to try to send anyone out across the lake to seek help,' prosecuting counsel Andrew Yaffe said.

'Joshua Creaglie and his guests initially seemed to accept that his father Alistair Creaglie's death was an accident, if an unfortunate and somewhat gruesome

355

one, his recent ill health potentially causing him to stumble and fall, breaking the ancient banisters and falling from a height.

'However, after Ms Thompson was *also* discovered dead, and it was found that the chimney in her room had been blocked, the attendees started to realize that two deaths in one night was unlikely. The storm was still making leaving the island impossible, so the occupants agreed that from then on, no one would go anywhere alone while they waited out the storm.

'Ms Thompson had recently written to the family explaining she believed she was a long-lost relative. This information had been planned as a reveal for additional interest later in the evening, because renowned ghost hunter, Silas Ivory, was filming the event for his popular online channel. Tabitha Creaglie, her husband, the deceased Alistair Creaglie, and the now-current Laird, Joshua of Creaglie, were all aware and on board with the plan, and had been delighted to meet this new, long-lost member of their family. But sadly the planned reunion never happened on camera, as she died before her identity could be revealed.

'After police had taken all the occupants of the castle to the mainland police station for questioning, the house was thoroughly searched.

'Traces of oleander leaves were found in Mrs Laroche's apron pockets, along with several boxes of high-strength Vitamin A capsules, which can cause serious health issues when taken in excess, in both the kitchen and Mrs Laroche's bathroom, along with the type of sleeping pills which caused the overdose of Lady Tabitha. The Vitamin A, which was found to be present in unusually high levels in the deceased's body, is believed to be the reason for the decline in health of Laird Alistair Creaglie over the weeks leading up to his death – beginning around the time of Sarah Laroche's employment. It is the prosecution's case that the Vitamin A is also likely to have been administered by Mrs Laroche.

'A bag of toenails, which were later found to have come from Alistair Creaglie, and a kit for DNA testing, were also found in Mrs Laroche's room, as well as press cuttings about the presumed death of Amelia, the Nineteenth Lady of Creaglie. It has recently become apparent, due to the testimony of her former partner Luca Fallowfield, that Amelia, the first wife of Alistair Creaglie, faked her own death before giving birth to Kayla Thompson. Kayla, in turn, was now clearly a potential heir to the Creaglie fortune. In spite of a widespread search, Amelia's current whereabouts is unknown and, indeed, it is possible that she is no longer alive.

'Sarah Laroche appeared to be suffering under the delusion that she is the half-sister of Joshua Creaglie and the daughter of the deceased Laird Alistair Creaglie, whom she had contacted in the past on this subject, using her maiden name.

'The prosecution's case is that Mrs Laroche pushed Alistair Creaglie from the upper gallery and then blocked the chimney of Ms Thompson's room, as well as putting oleander leaves in the fireplace after discovering that Ms Thompson was, in fact, Lord Creaglie's illegitimate daughter – a potential claimant to the inheritance she felt should be her own. The current Laird of Creaglie, Joshua, told the police he had become suspicious of Mrs Laroche's motives for being in the castle and believed that he himself could also be in danger.

'Sarah Laroche is also alleged to have laced Tabitha Creaglie's drink with sleeping pills. This was a drug which Lady Creaglie took for insomnia, but a higher dose than usual was found in her system. It is believed that the grapefruit juice in the Brown Derby cocktails, prepared and served by Laroche, could have also exacerbated the effect of the drug to ensure the dose was fatal.'

DNA tests have since revealed that Mrs Laroche is not related to the Creaglie family. Her true paternity remains unknown. She pleads guilty to DNA theft under the Human Tissue Act 2004, and not guilty to three counts of murder.

The hearing continues.

# Part Nine

# The Twenty-First Lady of Creaglie, Deceased

## 2026
Tabitha, the Twenty-First Lady of Creaglie

This was not how it was meant to turn out.

I thought I'd got the dose right – that I'd sleep, miss all the drama, be out of the way when that grasping young woman Kayla met her demise, but no.

Who knew that something as innocent as *grapefruit juice* can make sleeping pills – benzos – more potent? Certainly not me. So there you have it. That's why I didn't wake up. Ridiculous. All that planning and effort and then, of all things, foiled by *grapefruit juice*.

There was an investigation, of course – not just into my death, but also Alistair's and the girl's. Nothing at the time pointed to any wrongdoing by me or Josh – especially not by me, as I was unconscious for most of the evening, and then dead, which is about as good as an alibi there is. Josh told the police that he thought Sarah had been behaving strangely and, following the deaths, had searched her room and made the link between her and the woman who had written to his father, falsely claiming to be his daughter. He also said that he believed he would have been next on her kill list. Thanks to this the police found the things we'd planted – the Vitamin A with which I'd been dosing Alistair in the kitchen as well as some Josh had hidden in her cupboard along with some of my sleeping pills, and the oleander in her pockets. So that, along with the letters claiming she was a Creaglie that he showed them, meant she looked dodgy as fuck. As for the toenails she was apparently sending off for DNA testing (gross). That was all her. So she's only got herself to blame for that. It didn't take long for her to be arrested and charged.

Sarah was eventually acquitted in court, disappointingly, because much of the evidence was admittedly circumstantial. But, as far as I understand, the public at large are pretty much convinced of her guilt. I'm not sure what has happened to her now, but there was a lot of publicity and I think she'd struggle to find a job again.

I think enough time has passed now that Josh is unlikely to ever be investigated over the deaths. I am no lawyer but, as far as I understand, a new trial would usually require there to be new evidence. And apart from anything else, while Josh was questioned along with everyone else at the outset, no one ever really seemed to suspect him. And if it came to it now, as I am already dead, he could always pin it on me, as the young wife who had regretted her hasty marriage to a man more than twice her age. I wouldn't mind at all if he did. I have nothing to lose now. If the positions were reversed, I would do the same in a heartbeat.

Luca, the man who brought Kayla up, turned up for Sarah's trial and sat stony-faced throughout. Though it was clear that there is no love lost between him and the Creaglies, he had no real reason to believe anything other than the prosecution's version of events. That this weird housekeeper was responsible for the death of his 'daughter'. He has since launched a civil case against the Creaglies for what amounts to a failed duty of care for her when she was at the castle. It was settled out of court, and he's set up a foundation in Kayla's name to help support families of children awaiting transplants.

I miss being alive. And I miss Josh. But it could be worse because, who knew? It turns out that the dead and the living *can* communicate after all. Just like he's always said. We don't need that stupid Elvira woman here. I let him know my presence in my own ways when I feel like it. A breeze which feels like a caress. A warmth when I sit by him. He can't see me, but he can feel me still, I'm sure of it.

And there is one piece of happy news. Luca told Josh about Kayla's real reason for coming to the castle, and Josh has donated a kidney to her boy, Ezra. Josh is young and healthy so can cope but, more to the point, it makes him look good in the press. Why would anyone kill someone and then donate a kidney to their child? But because of the way Alistair's will was written, with Kayla dying before she could inherit, Ezra will never receive a penny. We talked about this when we were planning. His benevolence doesn't go that far.

Josh was right all along; there are ghosts in the castle. Most of the stories which were told as myths were – it turns out – actually true.

The hotel business and the monthly ghost hunts at Creaglie Castle are doing very well. Even the revelation of the infrasound machine we were using to make people feel uneasy which the police found during their search, hasn't put people off. Infrasound can't be heard by the human ear but it can affect people mentally, making them anxious or even nauseated. We hid machines in the cellar and above the nursery. Poor Ben was obviously affected the most out of our little group, though he did his best to hide it, bless him.

Eternity is long. But myself and Amelia, the Nineteenth Lady of Creaglie, pass the time by freaking out the guests. We have a lot of fun during the séances, pushing things around in ways the usually-fake mediums aren't expecting, and generally making a nuisance of ourselves.

Amelia doesn't know what Josh and I did, which is a relief because I doubt she would thank me for the part I played in killing her daughter. And she is grateful to Josh for donating his kidney. Even though she never bonded with her daughter Kayla in life, she's delighted that her grandson's life has been saved. Kayla is still here too, and Amelia is trying to get to know her, to make up for lost time. Some days Kayla seems to understand why Amelia did what she did, why she felt she had to leave her as a baby. To try to protect her from the Creaglie family. But it is, understandably, a difficult thing to come to terms with so, on other days, Kayla is angry at her treatment by Amelia and she makes her feelings known. The ghost hunters love that – the readings on their instruments, whatever they are, go through the roof. Alistair remains as a presence too but he stays away from us and the guests. He's more like a black hole, a mood-suck, not that different to how he was when he was alive in many ways.

One of the big streaming services made a three-part true crime documentary about the deaths, which has only added to the success of the business, as well as to the public belief that Sarah is guilty. Josh gave an interview for the documentary, while Sarah didn't. Ben has written a book based on his experience – yet more publicity for Creaglie Castle, and, from what I've gleaned from conversations I've heard at the castle and when they filmed for the documentary, his career has taken off too. His new specialism is haunted places.

Silas made a series of programmes for his channel about his time here. They are quite well made and very fair and balanced – he didn't come to a conclusion one way or the other about whether Creaglie Castle is truly haunted, but did concede that he'd noted a few 'interesting phenomena'. His channel has gone from strength to strength and I believe a mainstream series is in the offing for him too now.

Josh claims publicly that they don't use the infrasound any more, but I know they do – they've just moved the machine to somewhere it can't be found. They don't use the creepy singing triggered by a timer in the nursery though – you can't really do something so specific like that more than once.

I don't have the ability to read minds, but I can go where I please unseen, and unfelt, except when I want to make my presence known.

And for the first time, I feel quite at home in Creaglie Castle.

I might just stay here for ever.

# Acknowledgements

First thanks as always to my brilliant agent Gaia Banks for all the advice, reading of terrible half-drafts and general handholding way above and beyond the call of duty, as always. Thanks to everyone at HarperCollins who it is a privilege to work with, especially Kate Bradley and Morgan Springett for their brilliant editing and patience with all my annoying questions. Thank you to Penny Isaac and Meg Le Huquet for the meticulous copy editing and proof reading, and to Claire Ward for a particularly fabulous cover.

Thanks to beta readers Sarah Clarke and Fran Bevan, your input was invaluable. Thanks to the talented Knipe family for helping me out with the chess moves.

As usual thanks to my online friends who have been involved in donating their surnames to characters, pedantic discussions of grammar points (everyone seems to love those!) as well as generally keeping me entertained. Special thanks to the Witches and the Savvies.

Thank you to the crime writing community for being such fabulous and supportive people – massive thanks especially to those who have read and endorsed this or the previous books – every single one is appreciated.

As ever thanks to Alex for your general support, reading drafts of the book and generally listening to me boring on about plot points, but also for building my library for me literally as I write now – so excited!

And finally thanks to the bloggers, bookstagrammers and readers. I am so grateful for your support and continued enthusiasm for the books, and I'm always delighted to hear from you. Keep doing what you do!

# KARIN Slaughter's

# CRIME CLUB

© Alison Rosa

**Dear Readers,**

Welcome to *The Lake* by Catherine Cooper, a gripping tale that intertwines mystery, family secrets and the supernatural into a twisting thriller like none other. As you delve into its pages, prepare to be transported to the eerie and atmospheric Creaglie Castle, where every shadow holds a story, and every character harbours a secret.

The tension escalates when guests arrive for a ghost-hunting weekend, setting the stage for a series of shocking events that will keep you guessing until the very end.

You'll feel the weight of grief, the sting of betrayal, and the thrill of uncovering long-buried secrets. With twists and turns that will leave you breathless, *The Lake* is a gripping exploration of the lengths one will go to for love, revenge, and redemption.

Thank you for joining us on this thrilling journey through *The Lake* – I hope you enjoyed it as much as I did.

Enjoy!

Karin

# READING GROUP QUESTIONS

*Warning: contains spoilers*

---

1. How do the experiences of the Nineteenth Lady of Creaglie, shape her actions throughout the story? Do you empathise with her choices?

2. How do the relationships between mothers and their children influence their characters and decisions?

3. The characters in *The Lake* tell a lot of lies. How do these secrets impact their relationships with one another? Can you identify a moment where a secret significantly affects the plot?

4. How does Creaglie Castle serve as a character in the story? In what ways does the setting influence the events and the mood of the narrative?

5. There are some very wealthy, and some very poor characters in *The Lake*. Discuss how wealth and social status affect the characters' lives and choices.

6. What role do ghosts play in the story? How do the characters' beliefs about the supernatural reflect their personal struggles and fears?

7. How do power and control manifest in the interactions between male and female characters?

8. How do the characters grapple with their family histories and the expectations placed upon them?

9. Are there moments of redemption or forgiveness in the story? How do these moments affect the characters' journeys?

10. How do the characters' identities evolve throughout the novel? Discuss how Amelia, Tabitha, and Kayla each seek to define themselves in relation to their pasts and their families.

# Q&A WITH
# CATHERINE COOPER

*Warning: contains spoilers*

---

### I. What inspired you to write *The Lake*, and how did you decide on the central themes of isolation, family dynamics, and the supernatural?

I used to be fascinated by the supernatural as a child, and lately have had this interest rekindled largely by the podcast Uncanny. The stories are fascinating, but mostly I love how their experts come up with both supernatural and logical explanations for everything which happens. So I wanted to write a book where there *could* be a supernatural element, but everything which happens could also be explained logically. Isolation is always a useful device in a thriller, and as for family dynamics, there's always something to fall out over when a large inheritance is at stake!

### 2. The characters in your novel are deeply complex. How did you approach developing their backstories and motivations, particularly for Amelia and Sarah?

I tend to simply start writing and see how characters develop. I knew that Amelia would have to have no one to turn to when things went wrong, which is why she never knew her family, and then once she lost her child, it was obvious that that would have an enormous impact on her life and what she would decide to do next. Sarah had a strange childhood in that she never really spent time with other children so became overly obsessed with Thalia, her surrogate sister, and in turn, with the Creaglie family.

**3. Creaglie Castle plays a significant role in the
story. How did you envision the setting influencing
the plot and the characters' experiences? What
research did you do to create such a vivid and
atmospheric location?**

Creaglie Castle has been in the same family for generations so you
have the family's fierce pride in it, but also the ghost stories which
often come with an ancient and isolated place. I normally like to visit
the places inspiring the locations I'm writing about but this time
I didn't, partly because for a while I couldn't decide if it should be
in Scotland or Switzerland. I have visited and even stayed in a lot of
castles over the years, but other than that this time it was mainly
internet research.

**4. The theme of grief is prevalent throughout the
novel. Can you share your thoughts on how you
wanted to portray the different ways characters
cope with loss?**

I think any parent would agree that there is no possible worse thing
than the loss of a child, so it stands to reason that Amelia could
never get over it, especially as she felt herself to blame. For Luca it
was different as he never knew if Thalia was his child or not. Sarah
lost Thalia, the only friend she'd ever had, at a very vulnerable time in
her life, and this, compounded with her disappointment at not being
able to have her own child could, conceivably cause her to become
obsessed with the idea of family.

**5. What role do ghosts play in the narrative? Are they
purely symbolic, or do you see them as integral to the
characters' journeys?**

I'm not sure they're either. They're written so that they (arguably)
don't influence anything tangible which happens in the real world,
and could easily not exist outside of the readers' minds. Though I feel

Amelia really came into her own as a ghost, regaining the confidence and spark she lost while she was alive because of Alistair, and I liked the idea that she and Kayla could potentially reconnect. But equally you could take the ghosts out of story and it would still hold together.

## 6. Many characters engage in morally ambiguous actions. Who did you give the hardest decisions to?

Definitely Amelia. She didn't do anything wrong, she was a victim of circumstance. She took a huge risk leaving Alistair to try to protect Thalia, and then she left Luca to try to protect her second child. It didn't go well for any of them, but none of it was her fault.

## 7. Can you describe your writing process for *The Lake*. Did you have a clear outline, or did the story evolve organically as you wrote?

I would have loved to have had a clear outline, but I never do when writing, so it very much evolved as I went along. It took a while to settle on a location or an era – the past sections were initially going to be much earlier in time, and the castle started off being in Scotland, then moved to Switzerland, and then back to Scotland again. But as usual during the first draft I was very strict with myself about writing at least one thousand words per day – if it's not on the page, there's nothing to edit.

## 8. What do you hope readers will take away from *The Lake?*

As usual mainly I want to tell an entertaining story. If it makes people question their thoughts around the supernatural, whether they believe or not, that would be a bonus. And if anyone has any ghostly experiences to share, I'd love to hear them!

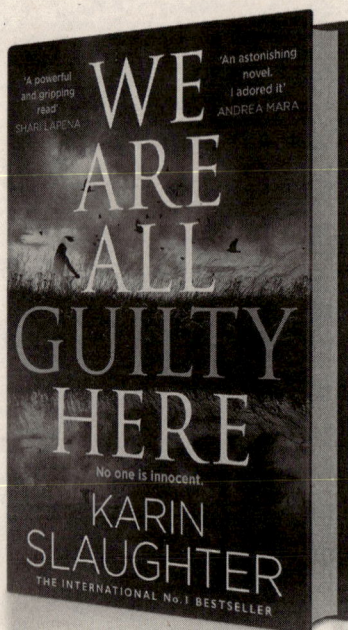

## No one is innocent.

**Welcome to North Falls. A small town where everyone knows everyone. But nobody knows the truth.**

Emmy Clifton has lived here all her life.
She thinks she knows her neighbours.

**She's wrong.**

She thinks it's just another hot summer night: a night like any other.

**She's wrong.**

When her best friend's daughter asks for help,
she thinks it's just some teenage drama. She thinks it can wait.

**She's never been more wrong in her life.**

As the town ignites in the wake of the girl's disappearance,
Emmy throws herself into the search. But then she realises:

**You never really know a town until you know its secrets.**

**Is Emmy ready for the truth?**

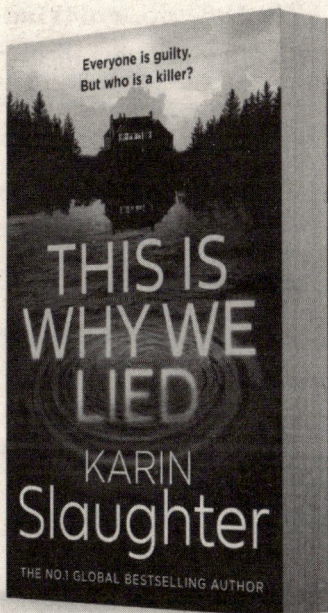

Everyone is guilty.
But who is a killer?

THIS IS
WHY WE
LIED

KARIN
Slaughter

THE NO.1 GLOBAL BESTSELLING AUTHOR

**Everyone here is a liar,
but only one of us is a killer...**

Welcome to the McAlpine Lodge: a remote mountain
getaway, it's the height of escapist luxury living.

Except that everyone here is lying. Lying about their past.
Lying to their family. Lying to themselves.

Then one night, Mercy McAlpine – until now the good
daughter – threatens to expose everybody's secrets.
Just hours later, Mercy is dead.

In an area this remote, it's easy to get away with murder.
But Will Trent and Sara Linton – investigator and medical
examiner for the GBI – are here on their honeymoon.

**And now, with the killer poised to
strike again, the holiday of a lifetime
becomes a race against the clock...**

**If you enjoyed *The Lake*, don't miss out on Catherine Cooper's other gripping thrillers . . .**

**Four friends. One luxury getaway. The perfect murder.**

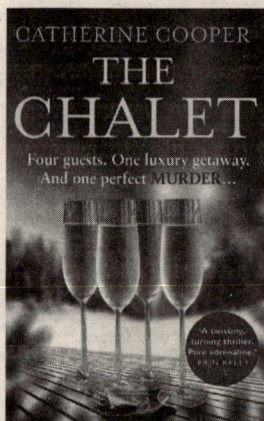

**French Alps, 1998**

Two young men ski into a blizzard . . . but only one returns.

**20 years later**

Four people connected to the missing man find themselves in that same resort. Each has a secret. Two may have blood on their hands. One is a killer-in-waiting.

**Someone knows what really happened that day.**

**And somebody will pay.**

**They thought it was perfect. They were wrong . . .**

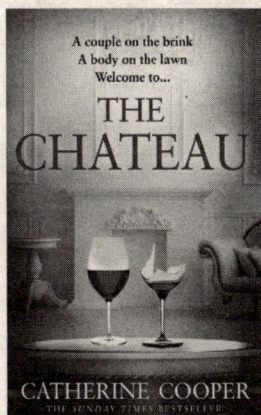

A couple on the brink
A body on the lawn
Welcome to...

# THE CHATEAU

CATHERINE COOPER
THE SUNDAY TIMES BESTSELLER

## A luxurious chateau

Aura and Nick don't talk about what happened in England. They've bought a chateau in France to make a fresh start, and their kids need them to stay together – whatever it costs.

## A couple on the brink

The expat community is welcoming, but when a neighbour is murdered at a lavish party, Aura and Nick don't know who to trust.

## A secret that is bound to come out . . .

Someone knows exactly why they really came to the chateau. And someone is going to give them what they deserve.

**A glamorous ship. A missing woman.**
**A holiday to DIE for . . .**

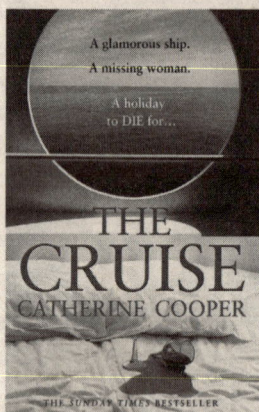

## A glamorous ship

During a New Year's Eve party on a large,
luxurious cruise ship in the Caribbean, the ship's
dancer, Lola, goes missing.

## Everyone on board has something to hide

Two weeks later, the ship is out of service, laid
up far from land with no more than a skeleton
crew on board. And then more people start
disappearing . . .

## No one is safe

Why are the crew being harmed?
Who is responsible? And who will be next?

**The perfect escape, or the perfect trap?**

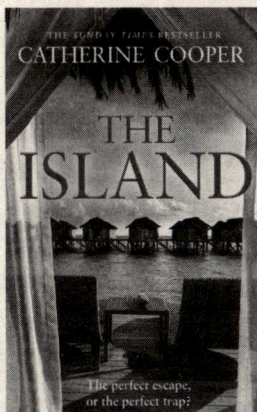

When a select group of influencers and journalists receive an exclusive invitation to a luxury resort in the Maldives, it seems like the ultimate press trip.

But when the island is cut off during a storm and people start dying, it looks like someone has murder in mind.

Are the guests really who they seem to be, or does each one of them have a secret to hide?

**Something they would kill for?**

**Beneath the glamour dark secrets lurk.**

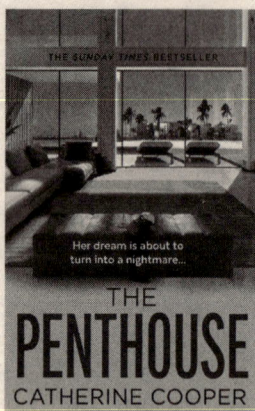

World famous singer Enola had it all – fame,
fortune, and a breathtaking penthouse view.
Then she vanished without a trace, leaving
the band's careers in ruins.

Fifteen years on, the remaining members are
reuniting for a series of concerts in Las Vegas.
But when mysterious accidents plague them, some
start to wonder if Enola is back for revenge.

**What happened all those years ago –
and who really knows the truth?**